Catalyst for Collapse

The GAIA Protocol Book Two

Harry Stoddart

Granite Oak Press

Catalyst for Collapse

Published in the United States of America

ISBN–13: 978-0-9878842-3-7 (Paperback)

ISBN–13: 978-0-9878842-2-0 (Ebook)

Contents

Start Here – Join My Reader Community

If you're enjoying the journey into the Catalyst for Collapse, I'd love to share even more with you.

Sign up for my newsletter and get exclusive access to:

The Shadow Emerges

Before she was La Sombra, she was a guerrilla fighter on a suicide mission. Injured, dehydrated, and pursued by the army, she dragged herself deeper into the jungle, refusing to yield. In the shadows of the cloud forest, a legend was born—one bullet at a time. **The Shadow Emerges** tells the untold story of how fear took human form.

Along with your free story, you'll also get:

- Early access to upcoming chapters and behind-the-scenes insights into the science woven in my stories.
- Exclusive background material and deleted scenes
- Updates on the next book in *The GAIA Protocol* series
- Occasional thoughts on climate, technology, and the future that inspire my writing

It's completely free, and you can unsubscribe at any time.

Scan the QR code below or visit www.harrystoddart.ca/signup/?source=CollStart

1

"Man, how much farther to this end-of-the-world waterfall?" Carter groaned, rubbing his calves. "My legs are toast."

Austin checked his phone. "My trails app says not far."

"Hey," Maureen pointed. "Is that the mouth of a cave?"

Mags squinted through the foliage. "Yeah. Looks like it. Spooky. Let's check it out."

They tugged flashlights from their packs and shone them across the opening. The beam lit a narrow cavern, tall enough to stand inside, a dark passage leading deeper into rock.

"That's kind of creepy," Maureen whispered.

Carter grinned, puffing out his chest. "What, you scared? Why don't I go first, big strong boyfriend style. Austin, you take the rear, keep the girls safe between us."

"Deal, bro."

They stepped inside, light bouncing across damp stone. A sudden flutter exploded overhead — wings scraping the air. The group ducked as a cloud of bats shot out into the fading light.

"God, I hate bats," Maureen said, pressing against the wall.

"They're just bats," Carter teased. "Nothing to—"

"Real funny," Mags snapped.

They pushed deeper. The cave air grew heavy, their voices echoing strangely, as if swallowed by the rock.

Carter yawned, then frowned. "Anybody else tired? Must be the hike catching up."

Austin's beam wavered. "No... listen. It's the air. It feels thick. Like it's pressing on my chest." His words slurred.

Mags swayed, hand braced to stone. "My knees... and my ears are ringing. Something's wrong. We need to get out."

Maureen's flashlight dipped. "I feel... dizzy. Can't... focus."

They turned in a scramble, beams jittering across slick walls, panic quickening their breath. The exit was in sight — daylight spilling thinly across the stone — but it looked farther than it should, receding with every step.

Austin yanked a satellite beacon from his pack. His thumb mashed the SOS. A hollow roar filled his ears, drowning out Maureen's shout. His vision tunneled, the edges closing to black.

He staggered, collapsing less than three feet from the opening.

The device blinked steadily in the dark.

2

The mist from the Fin del Mundo waterfall cooled Lucía's skin, the roar drowning out the chatter of six volunteers nearby. Evening light turned the Putumayo valley gold.

Then a gasp cut through the noise."¡Miren el agua!"

Lucía turned. At the base of the falls, the pool shimmered — then began to glow. A faint blue-green light pulsed beneath the froth.

The group scrambled to their feet, muttering in Spanish and Kichwa."It's poison," Esteban whispered."The spirits are angry," an older woman said, clutching her necklace.

The glow brightened, wrong and unnatural. Panic rose. Lucía stepped forward, voice cutting clean. "Tranquilos. We don't know what it is yet. Stay calm."

They quieted, but unease lingered. Lucía's hand brushed the grip of her machete. The forest felt too still.

A harsh rustle above made her glance up. A grackle landed on a low branch, belly flashing blood-red. Apamuy. Her grandmother's voice came back: *When Apamuy calls, the forest's breath goes wrong.*

The bird croaked once, a grating crrrck. Lucía spat. "Bad sign."

A distant engine shattered the silence. A battered motorbike skidded into the clearing, a man limping as he slid off. Behind him a young woman clutched a limp child.

Lucía sprinted to meet them. "What happened?"

“He went near the waterfall!” the woman sobbed. “He came back like this!”

They laid the boy down. His chest fluttered shallowly, lips pale, eyes glassy. Then he went still.

Lucía dropped to her knees, pressing hard into his sternum. “Breathe,” she snapped. Rhythm, pressure, sweat stinging her eyes. She’d kept comrades alive with worse — but this was no bullet. This was something unseen.

The mother’s wail rose over the roar of the falls. Minutes passed. The boy’s pulse slipped away. Lucía sat back, breath heaving, jungle silent as stone.

“¿Qué hacemos?” Camilo whispered.

Lucía’s gaze cut to the treeline. A flicker of red. The grackle again, watching.

She clenched her jaw. Only one person might make sense of this.

“Camilo,” she said, voice low. “Keep everyone away from the water. I’m making a call.”

3

Dr. Sabine Reinhardt pressed the heel of her boot into the red earth, firming the soil around the pau-brasil sapling. Sweat stung her temples and ran down the side of her face. She ignored it. The air smelled of loam and guava and leaf mold—real air, damp and imperfect, not the conditioned sterility of hotels, conference halls, and secure briefing rooms.

"This one will make it," she said.

Helio grunted and worked the dirt with both hands, fingers patient and sure. Eighty-six years lived in those hands. He didn't flatter. He planted.

Sabine let the rhythm take her. Dig. Set. Firm. Move on. There was comfort in work small enough to finish with your own body.

"You don't talk to them," Helio said.

She looked up. "The volunteers?"

"The trees." He straightened slowly and brushed his palms together. "You plant like you're filling out forms. Efficient. Quiet."

Sabine gave him a tired smile. "That sounds like criticism."

"It is criticism." He nodded toward the sapling. "If you want it to grow, tell it something. Promise you'll come back."

The leaves trembled in the faint breeze. For a moment she almost laughed. Instead, she crouched again, one hand resting lightly on the thin stem.

What promise do I have left?

Still, she bent close and said quietly, "Live. Even if we can't get it right, live anyway."

One corner of Helio's mouth twitched. It was all the approval she was likely to get.

Beyond the tree line, traffic murmured from the road. Somewhere higher up, a marmoset barked and then went silent. Volunteers moved in loose clusters among the rows—students, local families, activists, a few people who looked as if they had simply wandered in and found themselves handed a shovel. It was messy, underorganized, and real.

"How many trees have you planted?" Sabine asked.

Helio squinted toward the distant skyline. "Forty-six thousand. Maybe more. I stopped counting." He shrugged. "Trees don't ask for statistics. Just space and time."

Sabine smiled despite herself. "More effective than every conference I ever attended."

"That's not saying much."

A dry laugh passed between them.

Helio eased another sapling into its hole and glanced at her without lifting his head. "Tell me something, doctora. Why are you here with me, when you had the big stage? Paris. Cameras. The G20. You could have stayed there, talking to presidents and prime ministers." He pressed soil around the roots with both thumbs. "Instead you kneel in the dirt with old men."

Sabine tamped the soil slowly, buying herself a moment. "Because the big stage doesn't change what happens here."

Helio kept working.

"And because," she said, "the last time I stood in that spotlight, it nearly destroyed more than just me."

He looked at her then said, "Most people would kill for that kind of power. For the chance to be heard."

She brushed dirt from her palms and met his gaze. "Being heard isn't the same as having any control over what follows. And I was nearly killed because of that spotlight."

Helio studied her for a beat, then nodded once, as though filing the answer with the rest of the things he knew and did not intend to comment on.

"So now you hide here in my little project?"

Sabine looked down the line of new saplings, each one no taller than her knee. "Better to help something small take root than stand in the lights and watch everything burn."

It came out sharper than she intended. Helio said nothing. He only pressed the next sapling into place and handed her the trowel.

Nearby, a girl in muddy sneakers straightened and held up her phone. "Another ten for the leaderboard!"

A couple of the others cheered.

Sabine glanced over. "Leaderboard?"

"GreenPulse," the girl said, beaming. Soil streaked both forearms to the elbow. "It tracks your eco-score. Trees planted, plastic collected, water saved. You get credits and unlock tiers."

Helio made a low sound in his throat. "The craze. They log the work, the app spits out rewards. Training, recycled gear, sometimes cash. As long as they keep planting, I don't complain."

The girl stepped closer and held out the phone. The interface was sleek, bright, frictionless—leaf icons, progress rings, regional rankings, a small animation blooming across the screen each time a task was logged.

"Who runs it?" Sabine asked.

The girl shrugged. "Some global alliance, I think. Nonprofit maybe."

Sabine handed the phone back. "Looks efficient."

The girl laughed as if that were praise and hurried off to rejoin her group.

Sabine watched her go. The app had the look she had learned to distrust: elegant abstraction laid over messy human behavior, a polished system offering incentives while hiding the machinery underneath. Maybe it was harmless.

Maybe it planted more trees than it distorted. Still, the sight of it left a small cold place between her shoulders.

Then the Blackphone buzzed against her thigh.

Sabine went still.

Very few people had that number. Fewer still would use it.

She pulled it out and saw the name on the screen.

Lucía.

The old reflex hit before thought did: a tightening in the chest, a sharpened pulse, the body recognizing danger faster than the mind would admit it. She had not spoken to Lucía since Europe, since the collapse of everything she had once called work, since she had walked away from the ISMC, from classified briefings, from official responsibility, from the poisonous illusion that proximity to power meant influence over outcomes.

She had left all of that behind on purpose.

She answered anyway.

"Lucía?"

"Sabine." The voice on the line was taut and thinner than she remembered. Insects pulsed in the background. Water moved somewhere nearby. "Something's happening in the Putumayo. It's wrong."

Sabine closed her eyes.

"A child died," Lucía said. "No wounds. No fever I can see. Nothing that makes sense. And the water—"

Static tore across the line, swallowing the last few words. Then the signal steadied again.

"I need you to come," Lucía said. "I need someone who sees what others don't."

Sabine tightened her grip on the phone until the edge bit into her palm.

This was how it began. Not with declarations or headlines. With one frightened voice calling from far away and asking her to step back into the machinery she had barely escaped the first time.

She looked at the rows of saplings, at Helio bent over his work, at the volunteers laughing and passing buckets of soil. Small things. Real things. Things that did not require clearance or armed escorts or explanations to grieving families.

"I'm sorry," she said, and heard the strain in her own voice. "I can't."

The answer hung between them.

Lucía did not argue.

At last she said, "I'll send you what we found. You can pretend to ignore it."

The line went dead.

Sabine kept the phone in her hand for a moment after the call ended, staring at the dark screen as if it might light again and relieve her of the choice by making it for her.

It would. She knew it would.

Whatever Lucía sent, she would open it. Maybe not here. Maybe not in the next minute. But she would. The refusal had left her mouth; it had not reached the part of her that mattered.

A gust moved through the saplings, stirring the thin leaves in a single dry whisper.

At the edge of the tree line, something dark flickered between the trunks—slender body, long legs, a pale throat flashing white against black.

The bird stood perfectly still, watching.

Sabine felt the hairs lift along her arms.

Then it slipped into the undergrowth and was gone.

Around her, the volunteers were still talking, still digging, still laughing, but the sound seemed suddenly farther away. The grove had taken on a waiting quality, as if something had already crossed a threshold and was only allowing her a few final moments to pretend otherwise.

4

Karoline Reinhardt sat alone in the Berlin newsroom, her laptop casting a pale glow across the cluttered desk. Outside, winter pressed against the city, dark and muffled, but her mind had the restless charge that came when a story had not proven itself but refused to let go.

The video looped again on her screen.

At first it was only noise and motion: blurred green, rotor wash, a camera struggling to hold steady. Then the image resolved into a towering ceiba tree rising above the canopy, its trunk caught in the violent sweep of a helicopter spotlight.

"Descend immediately!"

The loudspeaker cracked so hard her speakers rattled. "You are trespassing on private property. This is your final warning."

The man in the tree lifted his chin and did not flinch.

He was young, lean, soaked through with sweat, one arm wrapped around the trunk as the canopy shuddered around him. From his pack he pulled a banner, snapped it open, and let the words unfurl into the rotor wash.

THE FOREST IS LIFE.

The cloth whipped sideways in the downdraft. Below him, workers in hi-vis vests stood frozen in a clearing hacked from the jungle, chainsaws hanging idle.

The spotlight pinned him against the trunk. He pressed one palm to the bark, then raised the satellite phone toward himself until his face filled the frame.

"My name is Yari Cuatindioy," he said. "I am Kamsá. My people have lived in the Putumayo longer than your machines, longer than Colombia itself. This forest is not property. It is life."

The helicopter dipped lower, rotors screaming.

"The law calls this Indigenous land," Yari shouted. "The companies call it profit. They think we are too small to matter."

He hauled the banner higher against the storm of air.

"We are not small. We are not silent. The forest is alive. It listens. And so do we."

The helicopter banked closer. The downdraft slammed the banner sideways. Yari braced himself against the trunk, jaw set.

The clip cut there.

Karoline dragged the cursor back and played it again.

This time she watched the clearing, not Yari. The cut lines through the trees. The lights. The machinery. The unmistakable geometry of a place being forced into industrial order.

In a second window sat the notes she had been building over the past week: local reports, permit fragments, activist posts, site chatter, and one strange mention from near Fin del Mundo about glowing water and a dead child. None of it was clean enough to print. Not yet. But the fragments were beginning to lean toward one another.

She grabbed her laptop and stood.

The newsroom was nearly empty, the hour late enough that the normal hum had thinned to distant keyboards and the soft mechanical breathing of climate control. Beyond the windows, Berlin lay dark and glassy under winter.

Her new editor sat in the glass-walled office at the far end, sleeves rolled, a tablet propped in one hand. She still thought of Julia sometimes at moments like this—Julia's steadiness, her instinct for when a story was real before the proof had fully arrived. Julia had left six months earlier. The loss still sat in the room.

Markus, the man in front of her was sharp, efficient, and far less forgiving.

Karoline set the laptop on his desk and hit play without preamble.

He watched the clip once through, expression unchanged. When it ended, he replayed the last few seconds.

"Strong footage," he said.

"That's not the point."

"No," he said. "The point is whether this is a story or an activist video with good timing."

"It's a lede."

"It's a man in a tree with a speech."

Her jaw tightened. "If they're using carbon capture language to cover ordinary extraction, that matters."

"Then bring me something we can stand on." He tapped the desk once. "Contracts. Internal decks. Permits that contradict public claims. Technical data. Something a lawyer can read without reaching for aspirin."

Karoline opened her notes window. "There are local reports of strange water near Fin del Mundo. One post mentions a child dead after exposure. I've got chatter around injection activity and site expansion, but nothing solid yet."

That made him look up.

"Glowing water?"

She nodded. "Probably contamination. Maybe gas migration. Maybe something else. But it's in the same zone."

His skepticism shifted, not gone but recalibrated. He looked at Yari frozen on the screen, banner twisted in the downdraft.

"That," he said, "is either nothing or your real way in. Not the rhetoric. The anomaly."

Karoline said nothing.

He handed the laptop back to her. "If there's something at Fin del Mundo, that's where the story lives."

She slid the computer into her bag and walked out before he could add anything else.

The newsroom felt darker now, the monitors less like tools than watchful eyes. She moved between the desks, through the glass doors, down the stairwell, and out into the Berlin night.

Cold bit immediately at her cheeks. Her breath fogged under the streetlight. She stopped under the awning for a moment and saw it again: the ceiba, the spotlight, the banner, the chainsaws waiting below.

Half a world away, someone near Fin del Mundo was posting about glowing water and a dead child.

Karoline felt it then—that small, hard click she had learned to trust. The moment a story stopped being interesting and became dangerous.

She stepped into the cold and started walking.

5

Dr. Martín Chasoy crouched at the base of a buttressed trunk, one knee in the wet leaf litter, the slim field tablet balanced against his palm. Sweat ran in a line down his spine beneath his shirt. The Putumayo forest pressed close around him—damp soil, orchid musk, insect hum, and the soft rot of things returning themselves to earth.

On the screen, his buried nanosensor grid pulsed through its usual rhythms.

For six months he had been mapping signal exchange through the mycelial mesh below the forest floor, training himself to recognize the ordinary variations: moisture shifts after rain, root interference, dead patches, nutrient surges, the little distortions caused by an animal stepping too close to a node. The network was never silent. It murmured constantly, a thousand small negotiations carried in chemistry, voltage, and response.

Today there was something different. Martín frowned and thumbed back through the last two minutes of data. One band on the display had begun to shear away from the rest—not random scatter, not the stuttering collapse of a failing sensor, but a clean irregularity layered inside the fungal baseline. He adjusted the filter and watched it separate more clearly.

A second rhythm.

He stayed very still.

If it had been one node, he would have marked it for inspection and moved on. If it had been broad-spectrum distortion, he would have blamed weather or interference. But the same pattern was appearing across multiple checkpoints, phase-shifted but coherent, as if something were moving through the mesh and teaching each node how to repeat it.

Martín tapped open the diagnostics. Battery stability normal. Node integrity normal. Signal latency within tolerance. He felt the skin along his forearms tighten. He remembered something his grandfather had told him when he was small enough to walk under a curassow snare without ducking, that the forest kept its secrets until it decided otherwise. When it spoke plainly, you listened. When it spoke strangely, you listened harder.

At the university he had learned to translate those instincts into cleaner language. Pattern recognition. Environmental feedback. Sensor anomaly. But the older warning lived underneath the newer one, and both were awake now.

He rose slowly, brushing mud from his knee, and turned in a slow circle with the tablet in his hand.

The anomaly strengthened to the south.

Not in one jump, but in a pull—subtle at first, then unmistakable once he watched three sequential nodes update. Node 14A. Then 14C. Then the riverbank cluster beyond them. Each carried the same irregular band, slightly stronger than the last.

Directional.

Martín slid the tablet into one hand and shouldered his pack. To the outside world he was Dr. Martín Chasoy, an environmental systems lecturer at the Instituto Tecnológico del Putumayo in Mocoa, Colombia where he also collaborated with the institute's natural-resources research group and was field lead on a monitoring program most officials only half understood. Here, moving between trees his family had known longer than any institution had known him, he was also his grandfather's grandson, taught to read ground, water, and silence before he ever learned to read a paper abstract.

He followed the signal downslope.

The trail was hardly a trail at all, only a thinning of undergrowth where runoff had carved a preference into the earth. Branches brushed his sleeves. Gnats found the sweat on his neck. Somewhere above him a monkey crashed through leaves, then was gone. He checked the tablet twice in twenty meters. The anomaly held, brightening as he approached the river corridor.

At the next sensor post, he crouched and checked the node housing by hand.

No visible damage. No condensation breach. No gnaw marks. The signal ran clean through it and onward.

Martín swallowed and moved on.

By the time he reached the shallows near the bank, his heartbeat had settled into that narrow, concentrated rhythm he knew from fieldwork—the body's way of making room for attention. He stepped through a patch of sedge and felt cold water seep over the toe of his boot.

He looked down.

At first he thought the light was a reflection. A torn piece of sky caught in standing water.

Then the puddle shifted.

Green and blue iridescence moved beneath the surface in thin living ribbons, not bright enough to cast light outward, but bright enough to be unmistakable against the brown of the mud. It gathered along the edge of the water and threaded around decomposing leaves like dye spreading through capillaries.

Martín stopped breathing for a beat.

He lowered himself carefully, one hand braced on his thigh, the other already reaching for the sample kit clipped to his pack. The tablet screen threw a dim glow across his wrist. The anomaly band was peaking now, close enough that the display had begun issuing soft haptic pulses against his palm.

No obvious petrochemical sheen. No diesel rainbow. No simple explanation announced itself.

He leaned closer.

A harsh cry split the canopy.

Martín jerked his head up just as a dark bird dropped from the branches and landed on the narrow antenna mast of the nearest sensor post. Its feathers flashed oily black. It cocked its head once, pale throat bright against the shadow of its body, then struck the metal housing with its beak.

The tablet shrilled.

The signal surged so violently that the display auto-scaled to contain it. The anomaly band spiked straight through the baseline, no longer layered quietly beneath the fungal chatter but riding above it, insistent, almost rhythmic.

The bird struck the mast again.

Martín stared at the screen, then at the glowing water, then back at the node as the pulses in his hand came faster.

This was no dead sensor. No field artifact. No ordinary contamination pattern he understood.

The forest had gone strangely still around him, as if the usual insect noise had pulled back to the edges to make room.

Martín felt, with sudden and irrational certainty, that he was no longer only observing a signal.

Something was trying to speak.

6

The highway narrowed to a cracked strip of asphalt before giving up altogether. Jose flicked on his signal out of habit and turned onto a secondary road that looked less built than carved—gravel, exposed roots, mud gone hard in the ruts. The SUV lurched hard enough to knock Karoline's shoulder against the door. Branches dragged along the windows with a dry, needling scrape.

"How much farther?" she asked.

Jose kept his eyes on the road. "Kilometers or time?"

She glanced over. "Are they that different?"

"The distance is not bad." He steered around a washout and dropped the right wheels into the next rut with a jarring thud. "The time depends on who wants to stop you."

Karoline steadied her notebook against her knee, then gave up and closed it. "How long until the protest?"

"If everything goes well, less than an hour."

She caught the phrasing immediately. "If?"

Jose did not answer at once. The jungle had begun to crowd the road so tightly that the branches seemed to lean in and listen.

"This is RegenX territory now," he said at last. "Out here, smooth is never guaranteed."

For the next forty minutes they crawled forward through dense green heat. The farther they went, the less the road felt public. There were no houses. No roadside stalls. No children. Only the track ahead, the pressed-in jungle, and the sense that they had already passed some point where turning around would not restore anything.

Then Jose said, quietly, "At the checkpoint, you are not a journalist."

Karoline turned to him. "What am I?"

"My wife's cousin. Visiting from Europe. I am showing you the ridge."

"And if I'm not?"

"Then we do not get through."

She stared at him. "They can't just decide that."

He gave her a brief look. "That is exactly what they do."

The road bent sharply. Beyond it stood a steel barrier arm, a prefab hut, and two pickup trucks parked at angles that made it clear no one passed without permission. Four armed men stepped into the road as the SUV rolled forward, rifles hanging low and easy in the practiced way that made them more alarming, not less.

Jose slowed to a stop.

One of the men came to Karoline's side and rapped twice on the glass before she lowered it halfway. He wore mirrored sunglasses despite the shade.

"You are on RegenX property," he said. "State your business."

Jose smiled and reached over with their identification. "My wife's cousin is visiting. I'm taking her to see the view."

The man looked at the cards, then at Karoline, then back at Jose. Another had already moved behind the vehicle. She could hear gravel crunch under his boots.

"No stopping," the first guard said. "No photos. No wandering. Straight through. If you're found trespassing, you'll be prosecuted."

"Entendido," Jose said.

The guard's gaze returned to Karoline and stayed there a beat too long, cold and inventorying. Then he stepped back and lifted a hand.

Jose drove on.

Neither of them spoke until the checkpoint disappeared behind them.

Karoline glanced into the side mirror. The barrier had already vanished behind dust and foliage. Still, she could not shake the feeling that passing through had changed nothing except that someone now knew she had.

"No press," she said.

"No assumptions," Jose replied.

A second checkpoint appeared twenty minutes later, smaller and looser: one truck, one man, one lifted hand after he recognized Jose's vehicle. They barely slowed.

That unsettled her more than the first one.

By the time they reached the ceibo, the road had run out.

The tree rose from the clearing like something that had been there before the argument and would remain after it. A banner hung against the trunk in black block letters:

THE FOREST IS LIFE

At its base stood a loose ring of men in rubber boots and mismatched work clothes. Not soldiers. Not mercenaries. Just people who had stayed.

One of them approached as Jose killed the engine.

"Who are you?" he asked. "Why are you here?"

"My friend wants to speak to Yari," Jose said.

The man glanced up into the canopy. "Can she climb?"

"No."

"Then she won't speak to him. He isn't coming down."

Jose tipped his head toward Karoline. "She's an international journalist. She wants his story."

The man looked at her properly then, not with checkpoint suspicion but with something narrower and more useful: risk calculation.

He held out his hand. "Card. Number. I'll pass it up. If he wants to talk, he'll call."

Karoline reached into her bag and gave him one.

"You're guarding him?" she asked.

"As best we can."

She looked around the clearing, then back down the road they had come. “You don’t look like much of a match for the men at the checkpoint.”

A thin smile touched his face. “We’re not.”

“Then what stops them?”

He glanced up into the branches. “Witnesses. Phones. Timing. If RegenX makes a move, Yari broadcasts from above. They want control. They don’t want another dead protester circulating by dinner.”

Karoline followed his gaze, but the canopy swallowed the upper limbs whole. Yari was up there somewhere, hidden in leaf and mist, above the reach of conversation and below the reach of safety.

The man tucked her card into his pocket.

“Take your pictures,” he said. “Get your story. Because once they know who you are, you won’t set foot here again.”

7

Jose guided them back onto the main highway, the tires humming over patched asphalt after the punishing road to the ceibo. For a few minutes neither of them spoke.

Karoline pulled out her phone. "I need to check in with my editor."

Jose shrugged. "Of course."

Markus answered on the second ring. "Tell me you have something."

"I have enough to know they're scared," Karoline said. "Checkpoints, armed company security, controlled access all the way up to Yari's camp. If I hadn't come in with Jose, I wouldn't have made it past the first barrier."

"And Yari?"

"Still in the tree. I left my card with his people. If he wants to talk, he'll call."

A beat of silence.

"Fine," Markus said. "Then listen carefully. The Fin del Mundo lead just improved."

Karoline straightened. "What happened?"

"I've got fresh images from the area. Same glow we discussed before, only clearer. And four American hikers launched an emergency beacon from near the falls."

"Do we know what happened to them?"

"No." Markus let that sit. "That's the point."

Karoline turned to Jose. "How long to Fin del Mundo from here?"

He frowned, thinking. "If we head through Mocoa and go up the back way, maybe three hours. Less if we switch to my bike."

She relayed it.

"Go," Markus said.

Karoline looked back through the rear window, though the ceibo and the checkpoints were long gone, swallowed by jungle and distance. "Yari's still the story."

"Yes," Markus said. "But he may not be the story that breaks first."

She said nothing.

"In Berlin we had a protest, some rumors, and a bad feeling," he said. "Now we have fresh images, a beacon launch, and possible casualties in the same zone. That's what gets click through."

Karoline pressed the phone harder against her ear.

"Get to the falls," Markus said. "Find out what happened. If Yari calls, you take it. But right now Fin del Mundo is where this is moving."

"All right," she said.

"Call me when you get there."

He hung up.

Karoline lowered the phone. The jungle outside looked unchanged, but the story had shifted underneath it.

Jose glanced over. "We're changing direction?"

"Yes."

"Toward the waterfall?"

She nodded. "How close to the hotel are we going?"

"My bike is on the next street over."

"OK. Drop me at my hotel for a couple of minutes, I need to change if we're riding a bike into the jungle."

Yari had brought her into the field. Fin del Mundo might tell her what the field was hiding.

8

Karoline was half way through changing her clothes when her phone chimed. She reached for it without looking, expecting Markus.

The subject line stopped her cold.

Glowing Water – Urgent Data

She finished pulling her shirt over head and read the short message.

Good evening, Ms. Reinhardt. I understand you are looking into the glowing water mystery in the Putumayo region of Colombia. I have gathered data I believe may be useful to you. The secure link below contains everything relevant to your investigation.

—A concerned citizen of the world

She stared at the screen.

Not the wording. The knowledge.

She had discussed Fin del Mundo with Markus. She had spoken to Jose. She had asked questions in the field. That was enough, maybe, in a place where enough eyes were always watching. Still, the message landed with a private, invasive force, as if someone had reached through the dark and touched the edge of her notebook.

She checked the sender information, then the routing, then the link itself.

Not clean enough to trust. Not sloppy enough to dismiss.

After a second round of precautions, she opened it.

The folder that bloomed across her screen was dense enough to make her sit forward. Maps. Geotagged photographs. Chemical tables. Seismic traces. Topographic overlays. Subsurface scans. Signal plots she couldn't immediately place. Not random junk. Too structured for that. But whether it was evidence or fabrication, she couldn't yet tell.

Karoline scrolled slowly, forcing herself not to jump at patterns just because she wanted one.

Whoever had sent this knew what she was looking at, or knew how to imitate someone who did.

She exhaled and let the laptop rest against her knees.

"This is either gold," she murmured, "or bait."

Markus could tell her whether it was usable as a story package. He could not tell her whether it meant anything. She needed someone who could look at the material and distinguish data from performance.

Her thumb hovered over her contacts.

Then stopped at Sabine.

Karoline stared at the name for a long moment.

She still had not told her sister she was in Colombia. Had not explained why. Had not asked whether she wanted to know. Sabine had retreated from enough already. Karoline knew that. But she also knew there were very few people alive who could look at a strange pattern and resist both panic and easy explanation.

She pressed call.

Sabine answered on the second ring. "You're calling at a reasonable hour. That's suspicious."

Despite herself, Karoline smiled. "No ocean between us this time."

"Depends where you are."

"I'm in Colombia."

A pause.

"And I'm in São Paulo," Sabine said. "So not no ocean. Just trees instead of water. What happened?"

Karoline looked back at the screen. “I just arrived and someone sent me a data dump. Anonymous. They knew I was asking about glowing water.”

Sabine said nothing.

“There are maps, chemistry tables, subsurface scans—at least I think that’s what they are. Seismic-looking traces. Signal plots. It could be real. It could be garbage dressed up to look real. I can’t tell.”

“Why are they sending it to you?”

“Good question.”

Another pause, shorter this time. Karoline could hear Sabine thinking, withdrawing and leaning in at once.

“Line,” Sabine said, “that isn’t my field.”

“I know.”

“I’m serious. Climate modeling is not geochemistry. It isn’t geology. I haven’t spent years in subsurface datasets.”

“No, Bine,” Karoline kept her voice level. “But you do know what real systems look like when they start behaving strangely.”

She could hear that land.

Sabine let out a breath. “You always did know how to make a thin argument sound reasonable.”

“I learned from professionals.”

“That is not flattering.”

Karoline’s smile faded as quickly as it had come. “I’m not asking you to solve it. Just look. Tell me if it’s nonsense. Or if it isn’t.”

On the other end of the line, she heard a shift in ambient sound—movement, maybe, or Sabine standing up and walking away from someone else.

“I’m trying very hard,” Sabine said, “to build a life that does not begin with anonymous files and bad instincts.”

“I know.”

“I mean that, Line.”

“I know.”

The silence that followed was not empty. It was history, strain, affection, and the accumulated cost of everything they did not say.

At last Sabine said, "Send me the link."

Karoline closed her eyes briefly. Not relief exactly. Something tighter than that.

"You'll look?"

"I'll look," Sabine said. "That is not the same as getting involved."

Karoline glanced at the files again, the graphs and overlays and unlabeled traces waiting in neat rows. "Right."

"And if it's nonsense," Sabine said, her voice sharpening just slightly, "I am going to tell you it's nonsense."

"That's why I called you."

A beat.

"How secure is the link?"

"Not secure enough for my taste."

"That's an alarming answer."

"It's been a strange day."

"I gathered that."

Karoline hesitated, then said, more quietly, "I'm glad you picked up."

Sabine's answer took a second longer than the others. "Send it before I change my mind."

The line clicked dead.

Karoline sat motionless for a moment, phone still in her hand. Then she forwarded the file package through a secure relay and watched the progress bar crawl across the screen.

When it finished, she looked back at the anonymous message.

A concerned citizen of the world.

No. Not concern. Intention.

Someone wanted this seen. Someone wanted it seen by her. And now, whether Sabine liked it or not, by Sabine too.

The roar of a motorcycle broke Karoline's deep thought.

9

Initially, Karoline didn't understand why Jose thought the motorbike was the right choice for this trek. The road was mostly paved and twisty as they rode the switchbacks up the ridge. It wasn't until they left the main road and headed along the ridge towards the falls that the path quickly narrowed to mud, stone, and exposed roots under the tires. The canopy closed over them in patches, turning the light green and uncertain. Branches whipped her helmet and shoulders until one snapped hard across her visor and she smacked Jose's back.

He braked at once and dropped a boot to the ground.

"What is wrong, señora?"

"My spine is filing a formal complaint," she said, pulling off one glove long enough to rub her lower back. "How much farther?"

Jose looked up the track, as if distance in a place like this could be read off leaves and slope. "Another 15 minutes maybe."

She nodded to him, "I hope you're right. My back isn't going to handle much more of this."

"In the jungle, it is never distance." He nudged the front wheel around a rock.

Karoline muttered something unprintable and was about to wave him onward when Jose went still.

He lifted one finger to his lips and pointed into the branches above them.

A grackle perched high in the canopy, black feathers catching the broken light. As it shifted, its belly flashed a deep, improbable red.

"Watching us," Jose whispered.

Karoline squinted through the leaves. "It's just a bird."

"In our stories, when the forest is wounded, it sends a watcher." He did not take his eyes off it. "If it follows you, be careful."

She gave a soft, skeptical laugh, but the bird did not move. It seemed less perched than stationed there, as if it had arrived first and was waiting for them to catch up.

Jose kicked the bike back into gear.

The trail cut along a rock face a few minutes later, and the temperature dropped abruptly. On their left, a dark opening yawned in the stone.

Jose slowed. "This is where the rescue beacon was traced."

Karoline swung off the bike before he had fully stopped. The cave mouth was larger than she expected, a black wound in the hillside, cold air breathing out of it. She crouched and swept her flashlight across the ground.

A torn backpack strap lay half-buried in the dirt. A crushed water bottle. Scuffed earth where boots had slid or scrambled toward the opening. Not staged. Not clean. The remains of panic had a look of their own.

Her stomach tightened.

"Where are they?"

Jose stayed by the bike, listening to the forest the way he always seemed to. "They say rescue crews came."

"They say?"

He looked at her. "No one saw bodies leave. Only a truck." Karoline swung the beam once more into the cave, but the light vanished a few meters in, swallowed whole.

A harsh croak broke the silence.

The grackle sat above the cave mouth now, red belly dark in the shade, head tipped slightly as if considering them.

Karoline lowered the flashlight. For one irrational moment, she had the sense that the cave, the bird, the missing hikers and the glowing water were linked by something she could not yet name

She climbed back on behind Jose without speaking.

The trail rose again, then opened so abruptly that she caught her breath.

Fin del Mundo.

The river hurled itself over the cliff in a blue-green plunge, the water bright with that same impossible glow she had seen in the images—more vivid here, alive inside the plunge pool and the racing current below. Mist drifted upward in slow veils. The place should have been beautiful. Instead, it felt wrong in a way her body recognized before her mind could name it.

Jose crossed himself.

"Bad omen," he said. "The animals avoid this place."

Above them, the grackle shifted and gave a single rough cry.

Karoline lifted her camera and took the shot anyway: the glowing falls, the mist, the dark bird balanced above it all.

Then she crouched near the bank.

"Karoline," Jose said.

She barely heard him. Up close, the glow moved in strands and pockets, not like reflected sky, not like oil, not like anything she trusted. If the anonymous files were real, this was the first thing she could actually hold against them. Evidence. Something to test. Something that belonged to the world and not just to rumor.

She took the sample bottle from her pack.

Jose was beside her now. "Be careful, it's dangerous."

"I know."

"No. You do not." His voice sharpened. "The ground is bad."

She looked at the water, then at the bottle in her hand. If she went back with photographs alone, someone could call it light, algae, trick photography, whatever they liked. A sample was different. A sample could argue.

She edged forward, one boot testing the mud, then another. The bank looked slick but firm enough. She leaned out, arm extended.

The ground gave way.

There was no warning, only motion. Mud sheared out beneath her boot and the slope vanished. The water hit her leg with a force that felt almost sentient, shockingly strong, and immediate. The bottle flew from her hand. She went down to one knee, then farther, the current dragging at her hip as if it had been waiting for her weight.

She grabbed for the bank and came up with roots and mud. Both tore free.

The water climbed to her waist as she was sucked in with a force that kept building instead of breaking. For one crazed instant she understood how easy it would be to disappear here. No clean scream, no cinematic plunge. Just a body taken and folded under glowing water.

Jose hit her from the side hard enough to bruise, one hand locking in the back of her jacket, the other digging for purchase. His boots slid once, caught, slid again.

"Hold!"

She tried, but there was nothing to hold. Mud came away in her fists. The river pulled harder.

Jose swore and heaved with his whole body. The jacket cut into her throat. Something in her shoulder screamed. Then the current lost her and she came free in a rush, both of them crashing backward onto solid ground.

For a few seconds neither moved.

Karoline lay flat on her back, sucking air, the sky spinning above her in pieces between branches and mist. Her flashlight was gone. So was the sample bottle. Her legs shook so badly she could feel it in her teeth.

Beside them, the river went on glowing.

Jose rolled onto one elbow and looked down at the water with naked dislike. "The river did not want to give you back."

She might have laughed on another day. She did not laugh now. She looked at Jose, then at the river. Then she pulled another sample bottle from her pack, crawled to the bank, and reached down to fill it. This time the ground held.

By the time they started back, dusk had collapsed into full dark.

The motorbike's headlamp cut a narrow cone through the brush as they worked their way back to the main road and began their descent. The turns came tight and blind, one after another, the uphill wall on one side and a drop into blackness on the other. Jose rode more slowly now, the earlier impatience gone. Karoline held tighter than before.

Ahead, red lights appeared around a bend, then vanished.

Jose straightened. "Truck."

They rounded the curve and found it: a pale tanker crawling downhill, brake lights pulsing red through the dark. Anonymous. No company markings she could see. Too large for the road and entirely comfortable on it.

Jose eased back and matched its speed.

At first Karoline thought the problem was fear.

Then she realized she could not get a full breath.

She inhaled and waited for the ordinary relief. It did not come. The air entered, but something in it felt thin, unfinished, useless. She pressed closer to Jose's back, as if proximity might steady her.

The truck braked into the next curve. Jose braked too.

Her head felt light.

Another bend. Rock wall to the left, jungle and open dark to the right. The tanker's lights smeared briefly, as if she were seeing them through water.

"Jose," she said.

Or meant to. The name came out soft and incomplete.

He shifted down and tried to widen the gap.

The air changed again.

Heavier here. Trapped.

Karoline's pulse climbed fast and shallow. The curve ahead flattened oddly, depth draining out of it. She knew something was wrong with terrifying clarity and almost no ability to hold the thought in place long enough to use it.

Jose corrected their line once. Then again.

This time the bike lagged.

Not a skid. Something slower. A delay between intention and response.

Jose swore under his breath and squeezed the brake harder.

The truck slowed harder too.

They entered a cut in the road where the rock rose close on the left and the trees fell away into darkness on the right. The air in the notch felt cold against her face and impossibly dense.

Her vision tunneled.

Jose leaned into the next turn.

The bike did not follow.

The front tire clipped loose gravel near the edge. The rear slid sideways. For one suspended instant they were no longer descending but hanging, the road dropping away beneath them while gravity made up its mind.

Then it did.

Karoline felt herself lift free of the bike before she understood she had been thrown. Leaves slapped her face. Branches tore at her jacket and hair and arms. Something struck her shoulder hard enough to flash white through her skull. Something caught her leg and twisted it. The fall broke in violent stages—impact, spin, scrape, another impact—until the jungle floor rose up and hit her for good.

Darkness took her.

When she came back, the earth was under her cheek and the jungle was breathing around her.

She dragged in air—real air this time, wet and heavy and usable—and pain lit up everywhere at once. Shoulder. Ribs. Hip. One knee burning. Her mouth full of dirt.

For a few seconds she had no idea where up was.

Then sound returned.

A dull impact from somewhere near the road above. Not sharp. Not explosive. Just heavy and final.

Then the truck's engine, labouring briefly as it took the next bend. Brakes hissing. Weight moving on.

Leaving.

"Jose!"

Her voice vanished into the trees.

No answer.

She tried to move and nearly blacked out. Above her, the road had erased itself. No headlamp. No taillights. No shape of the bike. Just a scrap of darkness where the slope climbed back toward what had thrown her off it.

Then even the truck was gone.

The insects came back first, loud and indifferent.

Karoline lay still, listening for Jose, for an engine, for voices, for anything human.

There was nothing left to hear but her own breathing.

10

Sabine Reinhardt had been reading without taking in a word for the last ten minutes.

The novel lay open in one hand, face-down enough to mark her place if she gave up pretending. Beyond the balcony doors, São Paulo moved in its usual distant register—traffic, a motorcycle somewhere below, the city refusing the idea of sleep. On the nightstand sat a heavy tumbler of Kräuterlikör, half-drained. She took it in small amounts, not for pleasure exactly, but for ritual. Bitter herbs, a taste of home, something measured and familiar at the end of the day.

Her phone buzzed against the wood. Sabine glanced at the screen and exhaled through her nose. Her sister, Karoline. Her thumb hovered over decline. Karoline had never believed in time zones, boundaries, or the possibility that other people might be asleep. Sabine almost let it ring out.

Almost.

Something tightened in her chest. She picked up.

"You never check the time," she said. "Line, do you know what hour it—"

"Bine..."

The word was thin, frayed, wrong.

Sabine sat up.

"It's me," Karoline said, her voice barely holding together. "Motorcycle accident. My leg's bad."

The tumbler rocked on the nightstand as Sabine set the book aside too fast. "Line? Where are you?"

"In the jungle." A breath, sharp and uneven. "I got a sample. The glowing water. I'm hurt."

Static tore through the line. Sabine pressed the phone harder to her ear, as if force could clear it.

"Karoline, listen to me. Tell me where you are."

"One road. Narrow. Twisting." Karoline's voice dipped, then came back thinner. "Jose was with me. I haven't heard him move."

Sabine swung her legs off the bed. "Are you alone right now?"

"I don't know."

The answer hit harder than panic would have.

"Can you send a pin?"

"No signal for that." Another ragged breath. Then, quieter: "I'm sorry, Bine. I love you. Tell Mutti I love her."

Sabine was on her feet now. "No. Don't do that. Don't say it like that." She crossed to the desk, already grabbing a pen, searching uselessly for paper while the room narrowed around the sound of Karoline trying to stay conscious. "Stay with me. Keep talking."

Silence crackled.

Then: "Cold."

Sabine shut her eyes for one second. Not to steady herself. To stop the wrong thoughts from taking shape.

"Line, listen carefully. You are not saying goodbye. Do you understand me?"

A sound came back that might have been a laugh or a swallowed cry. Then the line broke apart again.

"Karoline?"

Nothing.

"Karoline."

Still nothing.

Sabine pulled the phone away and looked at the dead screen as though it had personally failed her.

The apartment had not changed. The book was still on the bed. The bitter herbal smell of the liqueur still hung in the room. The city still murmured outside.

But retreat was gone.

She had built this life out of small, manageable things: rented rooms, planting days, routines that ended before they could widen into obligation. She had told herself that small acts of repair were enough. Honest work. Bounded work. Work that did not open the door to armed escorts, classified briefings, or the old catastrophic scale of things.

Now Karoline was injured somewhere on a mountain road in Colombia, and none of Sabine's careful limits meant anything.

She was already moving before the thought had finished. Shoes. Charger. Passport. The body knew before the mind agreed.

At the edge of the bed she stopped just long enough to press her fingers hard against her brow.

Too many risks. Too many ghosts. Too many ways back into a life she had left on purpose.

Then one name surfaced, clean and immediate.

Lucía.

Sabine grabbed the phone again and started to scroll through her contacts.

11

Sabine scrolled, found Lucía's number, and called.

The line clicked almost at once.

"Sabine?" Lucía said. Her voice was alert, not surprised. "What happened?"

"Karoline's hurt," Sabine said. "Badly. Near Fin del Mundo. How close are you?"

In the background she heard insects, distant voices, the muffled movement of people already in the field.

"We're back near the planting site," Lucía said. "Maybe twenty minutes from the falls, depending on which road."

Sabine pressed a hand against the desk. "Motorcycle accident. She said her leg was bad. She thinks Jose may be dead."

A beat. Then Lucía swore softly, already shifting into action. "Did she say where?"

"Not clearly. A narrow road. Twisting. She said they'd been at the glowing water. She got a sample."

"They came in the back way, then." Lucía was thinking aloud now, fast and controlled. "To avoid the main checkpoints. There are only a few roads bad enough to match that description."

"Could she be anywhere else?"

"If she was coming back from Fin del Mundo, not many places." Voices sharpened in the background. Lucía must have turned away from the group, because the next words came clearer. "Did she say whether they went over the side or stayed on the road?"

"No. The line was breaking up."

"All right." A pause, brief and practical. "I've got six with me. We start at the upper approach and sweep down. If the bike went off, we'll find the break in the brush."

Sabine closed her eyes for half a second. "Thank you."

"Don't thank me yet."

Sabine steadied herself against them. "I'm coming tonight. First flight I can get."

"Good. If she calls again, keep her talking as long as you can. Landmarks, sounds, anything. And send me every detail you remember from the call."

"I will."

"Then let me work."

The line went dead.

Sabine lowered the phone and stood still for one beat in the suddenly quiet room.

Then she turned toward the suitcase in the corner.

It had been sitting there untouched for months, half-hidden. She crossed the room, pulled it upright, and reached for the zipper.

12

Lucía snapped the decision into place. "Lights on. All of you, in the Jeep. We're heading downhill."

She didn't wait for questions. She swung onto the running board, boots slick with mud, one hand gripping the roll bar while the other swept her flashlight along the road's edge.

"Motorbike accident," she said. "Two riders. Survivors—if we're lucky."

The crew scrambled in behind her. The engine growled low as the Jeep eased forward, headlights tunneling into wet leaves and hanging vines. The road dropped steeply, the clay surface glazed from earlier rain.

"Slow," Lucía said. "Sweep the jungle as we move. If you see anything worth stopping for, shout. ¿Entendido?"

"¡Sí!" came the reply.

The Jeep crawled downhill, tires slipping once, then again. The driver corrected, jaw clenched.

Lucía slapped the roof. "Despacio. One mistake and we add bodies."

The jungle pressed close, branches brushing the vehicle, shadows leaping with every bend. Normally this stretch was loud—frogs, insects, distant monkeys—but tonight the soundscape felt thinned, as if something had been scooped out of the air.

"I see something!" someone shouted.

The Jeep braked.

Lucía dropped to the road, light already cutting ahead. Twisted metal lay half in the brush, half on the shoulder—a motorbike frame, bent and rusted, vines already threading through it.

For a moment, her pulse spiked.

Then she saw it properly.

Old damage. No fresh gouges. No blood.

She exhaled sharply. "Not ours."

A few nervous laughs followed, quickly strangled.

"Back in," she ordered. "That's a ghost. Don't let it distract you."

They rolled on.

The road tightened into a series of hairpins, each turn sharper than the last. Lucía leaned farther out now, scanning both the road and the drop beyond it. The slope fell away brutally—dense bush plunging down at an angle that would turn a stumble into a headlong slide downhill.

Another shout. "There!"

This time the Jeep stopped without being told.

Lucía's beam landed on shattered plastic and chrome just past a hairpin. Fresh skid marks scarred the clay, curving wide, then ending abruptly.

Jose's motorbike lay crumpled against the embankment, front wheel folded inward, frame twisted as if the road itself had grabbed it.

"Here," Lucía said quietly.

They spread out. Lucía crouched at the skid marks, fingers brushing the mud. The bike had entered the turn too fast—or too late. The line was wrong. Hesitant.

"Lost it," someone muttered.

"Maybe," Lucía said, not convinced.

Jose lay several meters away, thrown clear. One look told her enough, but she knelt anyway, fingers at his neck, then his wrist.

Nothing.

Her head dipped for a second. "Lo siento, hermano."

She stood. "Cover him. Poncho. Ahora."

As the body was respectfully shrouded, Lucía scanned the area again. One bike. One body.

"Where's the other rider?" someone asked.

Lucía didn't answer immediately. She walked the scene, slow, deliberate. No second body near the crash. No obvious trail leading away from the road.

"You're sure he had a passenger?" the volunteer pressed.

"Yes," Lucía said. "Which means she should be here."

But she wasn't.

Lucía moved back toward the hairpin, light sweeping wider now—not just the road, but the edges. Her beam dipped over the side and vanished into black.

The drop was severe. Steeper than it looked from above.

Her stomach tightened.

"She could have gone over," someone said softly.

Lucía studied the embankment. No clear break. No obvious slide marks.

"Or she could have walked," another voice offered.

Lucía shook her head. "If she walked, we'd see it. She's hurt. Something's off."

They fanned out along the road, scanning shoulders, ditches, culverts. Minutes stretched. The quiet pressed harder.

Then—"Blood!"

Lucía moved fast. A smear on leaves near the edge. Fresh.

Her light followed it downslope.

The ground dropped sharply, vegetation dense and tangled. This wasn't a place anyone chose to go.

"She fell," Lucía said. "Or slid."

They descended carefully, grabbing roots, sliding more than stepping. The slope forced them below road level almost immediately; the Jeep lights vanished above, leaving only their beams and the oppressive dark.

Broken branches appeared first. Then another smear of blood. Then a torn strip of fabric snagged on thorns.

Lucía held it up. "This might be hers."

The trail was uneven—disturbed plants, scuffed soil, signs of movement that didn't follow a clean line.

"She's alive," someone said, hopeful.

Lucía nodded, but said nothing. The marks weren't steady. They wandered, doubled back in places. As if the person making them had been disoriented.

"She didn't fall straight down," Lucía murmured. "She moved. Not far. But not clean."

They searched outward, calling softly now.

"Karoline?"

Only jungle answered.

A young volunteer crossed himself. "Santa María..."

"Focus," Lucía snapped. "Eyes low. Look where someone would crawl."

Her light caught a shallow depression beneath a bush—flattened leaves, smeared with blood. A place someone had hidden.

Lucía crouched, fingers brushing damp earth.

"You rested here," she thought. "Or passed out."

But again—no body.

The silence deepened. Normally the night here pulsed with sound. Now even the insects seemed reluctant.

A sudden rustle made several lights jerk upward.

A frog froze on a branch, eyes reflecting white.

Someone cursed under their breath.

"False alarms waste time," Lucía said. "Keep moving."

They widened the search, spiraling downslope, calling her name in low, controlled voices.

Minutes passed.

Then—barely audible—a sound.

Not a voice.

A cough.

Thin. Broken.

Human.

Lucía's hand came up instantly, fist clenched beside her temple.

The group froze. Lights dipped. Breath stilled.

The jungle leaned in around them, heavy and watchful.

Something—or someone—was still alive

13

Karoline dragged herself forward through the thicket, one arm at a time.

Everything below her ribs had narrowed into separate territories of pain. Her shoulder burned. Her hip throbbed. Her leg was worst of all, a bright, sick pulse that flared each time a branch caught her or the ground shifted under her weight. The jungle smelled of wet leaves, mud, and something fouler underneath.

Not dead, then.

That thought arrived without comfort. Only fact.

Her hand slid down her shin and came back wet. Blood. Good. Blood meant movement, heat, continuation. She pressed higher and had to stop herself from crying out.

Keep moving.

A twig snapped somewhere nearby.

Karoline froze, cheek pressed to the mud, breath held so long her chest trembled. Nothing followed. No footstep. No voice. Only the rush of blood in her ears.

She tried to rise and nearly blacked out. The moment she put weight on the leg, pain shot white through her body and dropped her back to the ground.

Right. Crawl.

Her hand swept blindly through leaves and roots until it struck canvas.

The satchel.

She pulled it to her chest and held it there for a second, not because it made sense, but because she had lost almost everything else. The sample was still inside. Or the notes. Or something that had mattered enough to carry this far. That was enough.

Then light moved through the foliage ahead.

Not moonlight. Beams.

Karoline flattened herself instinctively and clawed sideways under the drooping branches of a bush, dragging the satchel with her. Her pulse hammered so hard it seemed impossible the lights wouldn't hear it.

Voices.

Too far to make out words at first. Then closer. Men, maybe. Or one man and others behind him. Searchers. Hunters. Company security. Rescue. The jungle gave her no help in telling the difference.

She held her breath and tasted dirt.

The lights shifted away.

For one second she thought they might pass.

Then the cough she had been fighting tore loose from her chest.

The beams stopped.

A woman's voice called through the dark. "Karoline?"

She shut her eyes.

No. Don't answer. Don't be stupid.

"We're here to help you."

The voice came again, closer now, cutting through the fog in her head not because of the words but because of the shape of them. Familiar. Not safe yet. But familiar.

Leaves rustled. Footsteps slid and caught on the slope. A hand touched her shoulder.

Karoline screamed.

"Karoline." The voice dropped low and firm. "It's Lucía."

Everything inside her stalled.

Lucía.

Not a trick, then. Not company men. Not the road finishing what it had started.

Karoline turned her head enough to see her: flashlight glare behind her, mud on her knees, one hand already reaching to steady her, the other signaling the people upslope.

"Why are you here?" Karoline heard herself ask, though the question barely had enough breath behind it to be called a voice.

"Sabine called me," Lucía said.

Sabine.

Karoline swallowed and tried again. "Tell her—"

"You can tell her yourself," Lucía said. Not harsh. "First we get you out."

Karoline tightened her grip on the satchel. "I'm hurt."

"I know."

"Jose—"

Lucía's face changed for a fraction of a second. Enough. "We found him."

Karoline stared at her.

Lucía did not lie, and she did not explain. Not yet.

Hands were moving around them now, careful, controlled. Someone cleared branches. Someone else brought a light lower. The bush that had hidden her a moment ago suddenly seemed flimsy and ridiculous, a child's shelter against the whole jungle.

Lucía crouched closer. "Can you move at all?"

Karoline tried to answer, but what came out was a broken sound halfway between a laugh and a sob.

"Fine," Lucía said. "Don't. We'll do it."

They eased her out from under the branches. Mud smeared her arms. Wet leaves clung to her jacket and hair. The world lurched sideways once, and Lucía's grip tightened before she hit the ground again.

Above them, wings beat suddenly through the dark.

A harsh croak ripped across the slope.

Karoline looked up.

The grackle wheeled once through the lamplight, black body cutting across the beams, red belly flashing and gone.

Her vision blurred around it. For one irrational instant she thought of old woodcuts, black cloaks, childhood Germany, death given a silhouette and a name.

"Der Sensenmann," she whispered.

Lucía leaned closer. "What?"

Karoline tried to shake her head, but the motion dissolved before it was complete. The satchel slipped in her hands.

Then the light, the voices, Lucía's face, the whole wet breathing jungle tilted away from her at once, and she let go.

14

Sabine paid the driver, left the change in his hand, and crossed the hospital parking lot at a run.

It had taken the night and the better part of the morning to get from São Paulo to Mocoa, but fatigue had no real claim on her now. The hospital doors opened onto a lobby crowded with anxious families, plastic chairs, damp shoes, and the layered smells of antiseptic and jungle rain. At the reception desk, under a hard fluorescent glare and a wobbling ceiling fan, a nurse was fielding questions with the flat endurance of someone too exhausted to care who was asking.

"I'm here for my sister," Sabine said.

The nurse glanced up. "No hablo inglés."

Sabine swallowed irritation. "Posso ver mi hermana?"

The woman's expression did not change. "Identificación, por favor."

"Mi hermana. Karoline Reinhardt."

"Identificación."

Sabine was digging for her passport when Lucía came through a side door, clothes still marked with dirt and leaf stains from the search. She said something fast in Spanish to the nurse, took Sabine by the elbow, and steered her toward the elevator.

"What was that about?" Sabine asked as the doors closed.

Lucía hit the button. "She was making you work for it."

Sabine let that go. "How's Karoline?"

"Alive," Lucía said. "Weak, but alive. She lost a lot of blood."

"Is she going to be all right?"

"The doctors think so."

It was not reassurance exactly, but it was enough to keep Sabine upright for the time being.

The elevator opened onto a makeshift emergency ward assembled out of strain and necessity. Gurneys lined the walls. Monitors pulsed in uneven time. The air was thick with disinfectant, exhaustion, and the murmur of people praying quietly over the injured.

Karoline was in the far corner.

She looked smaller than Sabine expected. Mud had been cleaned from her skin, but the bruising had already begun to darken along one side of her face and neck. Sutures pulled a neat line along her thigh. Her satchel rested on top of the blanket, within reach of one hand.

As Sabine came close, Karoline's eyes opened.

"Bine," she said, the word rough and drifting. "You're here."

Sabine took her hand. "I'm here."

Karoline's fingers tightened weakly. "Did Lucía give you the sample?"

"Rest," she said. "You're safe. You're in a hospital."

Karoline's mouth moved in something like a smile. "If they know I'm alive, I'm not safe."

Before Sabine could answer, a doctor appeared at her shoulder in a stained white coat.

"Soy el doctor Andrés Muñoz," he said. "You are family?"

"I'm her sister."

He nodded and glanced at the chart. "She's hurt, but she was fortunate. Severe ankle sprain, partial ligament tear. No fracture. Lacerations to the thigh, abdomen, and arm, already sutured. Mild concussion. Shock. A lot of bruising, but no internal bleeding. She was lucky the wounds missed major arteries."

When he moved on, a younger woman stepped in to check the IV line. Her scrubs had been washed to a permanent grey-blue, and a strip of pink medical tape stuck to one wrist with notes.

"She's going to try to stand before the medication wears off," she said, adjusting the drip with quick, economical hands. "Don't let her."

"I heard that," Karoline murmured.

The nurse snorted. "Good. Then I won't have to repeat myself."

She checked the sutures, pressed lightly along the swelling at the ankle, then looked at Sabine with the calm of someone who had already seen worse things today.

"I'm Mila," she said. "Overflow and triage."

"Thank you for looking after her."

Mila gave a small shrug. "She did the dramatic part. I'm just here for damage control."

Something about the woman's competence—dry, unshowy, exact—steadied Sabine more than the doctor had.

When Mila moved away, Sabine sat down beside the bed. The chair creaked under her. Adrenaline was beginning to leak out of her system now, leaving behind the tremor underneath it.

Karoline turned her head slightly on the pillow. "You came fast."

Sabine looked at her. "You called sounding like you were saying goodbye."

Karoline's eyes shifted away. "I thought maybe I was."

Sabine should have said something softer. Something big-sister shaped. Instead she heard herself say, "Don't do that to me again."

Karoline gave the smallest breath of a laugh and winced at the cost of it. "I'll add it to the list."

Sabine brushed a strand of hair back from her forehead. "You went after glowing water on a jungle road with a motorbike?"

"When you say it like that, it sounds unwise."

"It was unwise."

Karoline closed her eyes. "The sample matters."

Sabine looked at the satchel. “I know.”

Across the ward, a man leaned near the doorway with his phone in his hand.

At first Sabine barely registered him. One more tired figure in a room full of them. Then his eyes lifted from the screen and fixed, not on Karoline, but on her.

Too direct. Too intent.

Their gaze locked for a beat.

He turned away at once and slipped into the hall.

Sabine was already half out of the chair when Lucía moved.

She had been standing behind the bed with the stillness of someone who never really stopped scanning a room. Now that stillness broke.

“Stay here,” Lucía said. “Watch Karoline.”

Then she was gone, threading through the ward between gurneys, IV poles, and startled relatives before Sabine could answer.

The hospital room seemed to tilt subtly out of alignment.

Karoline saw her face. “What?”

“Nothing yet.” Sabine kept her eyes on the doorway. “Rest.”

But the word safe was gone now, stripped cleanly out of the room.

***

Lucía caught the door before it finished swinging.

The corridor beyond was long, bright, and nearly empty. Fluorescent lights buzzed overhead. At the far end, a man moved through another set of doors without looking back.

Lucía went after him.

Her boots struck the tile hard, then quieter as she adjusted, forcing speed into silence. Halfway down the corridor she reached the next door and looked through the wired-glass pane.

There he was again—moving fast through a patient area, shoulders tight, head turning just enough to check whether he’d been followed.

Lucía slipped through and used the room itself for cover: a linen cart, then a cluster of nurses, then the shadow between two mobile screens. Each time he glanced back, she flattened, breath stilled, body disappearing into function.

He reached a door marked **SOLO PERSONAL AUTORIZADO**, swiped a keycard, and vanished through it.

Lucía lunged and caught the door with the side of her boot before it shut.

Heat hit her first, then steam. The restricted corridor opened into the hospital's service spine—laundry bins, exposed pipes, detergent stink, machinery hammering behind walls. The man was already at the far end, moving toward a rectangle of daylight at the loading dock.

Lucía broke cover and ran.

He heard her. Pushed harder. A keycard flashed once from his hand and skidded across the wet floor as he shoved through the final door.

Lucía reached the dock in time to see a car fishtail across the gravel lot, tires spitting stones. For a fraction of a second she caught the man's face in the rear window—flat, alert, already memorizing her as the vehicle shot through the gate and disappeared into the road beyond.

She stood still just long enough to pick up the dropped keycard.

Then the intercom came alive overhead.

"Código azul. Código azul. Habitación—"

Lucía was moving before the room number finished.

It was Karoline's.

15

The code blue hit like a blow.

Alarms tore through the ward—sharp, overlapping, immediate—followed by the clatter of wheels and shouted orders bouncing off tile and glass. Sabine was on her feet before she knew she had moved, eyes snapping to Karoline's monitor.

Green. Steady. Still there.

A crash cart rattled past the doorway. Bodies crowded the corridor in a blur of scrubs and urgency. Someone barked instructions in Spanish. A door slammed. Another alarm joined the first.

Sabine stepped into the threshold, trying to see through the surge of motion. No clear line. No familiar face. No Lucía.

A cold knot tightened low in her stomach.

She turned back to Karoline and forced her voice level. "It's not you."

Karoline lay rigid against the pillow, fingers twisted in the blanket. "It sounds like it is."

The alarms faded as abruptly as they had begun. The rush moved past. Voices dropped. Footsteps receded into another part of the ward. The quiet that followed felt thin and unreliable, like the air after a storm that had not actually passed.

Then Lucía stepped into the room.

She did not sit. She stayed near the door, attention moving between the corridor, the window, and the room. "That was close," she said. "Too close."

Karoline let her head sink back against the pillow, then looked at Sabine. "Bine."

Sabine crossed to her at once. "I'm here."

"No," Karoline said. "You're hovering."

Sabine almost argued, then stopped. Karoline was right. She had been straightening blankets that did not need straightening, checking the IV, watching the monitor as if vigilance itself could hold the world in place.

"You can't keep me safe by sitting here," Karoline said. Her voice was thin from pain and medication, but it carried. "Not if this is bigger than me."

Lucía said nothing.

Karoline's eyes shifted to the satchel at the foot of the bed. "That water isn't glowing by accident," she said. "And men don't watch hospital rooms by coincidence."

Sabine followed her gaze. Karoline was right.

Karoline reached out and caught her wrist. The grip was weak, but deliberate. "Please. Look at it. Before somebody else ends up on a gurney because I dragged that sample out of the river."

Sabine did not answer immediately.

Everything in her wanted to stay at the bedside, to narrow the world again to blood pressure, temperature, the rise and fall of Karoline's breathing. Small things. Manageable things.

But that had never been enough.

She nodded once. "All right."

Sabine pulled the rolling tray closer and set the sample on it. In the low hospital light the vial looked more wrong than bright, as if the glow were not illumination but persistence.

Karoline watched from the bed. "Factory runoff?"

Sabine raised her phone and zoomed in on the vial. "If this were just chemical contamination, it would look more uniform than this."

"Meaning?"

"Meaning something's suspended in it. Clumped, maybe organic. I can't tell from this."

"So what now?"

"Now, I need real optics. Real lab equipment."

Sabine looked up. "Lucía, is there anyone local who could help?"

Lucía came off the wall and crossed the room. "There's a local scientist. Martín Chasoy. He works with the Indigenous Guardians—forest monitoring, water samples, that kind of thing."

"Can he handle this?"

"If anyone nearby can, it's him."

Sabine glanced back at the vial. "Then he's our best chance."

"Let me call him and ask. But we need to get out of here."

Lucía was already on her phone, voice low and clipped. Directions. Urgency. A safe location outside town. One driver, maybe two. Then she made a second call. This time her tone shifted—still fast, but more familiar.

When she ended the call, Sabine said, "We need to split up."

Lucía looked at her sharply. "No."

"There'll be no place for Karoline to rest at Martín's lab."

"And there'll be no way for me to keep you both safe if we split."

"Karoline can't stay here, and we're wasting time if we move her twice." Sabine kept her voice low, but the force in it surprised even her. "You take her to your contact. I go to Martín."

Lucía's jaw tightened. "You do not know the routes. You do not know who is watching. And you do not know Martín."

"All true." Sabine pocketed the vial. "Still, it's the only lead we have."

"That is not enough."

From the bed, Karoline said, "She's right."

Both women looked at her.

Karoline's face was pale, but her eyes were clear again. "The hospital is burned. Let's find out what the sample tells us. Meantime, I can start looking through those files from the email."

Lucía stared at Sabine for a long second, weighing cost against time.

Then she exhaled once through her nose. “I can get two drivers.”

“Do it,” Sabine said.

Lucía held her gaze another beat, then started dialing.

Two paths. One vial. No safe version of the night left.

16

Sabine left the hospital alone in one of the cars.

She had insisted Lucía take Karoline to the safe house. Protection, extraction, routes, watchers—that was Lucía's work. This part was hers.

Dr. Martín Chasoy taught environmental systems at the Instituto Tecnológico del Putumayo in Mocoa, where limited equipment and chronic underfunding had made improvisation part of his scientific method. His lab sat at the edge of campus in a low concrete building with a patched awning and a faded sign: **LABORATORIO AMBIENTAL**. A single light burned inside.

Martín opened the door before she knocked.

He was younger than she had expected, early forties perhaps, with his glasses pushed up into his hair and one sleeve rolled higher than the other. He looked like someone who had been working too long and only noticed other people once they were already in front of him.

"Dr. Reinhardt?"

"Yes," Sabine said. "Thank you for seeing me."

He stepped aside.

The lab smelled of ethanol, damp soil, and overheated electronics. It was not tidy in the ornamental sense, but everything had a place. An aging fluorometer sat with one corner of its cover taped down. A centrifuge hummed softly. Filter papers hung above the sink to dry like laundry.

Sabine set her bag on the nearest bench and took out the vial.

"Collected near Fin del Mundo," she said. "I used my phone to zoom in but it's nothing normal that I can identify."

Martín looked at the vial, then back at her. "How not normal?"

"The light emission oscillates," she said. "Too coherent for simple decay. Too structured for noise."

That got his attention.

"All right," he said. "Where do you want to start."

She said, "Ideally, proper excitation and emission spectra, filtration by pore size to see whether the signal follows particulates, basic chemistry, and headspace gas if you can manage it."

Martín glanced toward the bench. "No gas chromatograph."

Sabine nodded once. "Can you give me reliable spectra, pH, alkalinity, conductivity, and direct dissolved CO_2?"

"Yes."

"Then we're still in business."

That almost earned a smile.

They moved into work without needing to negotiate it. Martín prepped the fluorometer while Sabine opened a blank log sheet and built a baseline table. The rhythm came quickly: one person handling the sample, the other watching for pattern and drift.

The first spectral run came back and the same pulse reappeared—slow, uneven, repeating.

Consistent.

Sabine felt that land harder than surprise. Strange things could still be accidents. Reproducible ones were harder to explain.

Martín leaned over her shoulder. "You saw this before?"

"At the hospital. I didn't trust my eyes."

"And now?"

"I trust it enough to be worried."

He nodded once.

While the second scan ran, he crossed to his desk and hesitated with one hand on the monitor.

"There's something else," he said. "I didn't mention it to Lucía because I wasn't sure how to describe it without sounding crazy."

Sabine turned toward him. "Try me."

He pulled up a map on his screen.

Terrain. River course. Fin del Mundo. A mesh of small tagged points spread around the area, each marked with an identifier.

"Nanosensors," he said. "Environmental monitoring nodes. Low power. Mostly passive."

Sabine stepped closer. "Monitoring what?"

"The electrical exchange between roots and nearby mycelial structures. Or trying to." He gave a brief, dry shrug. "Most days I collect noise and pretend it's progress."

He zoomed in.

Several nodes near Fin del Mundo pulsed in near-unison.

Sabine straightened. "That's synchronized."

"Yes."

"Shared power source?"

"No."

"Same substrate?"

"Not consistently."

She looked at him. "That shouldn't happen."

"I know."

Another window opened. This one showed a rolling trace with intermittent coherence surfacing out of baseline chatter.

"It comes and goes," Martín said. "When it appears, it aligns across independent nodes. Not perfectly. But enough."

Sabine studied the traces. "What frequency?"

"It drifts."

"How?"

He made a small motion with one hand, searching for the shape of it. "Not random drift. More like... correction. As if it's adjusting to hold itself together."

That pulled her eyes back to his.

He clicked again and brought up a time log.

"Two nights ago," he said.

A timestamp. Then a flat line. Then activity returning.

Sabine frowned. "A reboot?"

He nodded. "Not the whole array. Only the cluster nearest the falls."

"That's not a function you built in?"

"No." He met her gaze directly now. "And it wasn't triggered from my side."

Sabine looked from the node cluster to the vial on the bench, glowing softly under the hood.

"Did the node behavior start before the water lit up?"

Martín's pause was brief but not brief enough.

"Yes," he said. "A little before."

The fluorometer chimed.

Sabine turned back to the bench, more to give herself a second than because the machine required immediate attention. She wrote down the next set of numbers carefully, though her mind was already moving ahead of her hand.

"Keep logging the nodes," she said. "Don't alter their configuration. Don't ping them. Don't test for remote control."

"I already stopped."

"Good."

He glanced at the map again. "You think interaction changes the behavior?"

Sabine capped the pen. "I think we don't yet know whether this system is only transmitting through the network or learning from what touches it."

Martín looked back at the node traces. "That sounds worse when you say it out loud."

"It is worse."

He let out a breath that was almost a laugh. "I was hoping you'd say I was imagining it."

"No," Sabine said. "I think there is something to this."

For a moment neither of them spoke. The centrifuge kept up its soft whine. The ceiling fan ticked overhead. Beyond the windows, the campus had gone quiet.

Then something scraped outside.

Not loud. Not close enough to be sure. Just the faint sound of weight shifting where no weight should have been.

Martín looked toward the door.

Sabine did not move at all.

The sound came again.

Closer this time.

17

The car arrived without announcement.

A plain sedan eased to the curb across from the hospital—no markings, no plates Lucía recognized as local, just a man behind the wheel who did not look at his phone and did not look surprised when she opened the rear door. He was Indigenous, mid-forties, hair pulled back, posture relaxed in the way of someone who knew exactly where he was going.

Lucía met his eyes. A brief nod passed between them. Nothing more.

She helped Karoline into the back seat, then slid into the front beside the driver, angling herself to watch both the road ahead and the road behind. It was habit. Positioning. Karoline noticed but said nothing.

They pulled away.

Lucía tracked the city as it peeled back from them. Reflections first—storefront glass, darkened windows. A white SUV appeared once, then again three blocks later. Not following closely. Just present. A motorcycle lingered under a streetlight longer than it needed to.

Lucía registered both and said nothing.

The roads degraded in stages. Asphalt gave way to patchwork repairs, then gravel that rattled Karoline's teeth. Each jolt drew a tight breath from her. She pressed a hand to her ribs and stared out at the darkening landscape as the cell signal slipped from three bars to one, then vanished entirely.

The driver killed the headlights.

The sudden darkness tightened Karoline's chest. Lucía did not move.

Far ahead, a motorcycle parked at the roadside blinked a single flashlight—once, precise, deliberate.

The driver flicked the headlights back on and turned off the road.

"This is where the Guardians take over," he said.

The trail was barely visible, overgrown foliage folding in behind them. The car crept forward until three figures stepped out of the shadows, reflective sashes catching the headlights just long enough to be seen. Each carried a bastón de mando, the carved staff that marked them as acting with the community's authority. No weapons. No urgency.

They scanned the vehicle with the calm attention of people used to reading spaces quickly and well.

Lucía stepped out first. She greeted them formally, in Spanish, using terms that marked respect without claiming belonging. They acknowledged her with nods. Trusted, but not one of theirs.

One of them looked past her to Karoline.

"What danger follows her?" he asked.

Lucía did not hesitate. "Men with money, equipment, and no respect for territory."

These were not guards in the conventional sense. They were territorial monitors: community watchers who moved warnings, people, and information through the forest using radios, old phones, listening posts, and routes outsiders rarely saw.

A Guardian opened Karoline's door and offered a steadying hand. She accepted it, wincing as she straightened. His touch was gentle, clinical, and efficient.

Another Guardian produced a device that looked wrong and right at the same time—a carved wooden handle fitted around modern electronics. A listening wand. He swept it slowly around the vehicle.

It chirped. Not loud. Just a sharp digital click that changed the air.

The Guardian narrowed the sweep, moving closer to Karoline. The signal strengthened near her right side.

"What is that?" Lucía asked, her voice controlled but tight.

"A close signal," the Guardian said. "Artificial."

He asked Karoline to step forward. She complied, confusion giving way to unease as the wand passed over her arm, her bag, her jacket. The chirp spiked at a seam.

Lucía was already there, fingers probing the stitching. She found it—a paper-thin transmitter fused into the fabric. Not hospital-issued. Not accidental.

"That bastard," Lucía said. "At the hospital."

The Guardian sliced the seam open and tweezers plucked the tracker free, a sliver of metal no larger than a fingernail. He placed it on a flat stone and crushed it with another in a single decisive strike.

The wand swept Karoline again. Nothing.

"Now she is clean," the Guardian said.

The tension eased, but only by a degree.

"You are safe in our territory," another Guardian said.

They waved the car through and escorted it deeper into the forest. Lucía kept glancing back anyway.

The safehouse rose from the clearing on stilts—a wooden structure with solar panels on the roof and water barrels beneath. On one corner, an antenna array angled skyward: repurposed dish, metal plates, cables disappearing inside. It was not just a home. It was one of the Guardians' listening nodes, part of the improvised network they used to track chainsaws, engines, gunshots, patrols, and unfamiliar movement through the forest. In places where the state arrived late or not at all, this was how they kept watch.

The host emerged—older, steady-eyed. "My home is yours tonight. You are safe here."

Karoline nearly collapsed. Lucía caught her and guided her inside.

The interior was sparse and functional. A hammock chair. A wood stove. Shelves of herbs. On a small table sat a battered laptop, a solar charged battery pack, and several recycled phones mounted in a wooden frame, wires feeding a small amplifier. A screen showed a live audio waveform from somewhere out in the forest, rising and falling in real time.

"You've upgraded," Lucía murmured.

The Guardian nodded once.

A spike rippled across one of the screens. A faint mechanical crackle bled through the speaker. The Guardian adjusted a dial, listening without alarm.

Karoline lowered herself onto the mattress they had laid out for her. "What is all this?"

The man glanced at the equipment as if the answer were obvious. "We listen for what should not be here," he said. "Engines. Cutting. Vehicles. Sometimes voices."

He adjusted the antenna slightly, orienting it by feel more than sight.

"The network passes warnings from house to house," he said. "If something enters the territory, we try to know before it arrives."

Lucía absorbed the room again with new appreciation. Not improvised chaos. A system. Decentralized, quiet, resilient.

"The signals have been different these past nights," the Guardian said to her quietly.

Lucía looked over. "Different how?"

He considered the question. "Less like traffic. Less like machinery. Harder to place."

She checked the windows, the latches, the single-entry sightline. Approved it. The Guardian prepared tea for Karoline and set it beside the mattress.

Lucía sent an encrypted message to Sabine.

We're safe for now. No tails confirmed.

No reply.

Outside, the insects thrummed in the dark.

Lucía took her place by the window, watching the clearing.

Behind her, the network kept listening.

18

Sabine opened the door and looked out.

She did not step onto the walkway at first. She scanned the strip of concrete, the trees beyond it, the narrow slice of road visible through the fence.

Nothing moved.

Her driver stood by the car where she had left him, engine off, one hand on the open door. When he caught her eye, he gave the smallest shake of his head.

Nothing.

Sabine closed the door and went back inside.

The lab resumed around her at once: centrifuge hum, cooling glass, the careful draw of power through old equipment. The vial still sat beneath the hood, glowing faintly, unchanged by the interruption.

Martín looked up. "Anything?"

"No."

She crossed to the bench and looked at the display instead of the water. The oscillation was still there—slow, uneven, refusing to flatten.

"Talk me through the last few minutes," she said.

He did. No adjustments. No new inputs. A small drift, then the pattern settling again.

Sabine studied the screen. "If this were only the chemistry of the sample, I'd expect it to fade or hold steady."

"But it doesn't," Martín said.

"No." She looked at the vial. "It keeps finding the same rhythm."

He was quiet for a beat. "So the water isn't causing it."

"Maybe not." She adjusted the overlay on the screen. "Maybe the water is only showing it."

Martín stepped closer.

She pulled up the nanosensor data again and aligned the timestamps against the pulse.

"Here," she said, tapping the screen. "The node pattern starts before the visible glow."

Martín looked from the trace to the vial. "Then the glow isn't the event."

"No. It's the symptom."

He kept looking at the synchronized peaks. "But why would the water pulse with it?"

Sabine leaned in. "Because something bigger is setting the rhythm."

She tapped the node cluster. "Separate nodes should not drift into the same pattern unless something is coupling them—pulling them into step. The water isn't generating that pattern. The exudate is responding to it."

He looked back at the glowing vial.

"So instead of glowing steadily," she said, "it brightens and dims with the same larger oscillation."

Martín absorbed that. "Like the water is flashing to a beat coming from somewhere else."

"Yes," Sabine said. "The water just makes it visible."

He glanced at the map again. "That's worse."

"Yes."

She studied the traces in silence for a moment. The lab still offered the comfort of measurable things. For a moment she understood the temptation to stay here and pretend that measurement meant control.

Then she looked again at the node cluster.

"And the reboot?" Martín asked.

Sabine did not answer immediately. "It could be instability," she said. "Or the system trying to settle after drift."

Martín's eyes lifted to hers. "You say that like it's adjusting."

"It's adapting," she said. "That's not the same as intention."

He took that in.

Sabine straightened. "My working read is this: something is moving through that network and forcing separate nodes to behave like one system. The glow matters, but it may only be the visible part."

Martín glanced at the vial. "And the CO_2?"

"If dissolved CO_2 is elevated upstream, it could be changing the local chemistry just enough to make the exudate brighter. Not the cause. Just the reason we notice it here."

He nodded slowly. "Which means the falls are not the source."

"No. Just where the system becomes visible."

Sabine capped the vial and slid it back into her bag.

Martín looked up. "You're leaving?"

She checked her phone again. Still nothing from Lucía beyond the earlier confirmation that Karoline was secured.

"I want to check out the Guardians' listening network," she said. "It's human, technical, local. If this is affecting more than the sample, they may hear signs of it before we can measure them in here."

Martín looked around the lab, then back at her. He understood the implication immediately, and disliked it.

"You trust that more than this?"

"No." Sabine glanced once at the instruments, the traces, the fragile comfort of measurable things. "I trust that this isn't enough."

That was the truth of it.

She was leaving the place where the problem could still be narrowed and named, and moving toward the place where it might only be sensed in fragments. Everything in her preferred the lab. But preference was no longer the relevant standard.

"Run everything," she said. "Back it up twice. Don't touch the nodes."

"I won't."

"And if anything changes—frequency, timing, synchronization pattern—you log it before you interpret it."

That almost drew a smile from him. "You assume I interpret too early."

"I assume everyone does."

She went to the door.

Outside, the driver was still waiting at the car.

Sabine paused once on the threshold and looked back at the lab: the taped fluorometer, the hanging filter papers, the glowing vial's afterimage still ghosting in her vision, Martín already turning back to the screens.

A useful place. A necessary place.

She stepped into the night and got into the car.

The lab had taken her as far as measurement could.

What came next would have to be learned elsewhere.

19

Sabine arrived just after midnight.

The driver stopped short of the clearing and cut the engine. The safe house stood ahead on stilts, its outline softened by mist and foliage, one dim light burning inside. A Guardian met her at the steps, said nothing, and waved her in before turning back toward the forest as if the night itself required tending.

As Sabine crossed the threshold, the generator coughed and fell silent.

The lights did not die completely. They sank, just enough to make the room feel smaller. Outside, the forest pressed close, its sounds muffled by rain that had not quite started. Lucía was on her feet at once, listening rather than reacting.

"It'll come back," she said.

Karoline stirred on the thin mattress by the far wall and pushed herself upright with a wince. In the weak light she looked worse than she had in the hospital—pale, drawn, operating on stubbornness and very little else.

"You made it."

"Yes," Sabine said, setting down her bag. "What did you get through?"

Karoline reached for the laptop. "Not enough."

She opened it and turned the screen slightly. Folders bloomed across the display—too many of them, dates spanning years, file names that meant nothing until you opened them.

"I barely got started," Karoline said. "Permits. Transport summaries. Injection authorizations. Different agencies, different formats. Enough structure to know it's real. Too much mess to know what matters yet."

Sabine stepped closer, scanning quickly, not reading so much as orienting. "They still shouldn't all be in one place."

"We can't figure out who sent it?" Lucía asked.

Karoline shook her head. "Just an anonymous link."

Sabine kept her eyes on the screen. "Whoever sent it had access. That doesn't mean they understood it."

Karoline gave a tired breath that almost passed for a laugh. "Generous."

Lucía frowned from the doorway. "So is it useful?"

"Maybe," Sabine said. "But not like this. Not tonight."

She closed the laptop gently. "This needs daylight."

Karoline let out a long breath. "Good. Because I'm done."

A moment later, the generator caught again. The lights steadied. Outside, the rain finally began, soft and patient, as if it had been waiting.

They slept in fragments.

Morning came grey and damp.

Coffee boiled too long on the stove. Radios murmured in the next room. Rainwater still dripped from the leaves outside. Karoline sat at the table with her laptop open, painkillers lined beside her mug, her jaw set with the kind of resolve that came from having nowhere else to put the tension.

Sabine stood over the table. "Start with what repeats."

They worked differently in daylight. Slower. Cleaner. Sabine grouped files by function while Karoline cross-referenced dates. Lucía drifted near the edges of the room, watching the perimeter while listening to every word.

"Storage permits are clean," Karoline said at last. "At least on paper."

"They should be," Sabine said. "Look at the capture numbers."

She pulled up one report, then another from the same quarter. Karoline leaned closer.

"That's DAC - Direct Air Capture," she said. "Public-facing."

"And this is injected CO_2," Sabine said. "Same time window."

Lucía stepped in beside them. "That looks smooth."

Sabine nodded. "Too smooth."

Karoline looked from one file to the other. "Meaning what?"

"Real capture breathes," Sabine said. "Weather, downtime, maintenance, efficiency drift. This doesn't. It's too neat."

"So it's fabricated."

"Not necessarily." Sabine clicked into a power-allocation sheet. "Buffered. Blended. Curated for the report."

Karoline read the load figures and frowned. "These numbers are huge."

"They'd have to be," Sabine said, "if DAC were actually doing the full job they're claiming."

Lucía leaned one hand on the table. "And you think it isn't."

Sabine clicked open another file. "I think the story is doing more work than the plant."

Karoline scrolled farther. "Transport logs."

Sabine's eyes sharpened. "Those aren't pipeline records."

"No," Karoline said. "Truck routes."

Night timestamps. Repeating departures. Familiar origin points. Enough pattern to matter, not enough certainty to call it proof.

Sabine sat back. "This cache isn't evidence. Not yet."

Karoline looked up. "Then what is it?"

"A map." Sabine pulled up a glossy site rendering buried deep in the archive: steel, glass, water, clean angles, engineered serenity. "It tells us where to look."

"The DAC facility."

Sabine studied the image. "That place is a showroom."

Karoline frowned. "You really think the whole DAC story is cover?"

"I think it's social license," Sabine said. "A way to make continued extraction sound transitional instead of terminal."

Karoline folded her arms. "They claim it's the highest-yield DAC site on the planet."

Sabine gave a short, humorless breath. “Even if their system were twice as efficient as advertised, it still wouldn’t make the economics stop being ugly.”

Lucía glanced between them. “Explain that without the conference version.”

Sabine nodded once. “CO_2 in the atmosphere is diffuse. Expensive to capture. Then you still have to strip it, compress it, move it, and inject it. Every step costs energy. If that glossy facility were really carrying the load they claim, the power draw would dominate this whole region.”

Karoline looked back at the numbers on the screen. “But the energy profile doesn’t.”

“No.” Sabine tapped the file. “It’s too tidy. That’s the point.”

Lucía was quiet for a second. “So what’s real? The DAC, or the injection?”

“Probably both,” Sabine said. “Just not in the proportions they want the world to believe.”

Karoline stared at the rendering a moment longer, then said, “Sounds like we need a tour.”

Lucía nodded once. “They expect visitors. We won’t see anything they don’t want seen.”

Sabine met her eyes. “That doesn’t mean we won’t learn what they think matters.”

Karoline drafted the email carefully. Polite. Specific. Forgettable. She read it once, made one change, and sent it.

They did not wait long.

The reply came back within the hour.

Lucía let out a quiet breath. “That was fast.”

“They were ready,” Karoline said.

“They want this,” Sabine replied. “They think if we see the right things, we’ll stop asking the wrong questions.”

Karoline closed the laptop. “Then let’s go see what they’re proud of.”

20

The RegenX DAC facility's visitor center sat above the valley in glass and steel, its lines too clean against the raw green of the slope below. A brushed-steel sign hung on the chain-link fence at the gateway:

REGENX DIRECT AIR CAPTURE — PHASE III

Lucía let Sabine and Karoline step out first while she stayed a half pace behind, reading the site the way some people read weather—doors, sightlines, reflections, the intervals between cameras. Nothing aggressive. Nothing overt. That was what made it feel curated.

Karoline paused at the open door of the 4×4 for a fraction too long, one hand braced against the frame before she straightened. Sabine caught it. Karoline ignored the look and lifted her camera instead, settling the strap more carefully than she should have needed to.

A guide emerged from the main entrance wearing a company jacket and the kind of easy confidence that came from showing visitors only what had been chosen for them.

"Welcome to RegenX's Direct Air Capture facility," he said. "The highest-yielding installation in the world."

He turned and gestured across the valley. "But before we go inside, we should start with the energy source."

The reservoir lay broad and still below them, its shoreline cut too cleanly into the forest. Above it, the trees held dense and dark except for a large Spanish-style villa standing alone on manicured grounds.

"The Suyama Hydroelectric Project," the guide said. "Entirely RegenX-funded. Purpose-built to support this facility. No offsets, no public money, no burden on the local grid. Zero-carbon generation from end to end."

Sabine leaned closer to Karoline without taking her eyes off the water. "You still can't break the thermodynamics of DAC," she murmured. "Entropy doesn't care what the brochure says."

"Dedicated generation?" she asked the guide.

"Exclusively," he said. "We didn't want to compete with local demand. This system only works if the energy is as clean as the outcome."

Lucía watched the lake instead of the man. Water that did not move made her uneasy. She lowered her voice. "See the hacienda?" she said to the others. "That's where the American executives stay when they visit."

The doors sealed behind them with a soft, expensive sound.

Inside, the air was cool and dry, lightly scented with eucalyptus—clean in a way that felt designed rather than earned. They stopped before a two-storey wall of intake modules stacked behind glass, pale panels rising in disciplined ranks. Up close, each unit looked almost delicate: clean seams, uniform faces, the faint vibration of air being pulled through.

"This is the public gallery section," the guide said. "Representative modules."

Past the glass, the system continued far beyond the showroom wall. The same pale units stepped down the hillside in orderly fields, service roads cut between them, maintenance gantries bridging the gaps. The fans merged into a low, steady pressure that you felt more than heard.

"Modular contactors," the guide said. "Same unit repeated where we need density and where we need scale."

Karoline raised her camera and took the shot with her elbows tucked tight. When she lowered it, she shifted her weight off her bad side so subtly that only Sabine and Lucía noticed.

"This is the capture front end," the guide went on. "Ambient air, lightly conditioned. No pre-concentration. The atmosphere comes in as it is."

A schematic glowed to life beside them—arrows, molecules, color-coded flow paths.

"Fans move air across a solid amine sorbent. CO_2 binds at ambient temperature. Nitrogen and oxygen pass through."

Below the schematic, a live capture curve climbed in a line so smooth it was almost serene.

Sabine stopped.

Outside, a cloud crossed the sun. Humidity shifted. Somewhere deeper in the building, one of the fans altered pitch a fraction.

The line did not move.

"Capture varies with weather," the guide said, already turning toward the next stop. "But our control systems smooth short-term noise. Stable baseload from the Suyama hydro system helps."

Sabine kept her expression neutral and moved on.

They entered the regeneration gallery. The temperature rose slightly. Heat exchangers lined the walls, slim and architectural, their purpose half concealed by polished presentation.

"This is where the hydro matters most," the guide said. "Low-grade heat releases the CO_2 from the sorbent. Continuous power means continuous regeneration."

Karoline slowed. Her fingers pressed once, quickly, into her side.

Lucía shifted position without comment and took the inside line beside her.

The next space narrowed, glass giving way to reinforced concrete. Pipework braided overhead—stainless runs layered and color-banded, all feeding toward a central manifold the size of a delivery truck.

Karoline looked up at it. "That's a lot of input."

"Resilience," the guide said pleasantly. "We don't rely on a single capture pathway. DAC is a key input, but not the only one."

He gestured to one branch of the system, then another.

"Biogenic CO_2 from regional biomass processing enters here. Fermentation, anaerobic digestion, waste-to-energy. And finally, for balancing supply, legacy industrial CO_2. Fully documented. Fully permitted."

Sabine saw the shape of it then—not fake. Blended.

Karoline had stopped at a narrow door set flush into the concrete wall, marked only by a small placard:

INSTRUMENTATION ACCESS

She reached for the handle almost absently, like someone testing whether a wrong door would tell the truth more easily than a right one.

The latch gave.

The door opened two inches.

A soft chime sounded overhead.

Not loud enough to be called an alarm. Not gentle enough to be mistaken for anything else.

A status strip on the nearby panel shifted from green to amber.

The guide stopped talking.

Lucía did not move at first. She listened.

Somewhere beyond the wall, a lock engaged with a heavy metallic clack. A second later the guide's tablet vibrated in his hand. Farther down the corridor, a door that had stood open when they arrived slid shut with quiet hydraulic finality.

"Let's not go in there," the guide said.

He smiled as he said it, but the smile had narrowed.

He closed the door himself. The chime stopped. The amber strip returned to green.

"That section isn't part of the tour."

Above them, one of the dome cameras rotated with a smooth, deliberate correction and settled on their position.

Karoline took a half step back from the wall.

The tour resumed, but not in the same mood. The guide spoke faster now, as though the route had become something to complete rather than enjoy. Twice more his tablet vibrated. Twice more he glanced at it without breaking stride.

Lucía kept watching the building rather than the man. The facility had changed around them in small ways. Doors were closing earlier. Sightlines were shortening. At the end of one corridor, a pair of grey-jacketed staff stood talking beside a security panel they had not been near before. Neither looked at the visitors directly.

They ended in the observation bay above the injection interface, where thick lines ran out of sight toward the field.

"This CO_2 is permanently stored through retrofitted legacy wells," the guide said. "Secure formation. Stable caprock. Long-term sequestration."

Sabine barely listened. She was still looking at the inputs in her head—the too-smooth capture line, the multi-stream manifold, the polished story about clean atmospheric removal wrapped around something much murkier.

Lucía kept scanning reflections in the glass.

Karoline lowered her camera and said nothing at all.

They exited through a corridor of offsets, smiling staff photographs, and mission statements printed directly onto the wall.

By the time they reached the vehicle, the outer gate was no longer standing open. Two men in grey RegenX jackets waited beside it, speaking quietly to each other while a camera above the post tracked the lane.

One of them pressed a button. The gate rolled back.

Outside, the reservoir held the sky in one unbroken sheet.

"The capture curve was too flat," Sabine said as soon as the vehicle doors shut.

Karoline lowered herself into the seat with visible care, one hand braced on the frame. "And that room."

Lucía stayed turned toward the facility until the gate disappeared behind them. "We tripped something," she said.

Sabine looked at her. "Security?"

Lucía kept watching the road behind them. "Interest."

21

The ride back to the safe house was quiet only in the literal sense.

No one stopped talking. The DAC tour kept replaying in fragments—the polished guide, the too-smooth capture curve, the hidden door, the man from the hospital, the reservoir sitting below the site like a held breath. By the time they stepped back inside, the questions had stopped being impressions and started acting like tools.

Sabine dropped her bag on the table. "Open the spreadsheets again."

Karoline looked up from the cot, one leg stretched carefully in front of her. "We've already been through them three times."

"I know." Sabine pulled the laptop toward her. "Now we know what we were looking at."

Lucía stayed by the window, checking the clearing before turning back to them. "That tour changed something for you."

Sabine nodded. "They showed us the public story. I want to see where the private one breaks."

Karoline shifted, winced, and pulled the laptop closer anyway. "All right. But if this turns into one of your old math lectures, I reserve the right to bleed dramatically onto the keyboard."

A faint smile touched Sabine's mouth. "Math tells stories too."

"Yes," Karoline said. "But unlike normal stories, it insists on involving axes."

Sabine ignored that and pulled up the pressure logs.

"Here. Storage well pressure over time."

Karoline leaned in. "It looks almost flat."

"It only looks flat because of the scale." Sabine changed both axes to log.

The graph bent.

Not gradually. Sharply.

Karoline's expression changed. "That wasn't there before."

"It was always there," Sabine said. "We just hadn't taught the graph how to confess."

Lucía crossed the room and stood behind them. "Say that in words normal people use."

Sabine tapped the break in the slope. "Pressure should still rise as you inject more CO_2. Slower over time, yes, because the reservoir pushes back and the effective storage volume expands. But not like this. Not a drop that abrupt."

Karoline frowned. "So they kept pumping, but the pressure stopped behaving."

"Exactly."

"Leak?"

"Maybe." Sabine scrolled down. "But if it were leaking at that scale, some part of the monitoring regime should have noticed by now. And this shift starts almost three years ago. Too early. Too clean."

Karoline pulled up the injection volumes and compared them side by side. "Throughput doesn't crash."

"No." Sabine traced the screen with one finger. "Same general input pattern. Different pressure response."

Lucía folded her arms. "So what changes?"

Sabine sat back. "Either the underground behavior changes, or the CO_2 stream does."

"Or both," Karoline said.

Karoline pulled up the glossy DAC site rendering again—steel, glass, water, clean lines, engineered reassurance.

"The whole place felt like a showroom," she said.

"It is a showroom," Sabine replied. "A public-facing argument in building form."

Lucía glanced between them. "Then what do we still not know?"

Sabine looked at the map of the site. "What it does when no one's meant to be impressed."

That turned the room.

Karoline nodded slowly. "So we need eyes on it."

Sabine looked toward the Guardian at the listening station. "Do you have coverage near the DAC site?"

Rogelio Taimal looked up from his equipment. He wore his hair tied low at the nape, and even sitting still he had the balanced, economical stillness of someone used to boats and uneven ground. "Some."

"Can you put a camera out there?"

He did not answer immediately. He glanced at Lucía first, then back at the screen, then at Sabine. "Not tonight."

Karoline frowned. "Why not?"

"Because right now RegenX is still seeing too much." Rogelio tapped one of the relay maps. "Every fixed feed that stays up long enough blooms on their scanners. If we place a camera before the relay hardening is live, we risk losing the feed and the position."

How long do we need to wait?"

"A day." Rogelio adjusted a dial. "Maybe less, if the patch arrives when promised."

Sabine looked at him. "Patch from whom?"

Rogelio shook his head once. "A remote specialist. Indigenous channels sourced the need. The solution is coming in through a different path."

That was not an answer, but it was all the one she was going to get tonight.

Karoline leaned back and let out a breath. "So we wait."

Lucía corrected her immediately. "No. We prepare."

Sabine nodded. "Route options, approach angles, likely camera placement, and what we need the feed to answer."

Rogelio said, "If the patch works, I can run motion-triggered capture, short bursts only. Vehicles. Shift changes. Deliveries. Enough to start building a pattern."

Sabine looked back at the files on the screen, then at the memory of the silent curve, the door, the calm guide.

"The tour showed us what they want seen," she said. "The camera will tell us what they do when they think no one is looking."

22

The safe house had fallen into the kind of silence that only happened when everyone was listening to something that refused to speak.

Static hissed from the speakers on the table in thin, broken breaths. Rogelio Taimal sat hunched over the laptop, headphones crooked around his neck, one hand braced against the wood as if force might steady the signal. The onscreen map showed half the listening nodes along the eastern valley were still lit but useless—alive, recording, and effectively mute.

The new DAC camera was not one of them. That feed was still dark by choice, waiting for the hardened relay protocol.

Lucía leaned against the wall near the door, not relaxed so much as disciplined into stillness. Karoline stood with her arms folded tight, watching the screen as if annoyance alone might coerce it into clarity. Sabine had taken the chair nearest the far corner and regretted it now; from there she could see all of them, which meant she could feel the room's frustration gathering like heat.

Rogelio swore softly.

"What?" Lucía asked.

He clicked into another log, frowned, backed out, opened a packet trace. "It's happening again."

Karoline exhaled through her nose. "You keep saying that."

Rogelio pointed at the screen. "The forest nodes are still collecting. Batteries are stable. Local storage is active. But every time they try to push, the transmission hangs as soon as it is exposed."

"Exposed to whom?" Karoline asked.

"To anyone watching for the pattern," Sabine said.

Rogelio nodded once. "RegenX doesn't need the content. They just need to see where the signal keeps trying to rise and overpower it."

Lucía straightened. "How many have we lost that way?"

"Two confirmed. Maybe three." He rubbed a hand over his mouth. "Not because they found the devices right away. Because they found the area. Then the patrols started getting very interested in exactly the right trees."

Karoline muttered, "Comforting."

Sabine watched the traces stall and flare across the screen. The weakness of the network was not fragility. It was legibility. Every live transmission was a flare.

Then Rogelio stopped.

Lucía saw it first. "What?"

"The eastern arc just switched."

Karoline pushed off the table. "Switched how?"

Rogelio's hands started moving again, faster now. "The nodes aren't trying to uplink live. They're caching everything local, splitting the files, then waiting—"

"For what?" Lucía asked.

"For tiny random windows." He looked up, startled and almost admiring. "Too small to give a stable fix."

Sabine was on her feet without remembering the moment she rose.

On the screen, the traffic map no longer showed the old desperate reach of a fixed node trying to dump a full load before the jammer closed over it. Instead the transmissions came in thin flashes—a fragment here, another there, one gone almost before it appeared, then another reemerging elsewhere through a relay path that had not existed five minutes earlier.

Karoline leaned in. "Is that good?"

"If it holds," Rogelio said, "yes."

Lucía stepped closer. "If?"

He pointed. "If the burst windows stay short and irregular enough, RegenX can't build a confident triangulation. Not quickly."

Audio began spilling through in compressed chunks—truck engines, a metallic clank, voices too far off to parse.

"They haven't stopped the network," Rogelio said. "They can't catch what they can't see."

Sabine reached the table. "What changed?"

Lucía was watching Rogelio, not her. "We tested the patch."

Karoline looked over. "What patch?"

Rogelio opened the update log. It was bare. No branding. No header clutter. Just a short operational note attached to the new protocol.

NO LIVE UPLINK FROM FIXED NODES.CACHE LOCAL. SPLIT SMALL. BURST DIRTY.IF THEY CAN MAP THE PATTERN, YOU'VE ALREADY LOST.

Below it, the source tag.

LORENTZ

Sabine went cold.

For a moment she was somewhere else entirely—another crisis, another room, Alexei half-lit by a screen, telling her with maddening patience that no secure channel stayed secure forever and that if she wanted the next drop she should find him somewhere nobody serious would think to look.

The Iny Lorentz fan page.

Her laughing. Then not laughing.

One of my only guilty pleasures, she had said.

And now the name sat in front of her on a jungle safe-house laptop.

Lucía heard the change in her breathing. "Sabine?"

Sabine stared at the screen. "Where did you get this?"

"The protocol?" Lucía asked carefully. "Through the relay."

"Who named the source?"

Lucía's face sharpened. "We never asked."

Karoline looked between them. "Why does that matter?"

Sabine still could not answer her. Her throat had gone tight. The room had narrowed until all she could really see was the codename and the three clipped lines beneath it.

It was exactly the kind of doctrine Alexei would write. Compressed. Defensive. Nothing trusting.

Karoline stepped closer. "Sabine."

She forced the words out. "Alexei used my favorite authors as dead-drop names."

Silence.

"He's dead," Sabine said.

It came out flat and useless.

Lucía's eyes stayed on her. "You don't believe that?"

Sabine turned on her too fast. "I did."

Lucía said, "The help came through Indigenous channels. That part is true. We sourced the need. We carried the risk. But for the signal work—" She glanced at the screen. "There was a remote specialist."

On the screen, another batch of buffered files came through from the southern line. An image resolved in grainy gray: a service track, a truck bed, two men in reflective gear where no one should have been at that hour.

Rogelio swore under his breath. "It's working."

Of course it was.

Of course Alexei would come back into her life first as competence.

The secure relay chimed.

Nobody moved.

A new message appeared beneath the source tag.

Lorentz

TRIANGULATION WINDOW COLLAPSED ON TEST THREE.THEY DIDN'T GET A FIX.RUN EASTERN ARC AGAIN IN 12.

Then, after a blank line:

IF SABINE IS THERE, TELL HER I KNOW.

Sabine stared at the words until they blurred.

Karoline whispered, "Jesus."

Lucía's gaze stayed on Sabine. "Do you need a minute?"

A minute.

Sabine almost said no. What she actually felt was impact—anger first, hot and humiliating, that he had let her carry his death all this time while remaining close enough to reach through a jungle relay and choose that name.

Then relief, worse because it came uninvited.

Alive.

"He let me think he was dead," she said.

Her voice broke on dead.

Nobody looked directly at her then, which was its own mercy.

Lucía answered with the plainness of someone who understood pain and refused to decorate it. "Yes."

Sabine pressed the heel of her hand once against the edge of the table. The wood bit into her skin.

Rogelio rose awkwardly, suddenly fascinated by the field radio. "I should tell the ridge team to repeat the eastern test. And if this holds, we can put the DAC camera up tomorrow without burning the position."

Karoline nodded too quickly. "I'll go with him."

They moved for the door, grateful for the pretext.

Lucía stayed.

Sabine kept staring at the codename.

Lorentz.

Lucía said quietly, "Do you want me to shut the relay down?"

Sabine swallowed. If she said yes, she could keep the wound clean for another hour. Maybe two. Pretend operational necessity and personal devastation had not just collided in the middle of a jungle safe house.

But outside, RegenX was still moving. The forest monitors were still in the trees. The patch had just proved it could keep them hidden. And by tomorrow, if it held, the DAC camera could go up.

"No," she said.

Lucía studied her face, then nodded once and turned toward the door. At the threshold she paused.

"Later," she said.

The door closed behind her.

Sabine stood alone with the laptop.

The relay window glowed softly in the dark room. Beyond it, the jungle breathed. Static whispered through the speaker, thinner now, no longer blind.

She read the message again.

IF SABINE IS THERE, TELL HER I KNOW.

Her mouth twisted.

"You arrogant bastard," she whispered.

Outside, Rogelio's voice carried in clipped instructions. Another burst test. Another relay window. The work was continuing.

Inside, Sabine drew one ragged breath, then another, and sat down in front of the laptop.

Not because she was ready.

Because the work had not stopped for either of them.

23

By the next evening, the camera was live.

Rogelio did not announce it dramatically. He simply looked up from the listening station and said, "We have the first clean sync."

Sabine crossed the room at once. Karoline followed more slowly, one hand on the back of a chair to take weight off her bad ankle. Lucía was already there.

The footage was grainy night video from outside the DAC gate. Not beautiful. Useful. The angle was low and partially obscured by brush, which meant the Guardian had placed it well.

A tanker truck entered the frame.

It rolled to a stop, connected, stayed in place, then pulled away again.

Karoline went still. "That truck."

Lucía looked at her sharply. "You know it?"

Karoline pointed at the screen. "Same size. Same cab shape. Same tank profile. I'm almost sure that's the one we were behind on the mountain before the crash."

Lucía's face hardened. "Almost?"

Karoline kept looking at the footage. "Close enough that I don't like it."

Rogelio backed the video up. "Watch the wheel well against the gate post."

The tanker entered heavy and left riding higher.

"Delivering," Sabine said.

Lucía narrowed her eyes. "You're sure?"

"Not mathematically," Sabine said. "Visually? Yes."

Karoline frowned. "They never mentioned trucking CO_2."

"They wouldn't," Sabine said. "Pipelines sound permanent. Controlled. Industrial in a respectable way. Trucks sound messy."

Karoline was already back at the laptop. "There were manifests in the files."

"Find them."

Her fingers moved fast now. Folder. Date. Logistics. Haulage. A spreadsheet opened.

"Here," she said. "A few tankers every day. Biogenic CO_2 from the fermenter. Some smaller industrial sources." She scrolled farther, then stopped. "And one larger supplier."

Sabine looked over her shoulder. "Who?"

"ColPutumay Oil."

Lucía turned from the monitor. "An oil company is feeding the DAC site?"

Karoline looked up. "Apparently."

Sabine held out a hand. "Where are they?"

Karoline opened a map, entered the address, then plotted the route from ColPutumay Oil to the DAC site.

The line curved through the valley, climbed, and ran straight across the mountain road.

Sabine leaned closer. "That can't be the default haul route."

"It's what the map gives."

Lucía stepped in beside them. "Where did you crash?"

Karoline pointed.

The route ran straight through it.

No one spoke for a moment.

Sabine's phone rang.

She looked at the display. Martín.

She answered at once. "Tell me you have something."

"I do." His voice came fast, strained but controlled. "The glow responds to pH. As the pH drops, the signal intensifies."

Sabine turned away from the others to hear him better. "But most streams there run acidic."

"Yes, mildly. Not like this. The glow only becomes clearly visible below five."

Sabine stopped moving. "Nothing there should be naturally that low."

"No. Which means something is driving the acidity. I think it's dissolved—"

A violent noise tore across the line.

Metal? Glass? Something falling hard enough to make Martín break off mid-word.

Then silence.

Not static. Silence.

Sabine pulled the phone tighter to her ear. "Martín?"

Nothing.

"Martín."

Still nothing.

24

They never make it to the lab.

The road narrows first. Cones. Then a police truck parked sideways across the asphalt.

Beyond it, the street is washed in white light that feels wrong for the hour—too bright, too alert, as if the night has been forced open and told to stay that way.

Lucía eases the vehicle to a stop.

An officer steps forward with one raised hand. His uniform is clean. His face has already settled into the look of someone repeating the same answer for the fifth time.

"Road's closed."

"What happened?" Lucía asks.

"Gas explosion." He says it flatly. "Utility line. Building's compromised."

Sabine leans forward from the back seat. "Was anyone inside?"

The officer glances toward the lights, then down at a clipboard he is holding more for posture than use.

"Unclear," he says. "The building is generally empty at this hour."

Generally.

Sabine feels her jaw tighten.

"Do you have a list?" she asks. "Staff? Occupants?"

"Fire department's still assessing structural stability and air quality."

"That wasn't my question."

His eyes lift to hers then, tired but not careless. "No confirmed occupants. No confirmed injuries."

Behind him, something hisses softly.

Not flame. Pressure.

Sabine looks past his shoulder. She still cannot see the lab itself—only light, tape, shadowed movement, the edges of a scene already being contained.

"How long ago?" she asks.

The officer checks his watch. "About twenty minutes."

Twenty minutes.

Almost exactly when Martín's call had cut off.

Lucía gives the smallest nod and shifts the car into reverse. She does not argue. Does not ask one question too many. That, more than anything, makes the exchange feel finished.

As they pull away, Karoline turns and looks back through the rear window. She can't see the building. Only the lights. The tape. Figures moving with efficient purpose.

No one running. No one shouting names.

Sabine says nothing.

But later—when the road is behind them, the lights are gone, and the silence in the car has turned hard—she will understand what was wrong.

No one had said Martín's name.

And no one had asked for it.

25

They arrived back at the safe house without speaking.

Lucía was the first to break the silence, not with words but with procedure. She checked the windows, re-latched the back door, killed one lamp, then moved the spare radios from the shelf to the table.

Karoline watched her from the mattress, pale with pain and fatigue. "Is that supposed to reassure?"

Lucía didn't look up. "No. Just prepare."

Sabine stood in the middle of the room for a second longer than made sense, still seeing the roadblock lights every time she blinked. The officer's voice. Generally empty. No confirmed occupants. The careful absence where Martín's name should have been.

"No one asked who was inside," she said.

Lucía stopped what she was doing.

Karoline looked up. "What?"

"At the roadblock," Sabine said. "No one said Martín's name. No one asked for it."

The room tightened around that.

Lucía set the radio down. "Then we assume he wasn't there until proven otherwise."

Karoline shook her head too quickly. "We don't know that."

"No," Lucía said. "We don't."

"But we don't ignore timing either," Sabine said.

Karoline pressed the heel of one hand against her eyes. "I don't want this to be connected."

"That doesn't make it unconnected," Lucía replied.

Sabine lowered herself into the nearest chair. "We're not going to decide tonight that Martín was killed because of us."

"Not because of us," Karoline said. "Because of the story."

Sabine looked at her. "And we're not going to decide that either."

Lucía folded her arms. "We don't need certainty to tighten procedure."

That, at least, Sabine could not argue with.

"What changes?" she asked.

Lucía answered immediately. "No one moves alone. Phones stay off unless needed. Windows covered after full dark. Routes changed if we leave. And if anyone knocks, I answer it."

Karoline let out a breath that might have been a laugh on another night. "You really know how to make a place cozy."

Lucía's face didn't move. "Cozy got Martín a roadblock."

Silence again.

Sabine rubbed at the bridge of her nose. "We sleep for a few hours. In the morning we reassess with functioning brains."

"Sleep," Karoline repeated.

"Yes."

"My head won't shut up."

"About what?" Sabine asked.

Karoline looked toward the dark window. "Scale."

Lucía pulled the curtain tighter.

Karoline went on. "This afternoon we were still talking about polished curves and tanker routes and whether the DAC story was cover for something uglier. A few hours later Martín's call cuts off and his lab goes up. If those things belong to the same chain—"

"If," Sabine said.

Karoline nodded once. "If. Then this is bigger than I thought."

Sabine held her gaze. "That may be true. It still doesn't give you permission to turn guilt into evidence."

Karoline looked down at her hands. "I know."

Sabine's voice softened, but only slightly. "Good. Then don't."

Karoline leaned back against the wall and closed her eyes. "Okay, Mutti."

Sabine almost smiled. Almost.

They separated without pretending rest would come easily.

Four hours later, Karoline's phone began to vibrate on the table.

She reached for it in the dark, squinting at the screen. "Hallo."

"Karoline. It's Markus."

She sat up. Across the room, Sabine opened one eye.

"Do you know what time it is here?" Karoline asked.

"Do you know what time it is here?" he replied. "I'm calling because time matters."

Sabine rolled onto her back and stared at the ceiling.

"What do you want?" Karoline asked.

"Progress," he said. "Do you have something we can publish?"

"It's premature."

"The glowing water and the dead American hikers aren't front-page anymore. Your window is closing."

"Good journalism takes time."

"Time is currently measured in hours, not weeks."

Karoline swung her legs off the mattress, then stopped when pain reminded her what the last days had held. "Your lawyers will want certainty."

"Let me worry about the lawyers. What do you have?"

Karoline looked at Sabine, then away again. Putumayo. The DAC site. The route overlap. The crash. Martín's lab.

There was a beat of silence on the line.

Then Markus said, "You were nearly killed, you're hiding in a safe house, and you didn't call me?"

"You would have wanted to run it."

"Of course I would. Reporter nearly dies chasing a story is premium real estate."

"But I don't know if it wasn't an accident."

"There's no such thing as an investigative reporter accidentally dying," he said. "There are only deaths that cannot be explained with certainty."

Lucía, awake now, said nothing from her chair by the door.

Karoline's voice dropped. "If it wasn't an accident, I still don't know who did it."

"Oh, come on," Markus said. "They gassed you off the back of a CO_2 truck. If you'd gone over that road and died, everyone would have blamed the mountain."

Sabine turned her head toward the sound of Karoline talking.

"How did they know who I was?" Karoline asked.

"You went through a checkpoint. They saw your ID. Your driver borrowed a bike. You think Google stops at the equator?"

"It's still speculation."

"It's reporting under pressure. Write what you know. Flag the gaps. Don't invent certainty. But don't sit on it either."

"That's not my style."

"I know," he said. "It wasn't your last editor's either. She's not here anymore."

Karoline's face hardened. "Is that a threat?"

"It's a balance sheet. I need something by close of business. Berlin time."

The line went dead.

For a moment the room held still around the silence that followed.

Then Sabine said, "Wow."

Karoline gave a tired breath through her nose. "Yes."

"Is he always like that?"

"This is the first time he's let me chase a real investigation." Karoline rubbed her face. "Since he arrived, I've been stuck filing safe political pieces. My last real story was the engines. And your kidnapping."

Sabine sat up fully now. "Are you going to give him something?"

Karoline looked toward the window, where dawn had only just begun to thin the dark. "He made it clear I don't really have a choice."

"You always have a choice," Sabine said.

Karoline turned to her. "Not if the alternative is silence while they close every door."

Lucía spoke from the chair by the door. "Visibility cuts both ways."

Karoline nodded. "I know."

Sabine got to her feet and crossed the room slowly. "We still don't have proof."

"No," Karoline said. "But I have enough to make people look."

Sabine studied her for a long second. Her instinct was still to hold, verify, narrow, resist the violence of premature certainty. But the roadblock was still in the room with them. So was the unnamed absence around Martín.

"Then make them look at what you actually know," she said. "Not what you fear."

Karoline's expression changed. Not relief. Permission, maybe.

By the time dawn bled into the trees, she was at the small desk by the window with her laptop open and a mug of bitter coffee going cold beside her. She wrote the way she always did when she was afraid of getting something wrong: slowly first, then faster, shaving away every sentence that reached beyond what she could stand behind.

No accusations. No villains. Just facts, boundaries, and the blank space where the two no longer aligned.

Halfway through, she stopped and read aloud to Sabine what she had. "Too much?"

Sabine didn't move from her chair. "Only if it says more than you can stand behind."

Karoline held her gaze for a second, then turned back to the screen.

The sun was well above the trees by the time she finished. She read it once more, made two cuts, restored one sentence, then attached the file.

In the body of the email she typed:

Filed. This is as far as I can responsibly go.

She looked at it for a second longer.

Then she hit send.

26

Rogelio broke the silence first, resetting the band that held his hair at the nape of his neck.

"A contact at the hospital says Martín made it through the night in good shape," he said. "They kept him for observation. No major injuries."

The relief that moved through the room was real, but no one trusted it enough to relax.

Karoline let out a breath. Lucía looked away. Sabine was already reaching for her bag.

"Then we go now," Sabine said. "Before anyone decides he should be harder to reach."

Lucía glanced at her. "They may not let us in."

"We won't know unless we try."

On the way to the hospital, they passed what was left of Martín's lab.

The building was no longer a building so much as a blackened frame around absence. Steam drifted up from the wreckage. Firefighters moved through it with the flat efficiency of people who had already stopped expecting to find anyone.

Karoline lifted her camera and took two shots through the windshield.

"He's lucky," she said.

Lucía kept her eyes on the ruins. "If he'd been inside, he'd be dead."

A firefighter waved them on. "Road clear, señoras. Move."

They drove the rest of the way in silence.

At the hospital entrance, Lucía said, "Let me talk."

A few minutes later, she was leading them to the elevator.

"He's on a short leash, not a ventilator," she said. "If I weren't his sister, we wouldn't be getting in."

Sabine looked at her. "You're not."

Lucía gave a small shrug. "The nurse doesn't know that."

Martín was propped half upright in bed, wearing a hospital gown and an expression of deep personal offense. A bruise darkened one side of his forehead. Gauze marked his temple. Otherwise, he looked more inconvenienced than broken.

Karoline stopped in the doorway. "You look terrible."

Martín's eyes moved to the stiffness in the way she held herself and the bandaging at her foot. "That's rich."

Lucía set a hand on the bedrail. "He's lucid. Unfortunately."

Martín closed his eyes briefly. "They want to keep me another day."

"And yet here you are, alive enough to complain," Sabine said.

"Complaining is how I know I'm alive."

That was enough to let the room breathe.

Sabine stepped closer. "What were you doing outside?"

"Getting samples from the truck." He nodded toward the battered field notebook on the nightstand. "The real ones. The ones I didn't want sitting in the lab overnight."

Lucía folded her arms. "A decision that now looks wise."

Martín gave the smallest tilt of his head. "I have them. The notebook too. If the lab explosion was meant to erase the work, it didn't."

Sabine nodded once. "Good."

For a moment, that was enough too. He was here. Hurt, angry, inconveniently alive. The work had not burned with the building.

Lucía stepped back from the bed. "I'm getting coffee. Anyone object?"

No one did.

"Good," she said. "Four?"

Then Martín picked up his phone from the blanket.

"Speaking of terrible decisions," he said, tapping the screen and turning it toward Karoline, "you're internet famous again."

Karoline frowned. "What?"

Sabine took the phone first.

The headline above Karoline's byline was hotter, dirtier, and far more certain than anything Karoline would ever have filed.

Karoline swore softly in German before Sabine had even reached the second paragraph.

"That is not what I sent."

"No," Sabine said. "It isn't."

"He's spiced it up," Karoline said. "There are conclusions in there I never made."

Martín held out his hand for the phone again. "And he got exactly what he wanted."

From the next bed, a man muttered, "Could you keep it down? My mother's sleeping."

Karoline nodded once without looking at him.

Martín scrolled. "And RegenX is already responding."

Karoline looked at him. "Show me."

He turned the screen. A corporate statement filled it—smooth, clipped, ready far too quickly.

Sabine read it once, then again.

Her face changed.

"What?" Karoline asked.

"They had this ready."

"Meaning?"

"They don't want to argue water or bodies or what happened on that road." Sabine tapped the screen. "They want to argue that publishing any of it was irresponsible."

Martín took the phone back. "Which is smarter."

Karoline's jaw tightened. "He can't do that under my byline."

She reached for her sat phone.

Sabine saw the move immediately. "Karoline."

"He woke us in the middle of the night," Karoline said. "He can take my call in the evening."

"You can barely stand."

"I'm phoning Berlin, not running a marathon."

She pushed herself up from the chair, hissed once as pain shot through her foot, and caught herself against the wall.

Martín watched her. "Maybe wait until you can stand without looking homicidal."

"This sat phone is useless in here," she said, more to Sabine than to him. "I need a stronger signal."

"Karoline—"

But she was already out the door.

A minute later Lucía came back balancing a paper tray with four coffees and something wrapped in wax paper. She took in the room in one glance.

"Where's Karoline?"

Sabine looked at the closed door. "Calling Berlin."

Lucía set the tray down at once.

"How long?"

"Not long."

Lucía was already moving.

27

A succession of texts lit RegenX CEO Richard Stone's phone as he stood at the window with a glass of bourbon in his hand, the lights of the Houston skyline burning quietly beneath him.

Investigations had come and gone. So had the headlines. Richard Stone was still in Houston, still in charge, still rich enough to watch consequence thin out over distance and time.

You're not going to like this. Your favorite reporter from EcoLux is back.

He opened the link on a tablet.

The article was on a German news site under Karoline Reinhardt's byline.

Reinhardt again. Enough trouble last time to force hearings, statements, and expensive patience. Not enough to matter in the end.

He read the headline, then the first paragraphs, then skipped ahead and read the ending.

Too hot. Too certain. Berlin, not Karoline.

That was the first thing he knew.

The second was worse: underneath the editorial heat, he could still see her hand. The sequencing. The factual scaffolding. The places where she had almost certainly written with restraint and someone else had leaned on the language until it pointed harder than she would have allowed.

He read the middle again, more slowly this time.

There it was.

The hikers' deaths near Fin del Mundo had been pulled into the same frame as the glowing water. Her motorbike crash had been pushed from troubling coincidence toward implied consequence. What she might have filed as pattern and unanswered question had reached print as something much closer to accusation.

Someone in Berlin had sharpened the piece for outrage. They had not invented its direction.

He set the tablet down and picked it up again almost immediately.

The line answered on the first ring.

"She went through the checkpoint," Stone said. It wasn't a question. "I cleared the site visit."

"Yes," the man said. "You said transparency would drain the story."

"It usually does."

Stone kept his eyes on the skyline.

"She toured the DAC facility," the man continued. "Engineering walked her through the capture line, injection models, compliance framework. She asked the right questions. Nothing outside the expected range."

Stone said, "And yet this is what was printed."

A pause.

"What about the crash language?" Stone asked.

"The published version says the incident occurred after she visited Fin del Mundo."

"That is not what I asked."

Another pause.

"No," the man said. "We have no evidence tying the crash to the project."

Stone turned from the glass. "But someone decided to frame it that way."

"It appears so."

Stone looked back at the article.

The editor had done what editors did under deadline: closed uncertainty too fast, leaned on danger, made adjacency read like cause. Two dead hikers. A glowing river. A reporter injured on a mountain road after asking unwelcome questions. Corporate secrecy. Possible suppression. The piece stopped just short of direct accusation only because the law still existed.

And still, for all that, it was dangerous for a different reason.

"She did not write like someone dazzled by a guided tour," Stone said quietly. "Her editor sharpened it for outrage."

The man on the phone said nothing.

Stone read one paragraph again. A sentence about regulated exposure. Another about local silence. Another implying that whatever killed the hikers and sent Karoline Reinhardt to the hospital belonged to the same concealed system.

That was reckless.

It was also close enough to be a problem.

"She reported around the official language," Stone said. "Someone else turned the pattern into an accusation."

"We thought visibility would flatten this."

"We did."

Stone shook his head once. "Transparency flattens ignorance. Not knowledge."

The line went quiet.

He crossed to the desk and sat, reading the article again, more selectively this time. Putumayo. The glowing water. The dead hikers. The crash. The system behaving as designed.

Not the work of someone repeating outrage back to an editor. Someone had given her structure. Or evidence. Or both. The article had overreached in print, but it had not been invented.

"She did not build this from a controlled walkthrough," he said.

"No."

"Then find out what she learned after she left the site."

"We're trying."

"That is not what I asked."

The man stopped.

Stone's voice stayed level. "I want to know what she saw after the tour, who got her out of the hospital, and what made her connect dead hikers and a motorbike crash to a compliant storage project."

"Yes."

"And I want the tracker failure report."

Another pause. "The gown tag was discovered and destroyed."

"I know that."

The man said nothing.

Stone leaned back in his chair. "What I do not know is whether the crash was bad luck, or whether someone decided to improvise around a journalist I had explicitly cleared."

"No teams were authorized to—"

"I didn't ask about authorization," Stone said. "I asked whether someone freelanced."

The silence on the line lengthened.

"At this point," the man said carefully, "we don't have evidence of a sanctioned action."

"Which is not the same thing."

"No."

"Then find out."

"Yes, sir."

Stone looked again at the article headline. Still too hot. Still too sure. Likely not hers. But the damage was no longer in the headline alone. It was in the way the published version fused deaths, injury, and secrecy into a narrative the public would understand faster than the truth.

He said, "What do we have on the other woman?"

"La Sombra?"

"Yes."

"Fragments. Rumor. Some old reports that may be embellished."

"That's not an answer."

"No."

Stone's gaze stayed fixed on the screen. "Get me a better one."

"Yes."

"And listen carefully." He let the pause do the work. "I don't want Karoline contacted. No warnings. No pressure. No cleanup."

"Understood."

"No, you don't." Stone's voice sharpened by half a degree. "Pressure confirms relevance. Warnings create pattern. Cleanup is for mistakes already made." He looked back out at the city. "I want information."

"Yes."

"I want to know what she knows before she writes again."

The man answered immediately this time. "Yes, sir."

Stone ended the call.

For a moment he sat without moving, the article still open on his tablet in front of him, the skyline reflected faintly in the office glass.

The site visit had not failed.

It had done what it was supposed to do.

The problem was whatever had happened after.

He picked up the tablet again and read the article one more time.

They were still safe.

As long as she kept chasing the wrong story.

28

Karoline was watching the signal bars on her phone when she stepped out the side door of the hospital.

One bar. Then two.

She never saw the hand.

It clamped over her mouth hard enough to bruise, and something hard jammed into the small of her back. Metal.

"Don't scream," a voice rasped into her ear. "Don't fight."

Her feet stumbled on the curb as he drove her toward the street. The air smelled of disinfectant and diesel. Behind them, the hospital doors slid shut.

"Hey—what the hell are you doing?" another man hissed, rushing up. "This isn't—"

"Getting information," the first man snapped, tightening his grip.

"The boss said surveillance only."

Karoline felt the pressure at her back shift as they argued. Too close. Too distracted.

She drove her elbow backward as hard as she could and raked her heel down his shin.

He swore and loosened his grip.

For a fraction of a second, she had air.

"Stop her—"

She twisted free, half falling, heel skidding on the curb. Fingers caught her again, rougher now, angrier, one hand tangling in her jacket.

"Jesus Christ," the second man hissed. "You said this would be clean."

"It is."

"No, it isn't."

They dragged her faster now.

A battered sedan idled at the curb, engine knocking unevenly. Not a clean car. Not staged. Rust showed along one wheel well. The rear door flew open.

As they shoved her toward it, the driver twisted around, panic already on his face.

"Are you insane?" he hissed. "This was surveillance only. Cameras everywhere. You think no one saw you? You think they didn't get my plate?"

"Drive," the first man said.

"No. This is how we get caught. This is how—"

"Drive."

The door slammed. The car lurched forward too hard, tires squealing as it pulled into traffic.

No one had taken her phone.

That was when Karoline understood.

This wasn't sanctioned.

This was panic.

The hospital dropped away in the side mirror as the sedan accelerated, fast but not careful.

Someone had broken the rules.

29

Lucía was already moving toward the window. "You let her go alone?"

"She didn't give me much choice."

Lucía reached the glass and stopped.

"There she is," she said.

Then, instantly: "Shit."

Sabine was beside her before the word finished.

Through the narrow side-window angle, Karoline appeared only in pieces—the pale line of her face, the phone in her hand, the yellow hospital light cutting a hard edge along the wall. A man stepped in behind her. Then another.

One grabbed her arm. The other clamped a hand on her mouth.

Karoline twisted fast. Her mouth opened. Sabine heard nothing through the glass, but she saw the shape of the sound.

A dark sedan slid out of shadow at the curb.

Lucía was already turning away from the window.

"They've got her," she said, her voice gone flat with focus. "Call one-two-three. Watch which way they go. I'll text if I can."

Sabine grabbed for her own phone. No bars.

"My phone has no signal."

"Use the bed phone."

Then Lucía was gone.

Sabine lunged for the bedside table, nearly knocking over the water pitcher, and snatched up the receiver. Outside, in the last broken slice of parking lot visible from the window, she caught one more glimpse of Karoline being shoved into the back seat of an old car. The sedan jerked forward and vanished behind the angle of the building.

The line clicked alive in her ear.

"Emergencias, uno-dos-tres. ¿Qué pasó?"

Sabine shut her eyes for half a second and forced her voice level. "¿Habla inglés?"

A pause.

"Yes."

"My sister was taken," Sabine said. The words came out thin and exact. "From the hospital."

"Stay on the line. Where are you calling from?"

She gave the address, the hospital name, the side entrance, the direction the car had taken as best she could judge from the brief angle she had seen. She had to repeat the entrance twice. The operator kept her talking in that procedural tone people used when panic had already arrived and they refused to let it in.

"Police have been dispatched."

Sabine did not remember hanging up.

She only remembered running.

Out the room. Into the corridor. Past the nursing station, where someone called after her in Spanish. To the stairwell because the elevator was too slow. Down one flight too hard, shoulder clipping the wall on the turn. Through the lobby. Past the security desk, where a guard had only half-risen before she was through the doors.

The outside air hit her wet and warm, carrying the after-smell of rain off concrete.

The side entrance was brighter from ground level than it had looked from above. Too bright. The yellow security light threw hard shadows over the curb and the patch of pavement where Karoline had been standing less than a minute earlier.

The street beyond it was already empty.

No sedan. No Lucía. No sign that anyone had just been taken.

Sirens reached the hospital before the police cars did—faint at first, then swelling fast. Two units swung in with lights strobing red and blue across the white walls and wet road.

Sabine ran toward the first officer before he had fully stepped out.

"Señora, did you report a kidnapping?"

"Yes. My sister."

He took in her face, her breathing, the direction of her stare. "Where did it happen?"

"Here. By the side entrance." She pointed. "They grabbed her and forced her into a car. She's a journalist and they were angry about an article—"

"Just what you saw," the officer said, not unkindly. "Not what you think."

Sabine swallowed and forced herself back into sequence. "Two men. Dark sedan. They took her that way. Less than five minutes ago."

He was already repeating the description into his radio.

Another officer moved toward the hospital door, presumably for cameras, witnesses, whatever still existed in the wake of the car.

Sabine stood in the wash of flashing lights with the useless certainty that she should still be able to stop this if she moved fast enough.

But Lucía was the one moving.

She hit the parking lot at a sprint, yanked open the driver's door, and tore out onto the street hard enough to elicit a protest from the tires. At the end of the block she caught a glimpse of taillights cutting south.

"Rogelio," she said into the radio clipped at her shoulder. "You awake?"

A crackle. Then: "Sí, señora."

Lucía shot through the next intersection, eyes flicking over taillights, dark windows, any vehicle moving too fast or too carefully. "How close to Mocoa do you have ears?"

"We only cover the forested areas," Rogelio said. "South is where we have them."

Lucía filled him in while she drove—hospital, side entrance, dark sedan, two men, journalist taken, heading south. Fast, clipped, no wasted words.

"You don't need our ears," Rogelio said when she finished. "You need our eyes. I'll alert the Guardians."

"Tell them to watch for an old vehicle where it doesn't belong."

"Sí, señora."

Lucía cut around a slower truck and kept pushing south. The road lights were thinning now. Wet pavement held them in broken streaks.

"Where would you go?" she asked.

"I don't know," Rogelio said. "I'm not a criminal."

"If los petroleros were hunting you, where would you hide?"

That bought her a beat of silence.

Then Rogelio said, "There are three roads out of town. But only one gives you options."

Lucía already knew the answer before he said it.

"I'd head south," he said. "Into the monte."

"Even though it goes nowhere fast?"

"If you go into the mountains, there's one road and helicopters. Northeast is quicker, but you're exposed. South lets you disappear."

Lucía nodded once, though he could not see it.

Then Rogelio said, quieter now, "If I knew you were chasing me, I'd go anywhere but the monte. At least you can hear a helicopter coming. Nobody hears a shadow."

Despite everything, a thin smile crept across Lucía's face.

"Then they've already made their second mistake."

30

"Stone."

Richard Stone answered on the first ring.

"Boss, we have a problem."

"Then solve it, Mercer."

"Karoline Reinhardt has been reported missing," said Daniel Mercer, RegenX's Director of Protective Services, South America.

Silence.

When Stone spoke, his voice was level. "Was I unclear about not touching her?"

"No. You were explicit."

"Then why was she taken?"

A pause.

"Based on what the policía has so far," Mercer said, "it appears it was our people."

Stone said nothing.

"We're tracking who broke protocol."

"I told you not to touch her."

"You did."

"And yet."

The silence stretched just long enough to become its own reprimand.

"I'm going down there," Stone said.

"That's not advisable."

"Why?"

"If you appear now, it ties you to the disappearance. At the moment, we may still be able to frame this as random violence."

Stone exhaled once, slow and controlled.

"A journalist publishes a critical piece on our DAC unit and disappears the same day," he said. "No one needs help drawing that connection."

"We can still manage the optics."

"Optics aren't the problem," Stone said. "Absence is."

He turned from the window and crossed to his desk. For a moment he said nothing. Mercer could hear him thinking.

"I'll hold a press conference at the DAC facility," Stone said at last. "I'll answer the claims directly. I'll announce a new green initiative for Mocoa residents. We move the story."

"That invites questions," Mercer said.

"Good. People hide when they're guilty. Visibility reads as confidence."

Mercer was quiet.

"We'll contribute manpower to the search," Stone went on. "The policía are understaffed for jungle operations. Let them see us helping."

Another pause.

"There's still a protester in the ceibo tree," Mercer said. "You'll be asked about him."

Stone gave the faintest smile.

"Perfect."

"Sir—"

"I'll offer to meet him publicly. He wants attention. I'll give him attention."

"He's asking for Indigenous rights to be respected."

"Then find something he can call a win and I can forget tomorrow," Stone said. "A land-use concession. A paused access road. Something that sounds material and costs us nothing."

"And if he mobilizes people?"

"We manage that too."

Mercer let the silence sit a beat too long. “We can’t guarantee your safety if it gets crowded. Too many variables.”

Stone glanced back toward the glass.

“That’s why we built the security into the residence,” he said. “Set the meeting for one local time tomorrow.”

31

"Rogelio," Lucía said into the radio. "You out there?"

"Sí, señora."

"Anything yet? I'm crossing the Río Rumiyaco."

"No. Nobody in town saw a vehicle matching the description."

"What about the listening stations?"

"We don't listen near the highways," Rogelio said. "Too much noise. The ears only work where vehicles shouldn't be."

Lucía exhaled through her nose. "That's not helpful."

"The word is out along all three roads," Rogelio said. "Someone will see something."

"They'll use the road first," Lucía said. "Everyone does."

"And then?"

"Then they'll realize how exposed it makes them."

A beat of static.

"You've tracked a lot of people, señora," Rogelio said.

"Once I have a trail, I can relax," Lucía said. "Right now, I'm guessing."

She pulled out to pass, accelerating past a line of slower cars. Invisibility over speed. That was the rule.

She broke it.

A siren snapped her eyes to the mirror. Red and blue filled the glass.

"Shit."

She eased onto the shoulder and waved them past.

They followed her in.

Two officers stepped out with their weapons already raised.

"Exit the vehicle. Hands in the air."

"Officers—"

"Exit. Now."

Lucía complied. Cold air. Gravel under her shoes.

"Hands on the hood."

One officer kept his weapon on her while the other moved in fast and professional, patting her down.

"That was some reckless driving."

"Yes."

"Do you know how fast you were going?"

"Too fast," Lucía said. "Write me up and let's be done."

The officer studied her. "Where are you rushing to?"

"A friend. She's in trouble."

"You won't help her dead."

"No," Lucía said evenly. "I won't."

The second officer muttered to his partner. "Doesn't match the BOLO. Wrap it up."

The first officer stepped back and started writing the ticket. His tone softened, but only slightly.

"You see anything unusual on the road today?"

Lucía shook her head. "No."

"We're looking for suspects connected to a crime nearby."

"I'll keep my eyes open."

"Drive carefully."

Lucía nodded, already turning back to the car.

Nearly fifteen minutes gone.

She pulled back onto the road and headed south.

Rogelio's voice cracked through the radio.

"Señora Lucía."

"Sí."

"They stopped for fuel in Villa Garzón. You should be close."

Lucía looked at the empty road ahead. "I should be. But I'm not."

A pause.

"I had a conversation with the policía about my driving."

"That's unfortunate," Rogelio said. "You could have caught them."

"At least we know we're on the right road."

"Sí. But we'll lose the light soon."

Lucía slammed her palm against the steering wheel and pressed harder on the accelerator.

"That slows them more than it slows me."

She drove in silence, measuring distance in fading light instead of kilometers. Each village blurred into the next: concrete storefronts, televisions flickering through open doors, children being called inside for the night. With every mile, the road darkened and the jungle pressed closer.

"Señora," Rogelio said.

"Sí."

"I think we might have something."

Lucía eased off the accelerator. "What?"

"Engine noise east of El Porvenir. Deep off-road. We can't identify it."

"How clean?"

"Not triangulated. It was short."

Thin, then. Weak data. But it was the first lead that fit the direction she needed.

"I'm taking it."

She turned onto the secondary track, gravel snapping beneath her tires as the jungle closed around her. The canopy swallowed what remained of the light. Greens flattened into shadow. The air felt heavier here.

A low sound drifted through the brush ahead.

Lucía slowed and cut the engine.

For a moment her mind shaped it into what she wanted: an idling motor, muffled by foliage.

Then she listened again.

Not mechanical.

Heavier. Wet. Irregular.

She went forward on foot anyway.

Shapes resolved through the trees. Broad backs. Slow movement. Headlamps tipped low.

Cattle.

Two men followed behind them with sticks, guiding the animals through the brush. One of them noticed her and tensed.

"Easy," Lucía said quietly, keeping her hands visible. "I'm not the police."

The older man studied her, then nodded. "Evening."

"Evening. You see a car come through here? Older sedan."

The two men exchanged a glance. No hesitation. No calculation.

"No," the older man said. "Just us."

Lucía held his gaze a moment longer.

Nothing. Fatigue. Routine.

She keyed the radio as she stepped back toward the road.

"False alarm. Farmers moving cattle. No vehicle."

"Understood," Rogelio said. "The signal was brief."

By the time she reversed back onto the highway, dusk had thickened. The horizon was bleeding into shadow.

Time lost.

She accelerated south.

Her phone rang. Lucía answered on the first ring.

"Sabine."

"I finished with the police at the hospital. I'm moving toward you."

"You should stay with Martín," Lucía said. "You can't help here. You'll slow me down."

"I can be another set of eyes," Sabine said. "Another pair of ears."

Lucía let out a quiet breath. "I work best alone."

A pause.

"Stay in contact," Lucía said.

"I will."

The line went dead.

A moment later the radio crackled again.

"Señora."

"Do you have something?"

"We picked up a sound on the listening network that could be an engine running. Might be a diesel generator."

"Where?"

"Somewhere south of Route 45 after you cross the Putumayo River."

"That narrows it a little."

"Our network doesn't give us coordinates," Rogelio said. "Only general areas."

"How far south of the highway?"

"The river and the night distort the sound. West of the river and south of the highway. Nothing better."

"Fine," Lucía said.

A few minutes later her phone buzzed.

A screenshot from Sabine.

GreenPulse sync. Background location packet. Delayed 11 min. Confidence low.

Beneath it, two lines of text: Got this weird notification. Apparently Karoline's phone surfaced long enough to spit this out.

Lucía glanced at the map. The marked zone fell inside the same broad area Rogelio had described—south of the highway, west of the river. Not a location. Just an additional data point.

If they had Karoline's phone, it could be bait.But if they wanted to disappear cleanly, they would not have let anything sync at all.

She took a slow breath.

Calm. Invisible. Success.

Her headlights caught the yellow guardrails of the bridge over the Putumayo River, bright against the grey asphalt and the darkening green beyond.

Beyond the river, smallholder farms clustered close to the road. Scattered houses. Dogs. People. She slowed and scanned for breaks in the vegetation—old access roads, abandoned oil tracks, anything that cut south into the forest.

There.

She slowed, passed it, then reversed.

She got out and jogged back.

An old trail. Barely visible now. Overgrown. No fresh tire marks.

She returned to the car and drove on.

The tree cover thickened.

Lucía braked hard.

Backed up.

There.

Tire tracks plunging straight into the underbrush. Broken branches. Leaves torn wet and bright where they had not yet dulled.

Not hidden. Chosen.

She parked on the shoulder, killed the lights, and called Sabine.

"Have you found something?"

"A car drove straight into the jungle," Lucía said. "If there's a road in there, it hasn't been used in years. I'm parking on the highway and going in on foot."

A beat.

"Is that safe?"

"Probably not. But a stolen car is the least of our worries."

"I meant walking in alone."

"Alone is the best option. I'll radio Rogelio my position."

"I'm coming after you."

Lucía closed her eyes for a fraction of a second. "Try not to wake up the jungle. And don't use your phone. You'll blind yourself."

"How am I supposed to find you, then?"

"I'll hear you long before you see me."

Lucía ended the call, sent her position, and stood still for a moment with the engine off and the lights dark, letting the world settle around her.

Then she moved.

She followed the tire tracks into the jungle. With every step the shapes sharpened. Shadows gained depth. The forest stopped being a wall and became terrain.

Ahead, something resolved through the trees.

A shape too symmetrical to belong.

She left the tracks and circled wide, lowering herself as she closed the distance.

The car.

Same model. Deeply scratched. Dented. Mud and shredded leaves plastered across the doors and hood.

Lucía crouched beside the rear wheel and listened.

The exhaust ticked as it cooled.

The metal still held warmth.

She set two fingers against the body panel, then studied the ground. Footprints. Disturbed leaves. A clear line of movement in the same direction the car had been pointing.

A thin smile touched her mouth.

Someone knew where they were going.

Good.

The certain were easier to track than the lost.

32

Mercer set his phone face down on the table and looked at the assembled team.

"Who was assigned to Reinhardt this afternoon?"

"Óscar Vélez was lead," one of them said. "Diego Londoño on transport. Mauricio Peña as support."

Mercer nodded once. "Local contractors."

"Sí."

"They were briefed no contact?"

"Sí."

"Good," Mercer said. He did not sound relieved. "Pull the footage to confirm, but until we know otherwise, assume three freelancers decided to improvise."

He paused.

"Stone wants the asset recovered. Alive. Unmarked."

A beat.

"The contractors are expendable."

Mercer brought a map of the region onto the wall.

"If they were stupid enough to grab her, they'll think speed is safety." He traced the highway northeast with one finger. "Divert Overwatch One from perimeter patrol. Run Highway 45 north first. If they went this way, we intercept before here."

He tapped a point on the map.

"Fly the bird north another fifty kilometers past the intercept point. Make sure."

His hand shifted to the mountain road.

"Then check El Pepino on the way south. Slower terrain. Fewer exits. If they took it, we catch them before dark."

"And if we don't?"

Mercer didn't look up from the map.

"Then they were even stupider than I thought, and we have them boxed between here and the Ecuadorian border."

He let that sit a moment, then looked around the room.

"And if anyone asks, they aren't ours. Freelancers. No paper trail."

Silence.

"Keep the team small. Keep it quiet. Continuous updates. No contact. I don't want a digital trail tying us to them after the grab."

He turned off the map.

"They were doing site security," he said. "Until they weren't."

33

Lucía followed the vibration of the generator along the trail Karoline and her captors had left behind.

When the faint wash of light became visible through the trees, she cut a leaf and patched one eye.

She stayed in the deepest shadows as she approached. Over the generator she could hear voices from the central hut. One female, possibly Karoline. Two men. Maybe three.

She circled wide.

Generator in a shed. One main hut. One visible exit. No obvious trails except the one she had followed in.

No guard.

That bothered her more than a guard would have.

She moved closer through thick underbrush toward the rear of the hut.

A door creaked open. Dim light spilled across the platform and into the jungle.

Lucía froze.

A man stepped out and looked down at the boards by his feet. "Only room for one out here."

The door closed again.

Lucía let out a slow breath and kept moving until she could slide beneath the hut itself, ribs pressed into mud, the smell of rot and old river water thick in her lungs.

Above her, the floorboards were swollen and dark, warped by years of rain. Light leaked through the seams in thin blades. Every shift of weight overhead sent a shudder through the wood.

Boots thudded above her.

A table scraped across planks.

Hollow. Unsteady.

The hut had been abandoned for years.

Off to one side, the structure dropped toward a ravine. The balcony was only a few boards nailed into rotting wood, with nothing under it but air.

Someone stumbled inside.

Through the cracks Lucía caught a flash of Karoline—a hand striking the floor hard enough to shake dust loose into her hair.

"Why are you in Colombia?" the man from the door demanded.

"I hear the coffee's excellent."

Karoline sucked in a sharp breath through her teeth. The sound of a boot grinding bone followed.

"You could learn interrogation techniques from the Chinese," she said, tight but steady. "But they didn't get answers either."

"We can leave you here," a second man said. "No one would ever find you."

"That's better," Karoline replied. "Fear is more effective than pain."

The boards above Lucía creaked as the second man moved closer.

"What story are you chasing?"

A pause.

"I'm writing La Sombra's biography. I was meeting her."

Silence pressed down through the planks.

"Thought so," Karoline went on. "What was her rumored body count again?"

Boots shifted overhead.

A third voice, unsteady now. "Man, I gotta piss."

"Use the balcony," the first man said.

Lucía's pulse slowed.

Good.

Karoline spoke again, her voice drifting across the boards. “Fear works fast.”

Heavy steps moved toward the rear door. The hinge groaned.

Lucía slid her knife free—not to strike, but to brace herself if she had to move fast. Her other hand settled briefly on the Glock at her waistband.

“Fuck—my—”

The crack tore through the wood and into the ground beneath her. A scream ripped through the hut. One boot punched through the platform inches from Lucía’s shoulder, showering her with splinters and dust. The other leg twisted above, bone grinding on bone.

Blood began dripping through the gaps. Hot and fast.

“Don’t move him!” the first man barked. “Tourniquet first!”

The second man cursed as belt leather snapped free.

Lucía stayed still.

34

Mercer answered on the first ring. "Mercer."

"Sir, we have a problem."

"Then solve it."

"The ground teams are blocked by a landslide on 45, just south of Villa Garzón. The road won't reopen tonight."

Mercer's expression did not change. "Can they push through with the four-by-fours?"

"No, sir. It's a rock cut packed with mud, trees, and debris. They'd bury the vehicles."

Mercer looked at the map.

"Fine. Overwatch One lifts them across. I'll send fuel up from Ecuador."

"That'll take multiple trips."

"It takes what it takes," Mercer said. "They won't get far after dark. Everyone rolls the second they have wheels. I want this contained before Stone lands tomorrow."

"Understood."

"You fly with every load," Mercer said. "Recon both sides of 45 on each pass. They're somewhere between the slide and the landing zone."

"Roger."

"I want to know the second you have something that looks like a lead."

"Yes, sir."

The line went dead.

Mercer lowered the phone and studied the map again.

Good.

Let the policía dig in the mud

35

Yari lowered the ladder from the ceibo platform and waited while Eusebio climbed into the branches. When the older man stepped onto the platform, Yari caught his forearm to steady him.

"You came."

"You asked."

Yari let go. "Stone lands tomorrow. He wants a meeting."

Eusebio settled himself against the trunk. "Then he thinks he has already won."

"I wasn't asked," Yari said. "I was told. If I'm going to stand in front of him, I need demands he can't fake."

Eusebio studied him. "What demands?"

"Remove the checkpoints from our roads," Yari said. "And give us full access to the monitoring data. Not the polished reports. The real numbers."

"The checkpoints, yes," Eusebio said. "People understand checkpoints." He shook his head. "But the data? If the regulators can't get the truth out of them, why would they hand it to you?"

"Our analysts reviewed the filings," Yari said. "The numbers change depending on who is looking. We feel the heavy air. We see the ground giving way. The data says nothing is wrong."

Eusebio's mouth tightened. "When I was young, the lies were simpler."

Yari said nothing.

"But asking a tayra how it steals eggs gets you nothing," Eusebio said.

Yari gave a short nod. "Exactly. He'll refuse the data and grant the checkpoints so he can look reasonable."

"And if he refuses both?"

"Then we came in good faith," Yari said. "And everyone sees what he is."

Eusebio looked out through the branches toward the road below. "You won't gather people here without him knowing."

"He won't climb," Yari said. "He wants me to go to him."

"Where?"

"At the DAC facility."

Eusebio was quiet for a moment.

"That's where the cameras are," Yari said. "Where the regulators stand. If he refuses the data there—"

"No."

Yari stopped.

"That is his ground," Eusebio said. "His road. His guards. His story."

Yari's jaw tightened. "It would show we're not afraid."

"It would show you walked into his fence and called it courage."

The words sat between them.

Yari looked away first. "Then where?"

"La Hacienda," Eusebio said. "Above the drowned canyon."

Yari turned back.

"He thinks the road made that place his," Eusebio said. "Let him stand beside what he drowned."

"And if he refuses there?"

"Then we block the road."

Yari's expression changed.

"One road in," Eusebio said. "One road out. He thinks owning the road means owning the story. Let him test that."

"The helicopter will see people gathering."

"Our people moved before there were roads," Eusebio said. "If you need them there, they'll be there."

Yari nodded once. "That works."

Eusebio gripped the ladder and began his descent without another word.

Yari stayed where he was, one hand against the bark, listening to the old man move down through the dark.

Below him, the road ran toward the hacienda in a clean engineered line.

For the first time since Stone's message came, Yari looked at it and saw not access, but a choke point.

36

Lucía lay under the hut while the men tightened the tourniquet, hauled their injured companion inside, and slammed the door.

An anguished scream cut through the steady thrum of the generator.

The man who seemed to be in charge followed it with, "There's more where that came from. Tell us what you know and the pain stops."

"So we're back to pain?" Karoline said. "If you don't get your friend help, he's going to bleed to death."

"If you don't give us the answers we need, we're dead anyway."

"You should have thought of that before you grabbed me."

"There are many painful ways to die in the jungle. Snakebite. Fire ants. Jaguar."

"That's kind," Karoline said. "La Sombra's targets don't get to choose."

"Even La Sombra doesn't know this place exists."

"At least you understand she's more than a legend."

"Who gave you your information?"

"Government websites."

"You have private information. Who gave it to you?"

"There was nothing in my article that isn't in the public record."

"It's the next article the boss cares about."

"I haven't written it yet."

"Stop being cute."

A faint thump, thump, thump rose above the generator and grew louder.

"Shit, Vélez, what is that?" the second man asked.

"It's a fucking helicopter. Kill the generator. The light is visible for miles."

The second man burst out the door, missed one of the uneven steps, and hit the ground hard. He scrambled up limping and ran for the generator shed. The rotor beat swelled overhead. He threw the kill switch, and the camp dropped into black.

The helicopter passed low, loud enough to shake leaves, then faded behind the ridge.

The man stepped out of the shed.

Lucía never knew whether he heard the twig snap before she fired.

He folded and hit the ground.

She was already moving, back up the trail to where the hut steps and generator shed both sat inside her angle of view.

A branch cracked behind her.

Lucía turned and dropped in one motion.

"Don't shoot," a voice whispered. "It's me. Sabine."

"Sabine, you shouldn't sneak up on people like that."

"You said to be quiet."

"I didn't think you could be that quiet."

Sabine peered at her. "What happened to your eye?"

"Leaf patch. Night vision."

"Oh." A beat. "Was that you?"

"Yes. One down. One injured. Karoline and two men still inside."

"That's good."

"Not if there's one I haven't seen."

From the hut, voices called into the dark.

"Londo?"

Nothing answered.

"Hey! Londo, what was that?"

Silence.

"How do we get to Karoline?" Sabine whispered.

"We wait."

"It sounded like they were torturing her."

"They think the helicopter saw them. They're scared. Scared men move."

Sabine said nothing.

Lucía leaned closer. "Go to the generator shed. Stay hidden. When they're all out and clear of the steps, break a branch. Stay low."

Sabine hesitated. "Shouldn't I stay close to you?"

"No. Staying out of my way is helping."

Sabine slipped off into the dark.

Lucía settled at the corner of the hut with a clear view of the steps.

Minutes later the door opened.

The injured man emerged first, sidearm wavering in front of him.

"I can't see."

"Keep moving," Vélez said behind him. "We get out before anyone else arrives."

"But what about the gunshot?"

"We're dead if we stay here."

The injured man worked his way down the steps, good leg then bad. Vélez came behind him, holding Karoline tight in front of him as a shield, his gun jammed against her side.

He called into the jungle. "Whoever's out there, if you move, the reporter dies."

Lucía held still, safety off, finger ready.

The three of them edged away from the hut.

A branch snapped sharply near the generator shed.

Both men turned toward the sound and fired.

Lucía fired once.

The injured man collapsed.

Vélez heard the shot behind him and spun the wrong way. He shoved Karoline toward the noise, fired blindly, and bolted into the brush.

Karoline hit the ground hard.

Lucía was after him at once.

He crashed through the undergrowth, loud, fast, blind. She followed by sound more than sight, closing when he snagged on vines and lost a step.

Then she stopped, steadied, and fired.

He went down.

She moved in fast, kicked the gun from his hand, and when he reached for his belt anyway, fired again.

When she came back, Sabine was on the ground with Karoline in her arms. Both were crying, though neither seemed aware of it.

"Was that necessary?" Sabine asked. "He was down."

"It ended it," Lucía said.

"Ended what?"

"The part where he might still kill someone."

Sabine drew a breath as if to argue, then stopped.

Lucía knelt beside Karoline. "How bad?"

"I'm alive," Karoline said. "That's a start."

"Can you walk to the highway?"

"I can try. I think several toes are broken."

Lucía raised an eyebrow. "What else?"

"My shoulder." Karoline winced. "And some of the stitches from the accident have opened."

Lucía touched the shoulder lightly, then more firmly. The joint sat wrong.

"It's dislocated," she said. "We fix it now."

Karoline went pale. "Now?"

"Yes."

Sabine moved in beside her sister, hands hovering uselessly.

"Breathe," Lucía said.

She braced the shoulder blade with one hand and took the forearm with the other.

Sabine saw the movement a split second before it came. "Lucía—"

Lucía pulled.

The joint went back with a wet grinding pop.

Karoline screamed.

Her body folded forward, breath punched out of her. For a moment Sabine thought she might pass out.

Lucía kept one hand on the shoulder, testing the joint carefully.

"It's in."

Karoline dragged in a ragged breath. "Warn me next time."

"Warning makes it worse," Lucía said. "Your body fights."

Sabine stared at her, anger rising fast and sharp—then saw Karoline's arm resting naturally again instead of hanging dead at her side.

The anger had nowhere to go.

Lucía tore a strip from the dead man's shirt and made a sling.

"Can you move your fingers?"

Karoline flexed them weakly. "Yes."

"Good."

Sabine adjusted the sling once it was tied, cushioning Karoline's elbow with her jacket. Her hands lingered.

Lucía stood. "We need to build a litter."

They moved quickly. Lucía cut poles and stripped branches. Sabine helped lash the drag litter together. Within minutes Karoline was secured into it.

Lucía took the front position. "I drag first. Then we swap. Quietly."

"Why?" Karoline asked. "They're dead."

Lucía looked into the trees, not at either of them.

"Because the dead aren't the only thing in a jungle that watches."

Then she started up the trail toward the highway, dragging the litter, with Sabine following close behind.

37

Lucía stopped and raised a closed fist. Then she pointed into the dense underbrush beside the path and pressed a finger to her lips.

Once the three women were concealed, she whispered, "The car is ahead. I saw movement near it. Stay here."

Several minutes passed in cold, wet silence. Only the brush shifting marked Lucía's return.

"We have company," she whispered. "Hired men. Not policía. New plan. We head for the river and follow it out."

"How far?" Sabine asked.

"Too far. Move."

They cut away from the trail at right angles, Lucía leading, Sabine helping drag Karoline through the undergrowth until they had put distance between themselves and the shack.

"Rest," Lucía said.

Sabine bent over, dragging air into her lungs.

"Not long," Lucía added. "They'll find the bodies. Then they'll find our trail."

The next hours were brutal.

They settled into a rhythm: move until Karoline could not bear it, stop until she could. Lucía broke trail and held a bearing toward the river. With every cycle, Karoline weakened. With every stop, Sabine needed a longer rest.

Dawn seeped into the jungle.

Better light for Sabine and Karoline. Better tracking for anyone behind them.

Somewhere upslope, an unseen bird gave a harsh metallic call. Lucía looked up in time to catch the dark shape shifting between branches, a flash of pale throat in the weak light before it disappeared again.

Lucía called another halt and listened.

Birds were lifting behind them in small bursts, then resettling farther forward. A pattern. Moving toward them.

She turned at once. “Up. Now.”

“I’ve barely caught my breath,” Sabine said.

“They’re less than two minutes behind us.”

“How do you know?”

Lucía was already moving. “The jungle knows.”

They hauled Karoline forward.

The slope rose steeply, roots slick underfoot, the ground just soft enough to give at the wrong moment. Behind them came voices—too close now.

Sabine stumbled. The litter tilted. Karoline’s injured arm slipped free and struck the ground.

Karoline gasped.

“Sorry,” Sabine said, catching the pole before the litter rolled. She tucked the arm back in place.

Lucía glanced back once. “You good?”

“Yes,” Sabine said too fast.

“Karoline?”

Karoline gave a breathless, broken laugh. “Define good.”

“Don’t talk,” Sabine said. “Just breathe.”

“I’m bleeding again.”

Sabine saw the blood soaking through Karoline’s side and looked away at once. No space for fear. Not now.

Lucía raised a fist again.

Silence.

Then voices behind them. Closer still.

She scanned the hillside. Grey patches among the green. Exposed roots. Old slump scars. Wrong ground.

"We go across," she said.

Across meant unstable footing, but upslope would cost them time they no longer had.

Sabine nodded. "Go."

They moved laterally.

The litter jarred over a rock. Karoline cried out, then bit it off.

"I'm sorry," she whispered. "I'm slowing you down."

"You're not," Sabine said.

Another shout behind them.

The ground changed under Sabine's boots. Softer. Looser.

A shallow rut ran diagonally across the slope beneath the leaf litter. The downhill pole of the litter dropped into it.

"Lucía—"

The rut split open.

The crack ran fast along the buried seam, sharp as a rifle shot. For an instant the break between Sabine and the litter was no wider than a hand. Then the center lane liquefied.

The slope let go.

The litter slewed downhill as the earth beneath it turned to slurry. Lucía and Karoline were dragged into the moving mud in one violent surge.

Sabine lunged for them.

The slab under her feet sheared sideways instead of down.

She was hurled laterally, slammed into the buttressed roots of a ceiba while the main body of the slide thundered past in front of her.

Trees snapped.

Soil roared.

Sabine watched helpless as Karoline vanished into the moving earth.

"Karoline!"

Then her own ground collapsed.

The world became impact and motion—branches striking, her body spinning as the rotating slab beneath her broke apart and dropped. The air was driven from her lungs. She hit something hard enough to flash white-hot pain through her body.

Then everything fell away again.

38

The turboprop banked low over the green sprawl of the Putumayo basin and hit the short runway at Villagarzón hard enough to rattle the cabin. Heat shimmered above the tarmac. The engines wound down with a metallic whine.

Mercer was waiting beside a black Escalade when the door opened.

Stone descended first, sunglasses on, expression unreadable.

"Good morning, sir," Mercer said.

"Was it?"

They shook once and moved to the vehicle.

Inside, the doors sealed shut. Mercer pulled away from the runway.

"What do you know?" Stone asked.

Mercer kept his eyes on the road. "The situation is narrower than it was last night."

Stone looked out the window. "Define narrower."

"We found the kidnappers' hideout. Two bodies on site. One more nearby. The reporter was recovered there, then lost again."

Stone turned slightly. "Lost how?"

"Our men tracked the three women at first light—Karoline Reinhardt, her sister, and La Sombra. They were close when a slope failed under them."

"And?"

"They went into the slide. We lost three contractors in the same event."

Stone said nothing.

Mercer added, "No movement. No visual. No thermal. Overwatch made two passes before the ceiling dropped too low to be useful."

"So not confirmed."

"No, sir."

"But likely."

"Yes."

Stone leaned back.

"Natural causes create fewer complications," he said.

"Yes, sir."

"Who pulled them out of the hut?"

"No sign of additional personnel."

Stone let that sit.

Mercer said, "There may be more to the La Sombra legend than we assumed."

Stone did not answer that.

"What about the bodies?" he asked.

"Ecuadorian contractors. Clean separation. If they surface, they belong to no one."

"Good."

The Escalade rolled past a line of motorcycles and market stalls before Mercer spoke again.

"The village deaths are starting to turn our way. The medical examiner says probable gas accumulation in low ground. Possible volcanic or geothermal release. Nothing conclusive."

"And the glowing water?"

"Our analysts are calling it biological," Mercer said. "A fungal response under elevated dissolved CO_2. Strange, but no way to connect it directly to us."

Stone was quiet for a moment. "Who else knows?"

"Our people. Martín Chasoy came close."

"Came?"

"His lab exploded. Fire chief is calling it chemical ignition. He survived."

"Will he?"

"Unknown."

Stone gave a small nod. "Unfortunate."

They drove in silence for several seconds.

"And the man in the tree?" Stone asked.

"He agreed to meet at one."

"Where?"

"At the dam," Mercer said. "La Hacienda side. Above the reservoir."

Stone's jaw shifted almost imperceptibly. "He changed the ground."

Mercer nodded once. "Three friendly reporters are already on site. Local, national, and UP wire."

"Good. I want the dialogue on camera."

"And if he escalates?"

Stone looked out at the jungle.

"He can't," he said. "We control the road."

The Escalade turned off the highway.

"And Mercer?"

"Yes, sir?"

"If the women are alive—"

"We'll address it," Mercer said.

39

The hillside moved.

The earth dropped away with a sound like something ancient tearing open. Soil liquefied beneath their boots. Trees snapped in sequence. The drag litter twisted sideways.

Sabine shouted something—Lucía couldn't tell what—and then the slope gave way in full.

She lost her grip on the litter and felt Karoline sliding away with it as steady ground vanished. Mud flooded Lucía's mouth. Branches struck her face. The world turned sideways.

Then impact.

Hard. Sudden.

The slide roared past and over and then, as abruptly as it began, settled into choking silence broken only by falling debris and the distant rush of the river below.

Lucía forced her eyes open.

She was half-buried but upright, one arm wedged against a trunk that had held. The air smelled wrong—metallic and sour beneath the loam—and patches of vegetation on the torn slope above stood grey and brittle, roots exposed in soil that had slumped long before today.

She dug herself free and scanned.

"Karoline!"

A weak cough answered her.

Lucía slid down the churned slope, boots sinking into mud that had not decided whether it was earth or slurry. The litter had shattered, one pole gone. Karoline lay tangled in the torn tarp, half-covered in debris.

Lucía cleared her face first. "Stay with me."

Karoline's eyes opened. Disoriented. Alive.

"My shoulder—" she gasped.

"I know."

Lucía cut the remaining straps and checked quickly. The reopened sutures in Karoline's side were bleeding, but not fast enough to stop everything else.

"Sabine," Karoline breathed.

Lucía scanned uphill. Downhill. Nothing but churned earth and snapped timber.

"Sabine!"

No answer.

Only distant shouts from above the scar. Too far to see. Close enough to matter.

Lucía pulled Karoline free of the debris.

"What if Sabine's trapped?" Karoline said, her voice shaking.

Lucía looked once more at the broken slope, then toward the voices above it.

"Stable ground first," she said.

She dragged Karoline toward a stand of ceibas whose roots still held. Behind them another section of earth slumped into the ravine with a heavy, sucking slide.

Lucía did not look back.

Under the trees, she worked fast. A sapling. Vines. Cut branches. A new litter built with the economy of someone who had done this before.

"You need to look for Sabine."

"We need cover."

She strapped Karoline in and moved them deeper through the trees, threading between stumps and thickets until the slope eased and the ground felt less willing to betray them.

"We're far enough now," Karoline said. "You should go back."

"We need water."

"Where are we going to find drinking water here?"

"We'll find water," Lucía said. "It just won't be good water."

Karoline said nothing after that.

Lucía guided them into a narrow runoff ravine where a thin stream worked its way over stone and roots. She set the litter down, helped Karoline upright against a small tree, and cupped water to her own mouth first.

It tasted metallic and flat.

She brought a second handful to Karoline. "Worst tea you'll ever drink."

Karoline took a sip, coughed, and spat. "That's vile."

"It's still better than thirst."

Karoline swallowed the next mouthful. Then another.

When they stopped, she said, "I can stay here. Go look for Sabine."

Lucía listened to the jungle before she answered. The slope was still settling. The birds had not resumed.

"I'm finding the path to the river," she said. "If that takes me near the slide, I'll look."

Karoline's voice cracked. "She came because of me."

Lucía looked at her.

"I lost my brothers in the war," she said. "For a long time I thought that made their deaths mine."

A beat.

"It didn't."

Karoline's eyes filled.

"They chose," Lucía said. "So did Sabine."

"But if we can help her—"

"The best way to help her is to stay alive."

Lucía left her there and moved down the ravine.

The first gully narrowed into a sharp drop, too steep to lower Karoline without doing more damage. Lucía backed out, crossed the slope well clear of the fresh scar, and listened.

A low mechanical thrum.

Not jungle.

Rotor blades.

She dropped beneath a curtain of exposed roots where old erosion had undercut a tree and pressed herself into the leaf litter.

The helicopter came in fast from upriver.

It did not sweep wide.

It went straight to the landslide.

It hovered over the exposed scar, circling the raw earth and broken canopy. Then it made another pass. No ropes. No descent. No search pattern.

Not rescue.

It climbed instead, banked once more over the scar, and turned away.

Lucía stayed where she was until the sound was gone.

When she moved again, she cut farther across the slope and found a second ravine—steeper than she liked, but workable. Downhill would be possible with gravity. Uphill with the litter, impossible.

It would do.

On the way back, she climbed just above the edge of the scar to orient herself.

Her hand slipped against a trunk.

Mud smeared beneath her palm.

Lucía froze.

The mark had shape: the heel of a hand dragged downward, fingers spread, sliding. Dry on the surface. Still soft underneath.

She lifted her own hand and compared.

Different angle. Different pressure.

Someone had caught themselves there.

She scanned for more, but the churned earth and leaf litter gave her nothing.

She memorized the spot and descended toward Karoline.

"Found a way down," she said.

She did not mention the handprint. Not yet.

40

The hydroelectric dam loomed over the gorge, a poured wall stitched across what had once been a canyon. Behind it, the reservoir spread wide and glassy, reflecting the sky with unsettling calm. The old river lay somewhere beneath it—drowned, redirected, mastered.

Steel intake towers rose from the water in careful symmetry. Along the far bank, maintenance roads cut precise lines through what remained of forest. Transmission cables carried power toward the CCS site.

It was a place built to project inevitability.

A folding table had been set on the crest of the dam. Two chairs on one side. Two on the other. Cameras positioned just far enough back to suggest transparency without surrendering control. Security stood at a respectful distance—visible, disciplined, unblinking.

The wind moved lightly across the reservoir.

The water did not.

Stone stepped out of the Escalade without looking at it and moved toward his chair.

Mercer scanned the perimeter. Private security on the road. Two at the gate. Three near the retaining wall. Drone airborne.

Yari waited beneath a jacaranda near the terrace edge. No ladder. No platform. No tree this time.

He joined Stone at the table.

"You chose this place," Stone said.

"I did," Yari replied. "You built the road. You flooded the canyon. It seemed appropriate."

Stone smiled faintly. "We're standing on the future. A renewable energy asset that will power this valley for generations."

"We're standing beside land that held our dead," Yari said. "A river that fed our people. A dam that powers your extraction."

Behind the cameras, someone adjusted a lens.

Stone folded his hands loosely. "You asked for two things. Removal of checkpoints and access to monitoring data."

"Yes."

"The checkpoints can be reviewed," Stone said. "If they are impeding lawful movement, we can adjust."

"They are. And the data?"

Stone did not blink.

"Telemetry is subject to regulatory chain-of-custody. We do not release incomplete or proprietary datasets outside established channels."

"Our analysts reviewed your filings," Yari said. "The numbers change depending on who is looking. The ground feels wrong. The air feels heavy. Your reports insist nothing is wrong."

"That is because nothing is wrong."

"And the data?"

"No."

The wind shifted.

Beyond the outer fence, a low rhythm began. Not loud. Hollow. Deliberate.

Mercer's head turned slightly toward the treeline.

Yari did not.

Then the forest moved.

Not all at once. One figure stepped from the shade near the service road. Another appeared behind the retaining wall. Then three women emerged between the transmission pylons and stopped, hands at their sides. No banners. No shouting. Just people occupying ground that had been counted as empty.

Security tightened.

Mercer touched his sleeve. "All units hold."

The drone banked.

More people emerged—not rushing, not wavering. They had been there long before the engines arrived. A cluster of teenagers stepped onto the access road and stopped. An older woman followed and stood with them. Then more bodies filled the spaces between.

Within seconds the perimeter no longer felt private. It felt porous. Claimed.

The drumbeat deepened. Voices joined it—not slogans, but river names. Place names. Old names carried across the water.

One bottle struck the outer fence and shattered.

A guard flinched and raised his rifle a fraction.

Mercer stepped forward at once. "Down."

The muzzle lowered.

Stone's hand went once to his cuff.

Then stilled.

"You've made your point," he said.

Yari held his gaze. "I haven't started."

The gate groaned as hands pressed against it—not breaking, just reminding everyone that it was there.

Mercer leaned toward Stone. "Sir. Inside."

Stone kept his eyes on Yari a moment longer.

"We conclude," he said. "We will review the checkpoints."

"And the data?"

"No."

The voices rose. The drumbeat quickened.

This time Mercer did not wait.

"Residence. Now."

Security closed ranks. The Escalade repositioned, but the road was no longer clean. Bodies occupied space where empty access had been assumed.

As Stone was guided toward the residence entrance, he glanced once at the reservoir.

Still unmoving.

Behind him, the forest kept producing people.

41

Lucía and Karoline drank until their stomachs felt heavy with the metallic water.

Lucía checked the reopened sutures again. Still seeping, but clean. No thickening yet. No swelling beyond what she expected.

She lifted the drag litter and worked them down the ravine toward the river.

The descent was slow. Twice the litter slid sideways. Once Lucía had to brace her shoulder against a trunk to keep Karoline from rolling out. By the time they reached the bank, twilight had thickened into darkness.

The Putumayo moved broad and brown below them, carrying branches and silt in a steady glide. No boats. No engines. Just insects beginning their night shift.

Lucía scraped out a shallow hollow above the flood line and wove branches into a low screen.

"No fire," she said. "No light."

Karoline watched the river. "You should search for Sabine."

"It's too dark."

"You found me in the dark."

"They shone a beacon for me to follow."

Karoline said nothing for a while.

Then, quietly, "She came because of me."

Lucía kept listening to the jungle. Insects returning in pulses. Frogs starting up. The river unchanged.

"When I was sixteen," Karoline said, "I found out my grandfather was Stasi. Not rumor. Real. My mother hid it." She swallowed. "Later I published it."

Lucía did not look at her.

"I told myself secrets rot families. That dragging them into the daylight was the honest thing."

"And was it?"

Karoline let out something close to a laugh. "Maybe. It still broke her."

For a while there was only the river.

"I was good at it," Karoline said. "Finding what people wanted buried. I liked it."

Lucía glanced at her then.

Karoline's face had gone vague in the dark. Mostly voice now.

"If Sabine dies because she followed me here..."

Her voice thinned and failed.

After a while Lucía said, "When my brothers died, I went after the men I blamed."

Karoline turned her head.

"Some deserved it," Lucía said.

A pause.

"Some didn't."

Karoline stayed quiet.

"I told myself it was justice," Lucía said. "Sometimes it was. Sometimes I just needed someone else to hurt."

The insects swelled and dropped again.

"Do you regret it?" Karoline asked.

Lucía took a long time to answer.

"Enough."

Karoline let out a brittle breath.

Lucía adjusted the sling at her shoulder.

"You dig because you can't leave things buried," she said.

Karoline stared at the black line of water. "If I stop, I don't know who I am."

Lucía tightened the knot.

"Maybe," she said, "you'll live long enough to find out."

Karoline shivered.

Lucía pressed the back of her hand to Karoline's forehead. Warm. Not yet dangerous. The wound smelled wrong beneath the mud and river water.

"At first light," Lucía said, "I'll look for Sabine. If she's moving, she'll move toward water."

"And if she can't?"

Lucía looked upriver into the dark.

"Then I'll search close to where we lost her."

Karoline closed her eyes.

The jungle thickened around them.

Lucía lay back but did not sleep.

She watched the river and replayed the handprint in her mind.

Heel of the palm. Drag marks. Recent.

Not hope.

Data.

42

Inside the residence, Stone stood with a glass of bourbon and looked out at the sunset breaking across the reservoir and the intake towers below.

"Beautiful," he said.

Mercer did not answer at once. His attention was on the swelling noise outside and the live feeds shifting across his tablet.

Stone watched the reflected light on the water. "Some people still insist on standing in the way of progress."

"Your executive call is live in three minutes," Mercer said.

They moved into the boardroom.

The screens lit up:

Daniel Hargrove, CFO.

Megan Whitaker, COO.

Lucas Reed, CMO.

Stone sat at the head of the table.

"Keep this efficient," he said. "You've all seen the footage."

Whitaker spoke first. "Security says protest density doubled in the last twenty minutes. How many are we looking at?"

"Two hundred initially," Mercer said. "Now closer to six."

"That's not spontaneous," Hargrove said.

"No," Stone replied. "It's organized."

A sharp crack sounded through the residence.

Mercer looked to the wall monitor. A plastic water jug bounced off the inner fence. Then a rock. The drone feed jolted.

"Was that gunfire?" Reed asked.

"No," Mercer said. "Thrown objects."

Whitaker leaned toward the screen. "Why are they inside the service road?"

"They're not supposed to be."

On the feed, two protesters ran across the dam before security intercepted them. A third hit a maintenance ladder bolted to the intake housing.

"Get him down," Mercer said into his sleeve.

Stone did not look away.

"This is theatre," he said.

Another impact. This time glass, not shattered but failing.

Hargrove straightened. "How secure is the residence if the outer perimeter's compromised?"

"It's secure," Mercer said. "The perimeter is compressing."

The drone feed flickered out and returned.

When it did, the crowd was closer. The gate was no longer cleanly visible.

A guard shoved someone back. Too hard.

Reed swore. "If that goes viral—"

"It already is," Whitaker said. "Local feeds are live."

A louder crash came from the lower level.

Mercer's tablet chimed. He read the message once, then again.

"Sir."

Stone didn't move.

"Inner perimeter's been breached at the retaining wall."

A beat.

"They're on the terrace stairs."

Stone's jaw tightened. "Security will push them back."

"They are pushing," Mercer said. "We've lost distance."

On the screen, a protester reached the base of the residence before being dragged away. The crowd surged, then held.

One road in. One road out. Blocked.

Hargrove chose his words carefully. "Richard, this is no longer optics. This is liability."

Whitaker added, "If something ignites out there, if someone falls from the dam—"

"It won't," Stone snapped.

Another report came through Mercer's earpiece. His posture changed.

"Sir. We need to relocate."

Stone looked at him. "To where?"

"Safe room."

Silence settled over the table.

Reed blinked. "Is that necessary?"

"Yes," Mercer said.

Outside, the chant had changed. Rhythmic now. Unified.

A heavy thud rang through the structure. Metal, not glass.

Whitaker's voice dropped. "You cannot be physically present if this turns."

Mercer stepped closer. "Sir. Move."

Stone drained his bourbon, stood, adjusted a cuff, smoothed his jacket.

"This is unnecessary."

"Maybe," Mercer said. "But it's prudent."

Security entered fast but without panic. They left the boardroom while the executive team watched from thousands of miles away.

The hallway lights seemed brighter now. More artificial. More controlled.

Another impact shook the building behind them.

Ahead, a reinforced steel door sat flush with the wall.

Mercer keyed the panel. The lock disengaged with a heavy internal shift.

"Sir, once this seals, there are only two ways to open it."

"Yes," Stone said. "My palm or Houston."

He stepped inside.

The door sealed behind him with a thick, final sound.

Outside, the protest swelled.

Inside, the air was cool. Engineered. Silent.

The safe room was smaller than the boardroom but more elegant—sealed concrete disguised with walnut panels, recessed lighting, filtered air. A space built for continuity.

Stone removed his jacket and draped it over a chair.

The screens remained live.

Whitaker's face hovered in a bright Houston conference room.

Stone sat. "Where were we?"

Reed answered first. "We need contingency language. The protest is being streamed live and your media contacts are already asking for comment."

"Have we released the statement on the agreement?"

"Yes. But they're asking for comment on the escalation and the demand for transparency around the data."

"Then give them the usual response," Stone said, loosening his tie and reaching for water. "We release everything regulators require. What they want is proprietary. Competitive." He drank. "And find a better word than protesters. Eco-terrorists, perhaps. Insurgents."

Whitaker narrowed her eyes. "Richard, are you all right?"

"The lighting is different in here."

He set down the glass.

The air felt heavier than the boardroom.

Warm, perhaps.

He adjusted his collar.

A pressure built behind his eyes. Not pain. Fullness.

He took another breath.

Then another.

Neither helped.

"Turn up the ventilation," he said.

Mercer's voice came through the intercom. "Already at maximum, sir."

Stone felt the airflow on his face. It gave him nothing.

A faint tone chimed overhead.

He looked up at the environmental display above the main screen.

"Mercer," he said, irritation sharpening, "I'm getting an air-quality alert."

"Reviewing intake now, sir."

Stone stood.

The room tilted—not visibly, but inside him.

He put a hand on the table.

Whitaker was on her feet now. "Richard, sit down."

"I'm fine."

His voice sounded slower than he intended.

He drew in another breath.

No relief.

That annoyed him more than it frightened him.

"Mercer," he said, more forcefully now, "override the external intake."

"Attempting."

Stone crossed to the door.

The palm scanner illuminated.

He pressed his hand against it casually.

ACCESS DENIED — BIOMETRIC VARIANCE.

He blinked.

"What does that mean?"

Mercer did not answer immediately. When he did, his voice came thin through the speaker.

"Sir, your oxygen saturation and pulse are outside acceptable parameters."

Stone laughed once. Short. Disbelieving.

"Then adjust the parameters."

He pressed again.

ACCESS DENIED.

Heat climbed his neck and ears.

Whitaker's voice sharpened. "Richard, sit down."

"I am not fainting in my own residence."

He inhaled sharply.

That was when panic brushed him—not emotional panic, but physiological. His body wanted more air. He was breathing faster. He did not understand why.

The display glowed red.

"Sir," Mercer said over the intercom, and now the strain showed, "I need you to stay calm."

Stay calm.

Stone tried.

His heart was pounding. His hands had begun to tingle. The room did not feel small, but it had begun to feel close.

He walked back to the table.

Sat.

Stood again at once.

No position helped.

Whitaker was louder now. Reed had stopped talking entirely.

Stone tried to answer someone—he could not tell who.

"...ventilation," he managed.

"External intake may be compromised," Mercer said.

Compromised.

Stone's mind seized on it instantly.

The intake.Underground.Low elevation.Buried to prevent sabotage.

"It was supposed to be secure."

"No confirmed breach, sir."

His next breath did not clear the fog thickening behind his eyes.

He pressed his palm to the scanner again.

ACCESS DENIED.

"Mercer—"

The word came out broken.

"Whitaker," Mercer snapped, "remote override from Houston."

"It'll take a few minutes," she said. "The security fob is in the safe."

"Do it."

Houston.Distance.Time.

Stone leaned against the door. The cool metal felt steadier than he did.

His thoughts had started to slow.

Not enough to miss it.Enough to understand.

The intake.Underground.

His legs weakened.

He slid down the door to one knee.

Indignity hit him harder than fear.

He clenched his fists and pulled in air that still would not satisfy. It felt like drinking from an empty glass.

Whitaker was saying something. Reed too. Their voices had begun to flatten, lose edges.

"Richard, stay with us."

Stay.

He fixed his gaze on the walnut panel across from him. On the symmetry of the room. On the continuity he had built into it.

His last coherent thought was not of the protest. Not of the board.

It was of engineering.

His vision narrowed.

Sound receded.

He exhaled once.

And did not inhale again.

Outside the sealed door, Mercer stared at the monitor as Stone's vitals collapsed into a flat, unmoving line.

Inside, the air system continued to hum as designed.

43

Lucía woke at first light and slipped away while Karoline still slept.

The air was cooler. In the grey wash of dawn, the slope looked almost innocent. The torn earth had settled into quiet shapes, as if yesterday's violence had been imagined.

She returned first to the tree with the mud smear. The mark was still there: heel of the palm dragged downward, fingers spread. Not a fall. A catch.

If it was Sabine, she had changed direction fast.

Lucía angled toward the nearest intact grove, scanning for broken stems, disturbed moss, displaced leaf litter. She found a faint scuff, then a snapped twig at knee height, and followed it low and deliberate.

The trail tightened her chest with cautious hope.

Then it vanished.

No crushed ferns. No second mark. Nothing.

Lucía studied the last sign again.

She let the disappointment pass without indulging it.

A sharp metallic cry rose from a different copse upslope. Lucía caught a glimpse of a large black grackle taking flight.

She shifted direction.

The canopy thickened. Light broke into green shards. The ground softened underfoot.

A dark smear marked the underside of a broad leaf.

Blood.

Not much.

She did not call out. She listened.

The jungle held still.

Then came a sound.

Not a voice.

A wet, restrained cough.

Lucía froze.

It came again. Shorter this time. Choked off.

She moved toward it. "Sabine," she said quietly.

Nothing.

Then another cough, closer.

Lucía parted a screen of low branches and found her wedged beneath the buttressed roots of a massive tree, half-curled on her side.

Mud streaked her face. One sleeve was torn. Her breathing was shallow and wrong.

Her eyes opened at the movement. It took a second for them to focus.

"Lucía?"

Relief flickered there—and disappeared when Sabine tried to sit and failed.

Lucía crouched beside her. "Don't."

Sabine swallowed, then coughed again. This time Lucía saw the blood clearly, bright against the mud on her hand.

"Where's Karoline?" Sabine rasped.

"Alive. Hurt. By the river."

Sabine closed her eyes for half a second.

"How long have you been coughing blood?"

"Since last night." Her voice was thin. "It hurts to breathe deep."

Lucía laid a careful hand against her ribs. Sabine flinched sharply.

"What did you hit?"

"A tree, I think."

Lucía listened to her breathing. Guarded. Uneven. No obvious wheeze, but something was wrong deep inside.

"You stayed close."

"If I went farther," Sabine said, wincing as she shifted, "you wouldn't find me."

Lucía said nothing to that.

"Can you stand?"

Sabine tried. She got halfway up before another coughing fit doubled her over. More blood this time.

Lucía caught her before she dropped.

"How far?" Sabine asked when she could speak again.

"Far enough."

"I can walk."

"Until you can't."

Sabine gave her a look that was almost irritation.

Good. Irritation meant she was still present.

Lucía pulled Sabine's arm over her shoulders. "Then prove it slowly."

They started downslope.

Behind them, a strip of loosened earth sighed free and slid away. The hillside was still moving.

The return took longer than it should have. Sabine leaned heavier with every stretch, stopping twice to brace against trunks when the coughing took her. Lucía adjusted without comment, picking softer ground, doubling back once to avoid an exposed patch where the slope looked ready to go again.

By the time they reached the ravine, the sun had broken through the canopy.

Lucía came through the undergrowth first.

Karoline pushed herself upright against the tree. "Did you—"

Lucía stepped aside.

Sabine emerged behind her.

For one instant Karoline's face emptied with relief.

Then Sabine doubled over coughing, and Karoline saw the blood.

"Bine—"

Sabine tried to wave it off. “I’m fine.”

“You are visibly not fine,” Karoline said, already reaching for her with her good arm.

Lucía lowered Sabine carefully beside her sister. “Chest injury,” she said. “Internal, maybe. She walks, but not far.”

Karoline touched Sabine’s shoulder, then her face, as if confirming she was real. “I thought you were gone.”

“So did I,” Sabine said.

That was all. But it held.

Sabine bent her head against Karoline’s shoulder for one brief moment before the next cough made her pull away.

Lucía let them have those seconds. No more.

Then she straightened. “Stay hidden. I’m getting us out.”

She noted the flush in Karoline’s face, the tremor under her skin, the way Sabine guarded every deeper breath.

None of them were getting far on foot.

Lucía moved upstream and settled into shadow above a break in the bank where she could watch the river without being seen.

The first boat was a narrow canoe with two boys and a bundle of firewood. Too small. Too uncertain. She let it go.

The second announced itself before it rounded the bend: the sharp, uneven buzz of a two-stroke engine.

A peque-peque.

Lucía studied the silhouette.

One man. Fishing net at his feet. Fuel can behind him. No second rider. No alert scan of the bank.

Still, when she stepped out, she kept one hand raised and the other low near her holster.

The fisherman throttled down but did not come all the way in.

“What’s wrong?”

“Three injured,” Lucía said. “Landslide.”

His eyes dropped to the weapon at her hip.

She saw the hesitation and moved her hand away from it. Then she reclipped her holster slowly.

Behind her, Sabine coughed again. Wet. Raw.

That changed him.

He eased the boat in and grounded it on the mudbank.

Loading them was ugly.

Karoline could not manage the bank without biting back a cry at every shift of the sling. Sabine tried to help and nearly folded when the coughing seized her again. The fisherman grabbed Karoline under the good arm while Lucía half-carried, half-lowered Sabine into the bow. For a second the boat rocked hard enough that all three of them froze.

Then it steadied.

The fisherman looked from one sister to the other. "Hospital," he said.

"Yes."

He hesitated when Lucía asked for his phone, then handed it over.

She turned slightly away and dialed.

"Rogelio. It's Lucía."

A pause.

"You're alive?"

"Yes."

"Where?"

"Putumayo. South of 45. On the river."

"Did you find Karoline?"

"We found both of them."

Silence.

"And the kidnappers?"

"The jungle claimed them. Others came after us. Mercs. Helicopter too."

"RegenX?"

"I didn't stop to read the logo."

Another pause.

"What do you need?"

"Pickup at the 45 bridge. Straight to the hospital."

"For all of you?"

"For the sisters," Lucía said. Then, after a beat: "I'm coming too."

"I'll have someone waiting," Rogelio said. Then his voice changed. "You should know something before you get there."

Lucía looked at the river.

"What?"

"Everything changed last night."

The line crackled.

"Stone is dead."

Lucía said nothing.

Behind her, Sabine was coughing again and Karoline had started to shiver in earnest.

The fisherman turned the bow upstream.

The current fought them for every meter.

So would whatever waited at the bridge.

44

The safe-room locks released with a compressed hiss, and a pocket of stale air pushed into the hallway.

Stone lay crumpled just inside the door.

Mercer crossed the threshold at once and dropped beside him. Two fingers to the carotid.

Nothing.

"Get the AED."

He started compressions while one of the security men tore the unit from the wall cabinet and dropped it beside him. Pads on. Analyze. Shock advised.

They delivered one.

Stone's body jerked and fell back into the same dead slackness.

A second shock.

Then a third.

No rhythm. No pulse.

The EMTs arrived and pushed past Mercer with the blunt efficiency of people who already knew how this usually ended.

He moved aside and let them work.

Inside the room, the air remained cool, filtered, unnaturally still. No sign of struggle. Nothing disturbed except the body on the floor and the systems still humming as designed.

Then one of the medics swore softly.

Mercer turned.

The younger EMT had backed out of the room and braced a hand against the wall. His face had gone pale beneath the fluorescent wash.

"You all right?" Mercer asked.

The medic nodded too quickly, then stopped. "Dizzy."

His partner was already on his feet. "Mateo?"

"Probably nothing," the younger man said, though he did not sound convinced.

"Get him farther back," Mercer said.

The older EMT guided him down the hall and sat him on a bench. Someone handed over a portable oxygen cylinder. The mask went on. A few breaths later, color began to return.

Mercer watched the safe-room door.

Then he pulled out his phone and dialed Whitaker.

She answered immediately. "What do you know?"

"No pulse. No response. EMTs are working him."

A beat.

"And?"

"One medic got light-headed after entry. He's on oxygen now."

Silence for a fraction too long.

Then: "Until proven otherwise, this was a medical event."

"Yes."

"Cooperate with local authorities as required. Volunteer nothing."

"Understood."

"With Stone down, I'm acting CEO under emergency protocol."

"Yes."

Another pause.

"Anything else?"

Mercer looked back toward the safe room. One EMT still bent over Stone. The other sat on the bench in the hall, mask on, breathing slowly.

"No," he said.

"Learn what you can," Whitaker said. "And report back."

The line went dead.

Mercer stayed where he was, phone still in his hand, listening to the residence systems.

Everything sounded as it should.

That was the part he disliked most.

45

The fisherman ran the engine hard, the narrow hull shuddering as it fought the current. The bow slapped brown water, throwing spray that caught the light and fell back in a fine mist.

Lucía knelt near the stern, one hand braced on the gunwale, the other steadying Sabine's shoulder. Sabine lay half-curled against Karoline, her breath shallow, eyes half-open but drifting.

"Stay with me," Karoline whispered, brushing wet hair from Sabine's face. "Bine. Look at me."

Sabine tried. The effort cost her.

A cough seized her without warning. She turned, but not fast enough. Dark flecks stained the inside of her sleeve.

Lucía saw it and said nothing.

Karoline's face had gone pale beneath the jungle grime, except for the feverish color burning high in her cheeks. She swayed with the motion of the boat, jaw clenched as if that alone could keep her upright.

"You're shaking," Lucía said.

"I'm fine." Karoline swallowed. "Just get us there."

The river narrowed around a gravel bar, the current tightening under them. The fisherman leaned into the tiller, engine whining, eyes fixed ahead. On both banks the forest stood whole and indifferent.

Sabine's breathing hitched again. Not a cough this time—something thinner. A faint whistle on the inhale.

Lucía shifted her weight and found herself counting breaths.

Too fast. Too shallow.

"Bridge ahead," the fisherman called over the engine.

The concrete span came into view around the bend, low and plain against the sky. A pickup waited on the dirt shoulder above the embankment. Rogelio stood beside it, scanning the river.

The boat hit the bank hard enough to jolt all three women. Lucía moved first, rising into the wobble and hauling Sabine up under the arms.

Sabine tried to help and nearly folded at once, a broken sound catching in her throat.

"Easy," Rogelio said as he came down the embankment—then stopped when he saw her mouth.

Sabine's lips had gone dusky blue.

His expression changed.

Lucía shifted Sabine higher. "Take Karoline."

Karoline tried to climb out on her own and failed when the bank gave way under one boot. Rogelio caught her under the good arm before she fell back into the hull. She bit down hard on a cry, then forced herself up again.

The fisherman held the boat steady with both hands, boots sliding in the mud.

For a second the whole transfer threatened to come apart—Sabine sagging, Karoline slipping, the hull knocking sideways against the bank.

Then Rogelio found his footing.

Lucía half-carried Sabine up the embankment while Rogelio dragged Karoline after them. By the time they reached the truck, Sabine was coughing again, each breath thinner than the last.

They got her into the back seat first. Karoline climbed in after her and pulled Sabine against her shoulder, one hand locked around hers as if grip alone could hold her there.

The door slammed. The engine roared.

As the river dropped behind them, Sabine's head rolled against the seat. Karoline tightened both hands around hers.

The truck lurched as the tires spun from the dirt onto asphalt.

Fluorescent light would come next.

46

Fluorescent light came next.

It hit like weather.

After the brown river and the green dark closing over everything, the hospital seemed built out of glare and echo. White tile. Pale walls. Stainless rails. The air smelled of bleach, old air-conditioning, and something medicinal beneath it all, as if cleanliness never quite succeeded in overcoming the atmosphere.

The truck had barely stopped before orderlies were at the doors.

Lucía was out first. She came around the back just as they pulled Sabine from the seat. Sabine tried to help and failed. Her body folded wrong, all effort and no strength, and one of the orderlies told her gently in Spanish not to move.

"Careful with her chest," Lucía said. "She took a hard impact. Breathing's been shallow since."

That sharpened their movements. They got Sabine onto the gurney.

Behind them, Karoline had made it halfway out of the truck before the first real step undid her. She caught herself on the doorframe with her good hand and bit back whatever sound tried to come out. A nurse reached for her elbow.

"I can walk," Karoline said.

"No," Lucía said.

Karoline looked at her, eyes fever-bright in a face streaked with dirt and dried sweat. "I said I—"

Her foot touched the ground. Pain shot up her leg so visibly that the rest of the sentence died. The nurse put the wheelchair behind her and guided her down before pride could do more damage.

They took Sabine first.

Lucía kept pace beside the gurney while a nurse clipped a pulse oximeter onto Sabine's finger and another wrapped a cuff around her arm. Sabine's lips parted when they asked her name. It took her too long to answer.

"How long without water?" the nurse asked.

Lucía gave the best estimate she could.

"Any loss of consciousness?"

"In and out."

"Blood?"

"Some. After coughing."

They wheeled Sabine through swinging doors and into a curtained bay. Karoline followed more slowly, pushed by another nurse, muttering under her breath in German now, which told Lucía exactly how much pain she was in.

The emergency department moved around them with practiced indifference. Somewhere, a child was crying. Somewhere else, a monitor gave off a fast alarm until someone silenced it. A television in one corner played a game show with the sound off. People in scrubs passed with basins, IV bags, clipboards. The place did not feel safe so much as too busy to care who deserved what.

A doctor arrived at Sabine's bay. Mid-forties, tired eyes, hands that moved quickly without haste.

"What happened?"

"Collapse in the jungle," Lucía said. "Then river extraction. Dehydrated. Exhausted. Chest impact. Breathing worsened on the boat."

The doctor listened high, then low, frowning slightly as Sabine tried and failed to draw a full breath without wincing.

"Fluids. Bloodwork. Chest film," he said to the nurse. "Pain control after imaging."

Sabine made a small sound when they tried to sit her up enough to place the leads. Not a cry. She was too far past that.

Lucía stepped back to give them room.

Across the aisle, Karoline had become a different kind of problem.

Two nurses had cut away the lower leg of her pants, and one peeled back the dressing at her side while Karoline glared at both of them with the brittle hostility of someone still trying to negotiate with pain from a position of disadvantage.

"That needs to be cleaned," one nurse said.

"It's been cleaned."

"Not recently enough."

Karoline opened her mouth, then hissed through her teeth as the nurse pressed lightly near the reopened stitches. The skin around the wound was red and swollen.

The second nurse had taken off Karoline's boot and was now looking at the bruised, misshapen toes with professional displeasure.

"How long have these been like this?"

Karoline gave a short, ugly laugh. "Do you want the answer in hours or humiliations?"

The nurse didn't smile. "Either."

Lucía moved closer before Karoline could spend what little strength she had left on sarcasm. "Several days. Wound reopened. Fever started before the river."

Karoline shot her a look. "Traitor."

"You can hate me after they stop you losing the foot."

"I'm not losing the foot."

"No," the nurse said, examining the toes with careful fingers. "But you are going for imaging."

Karoline closed her eyes briefly, as if the room had become too bright to be worth looking at.

Rogelio appeared a minute later with two bags over one shoulder and stopped just inside the curtain line.

"How bad?" he asked quietly.

Lucía looked from one bay to the other.

"Bad enough," she said.

That was all he needed.

He set Sabine's pack near the foot of her bed and Karoline's camera bag beneath the chair. Karoline tracked the movement at once.

"My notebook's in there."

Rogelio nodded. "It stays with me."

She might have argued on another day. Instead she slumped back as the nurse wrapped a blood pressure cuff around her arm.

The doctor returned to Sabine after the first bag of fluids had begun to run. He checked the monitor, asked her to take a deeper breath, got halfway to an apology in his face when she couldn't.

"She's very dry," he said to Lucía. "And the chest pain is significant. At minimum, she stays for observation."

Lucía nodded.

"She kept going longer than she should have," he added.

Lucía looked at Sabine—at the damp hair clinging to her temple, the sharp line of collarbone above the blanket, the stubborn tension still visible around her mouth even now, as if some part of her refused to relinquish responsibility simply because her body had.

"Yes," Lucía said. "That sounds like her."

On the other side, Karoline's nurse was hanging antibiotics.

Karoline noticed and frowned. "What is that?"

"Something to help you make fewer bad decisions in the form of infection."

"I'm serious."

"So am I." The nurse adjusted the line. "You're running a fever, your wound is angry, and those toes need to be looked at."

Karoline let her head fall back against the pillow. "Everyone in this country is rude."

"Only the competent ones," Lucía said.

That got the ghost of a smile out of her.

Sabine stirred.

Lucía crossed back at once.

Sabine's eyes opened only halfway. They found Lucía after a moment and held there. Lucía had seen her afraid, furious, analytical, remote. This was rarer and harder to look at: stripped down enough by pain and fatigue that the performance of control no longer held.

"Karoline?" Sabine whispered.

"Alive," Lucía said.

Sabine's eyes closed again in visible relief.

"She's infected and furious," Lucía added. "So her personality remains intact."

That earned the smallest exhale through Sabine's nose. Almost a laugh.

Lucía leaned closer. "You are in a hospital. That does not mean you are allowed to become difficult."

Sabine opened her eyes again. "No promises."

Her voice was rough, but clearer.

"Good," Lucía said. "You need rest and fluids and a chest image."

Sabine blinked slowly, filing that away. "Karoline's shoulder?"

"Not the main problem. Infection. Toes. Fever."

Sabine's expression changed immediately.

"Don't," Lucía said.

"What?"

"You have the face you make before trying to get out of bed for someone else."

Sabine would have denied it on another day. Instead she let the accusation stand.

Karoline solved the problem for both of them by appearing at the edge of the curtain with her IV pole and a nurse in pursuit.

"You are not supposed to be up," the nurse said.

Karoline ignored her. "I wanted visual confirmation."

Sabine turned her head too quickly and winced.

Karoline saw that and stopped, whatever sharp remark she had prepared falling away before it formed. Under the fluorescent lights she looked wrecked in her own right—skin flushed with fever, hair matted from sweat and river spray, one foot bandaged and held at an angle that admitted more pain than she ever would.

"You look terrible," Karoline said softly.

Sabine looked at the IV line taped to the back of Karoline's hand, then down toward the bare foot she was keeping off the floor. "You too."

The nurse hovering behind Karoline made an exasperated sound. "Wonderful. They're both comedians."

Karoline ignored her and lowered herself into the chair beside Sabine's bed with extreme care. Then, after only the briefest hesitation, she reached out and took Sabine's hand.

Sabine looked at their hands for a moment before tightening her fingers weakly around Karoline's.

Neither of them spoke.

They did not need to. On the river, the silence between them had been fear. Here, under fluorescent hum and monitor beeps, it became the stunned fact of still being alive at the same time.

Lucía stood back and let them have it.

Rogelio moved to the doorway, making himself useful by taking up less space. The nurse finally surrendered and went to find a second chair rather than try to peel Karoline away from the bed by force.

For the first time since the fisherman had grounded the boat against the bank, there was nothing immediate left for Lucía to do.

That was when the exhaustion found her.

Not dramatically. Not enough to bend her. Just a slow descent of weight from the base of her skull through her shoulders, as if her body had been waiting for walls and witnesses before admitting what the river and the road had cost.

She rested one hand briefly against the metal rail at the foot of Sabine's bed and stared through the gap in the curtain toward the bright corridor outside.

No jungle. No water. No engines. Just linoleum, squeaking soles, a janitor pushing a yellow mop bucket, and the insane ordinary miracle of a place where people expected the night to continue in sequence.

A nurse came back with a chart and murmured something about X-rays for Karoline's foot and checking the wound again once the antibiotics had time to start. The doctor said something about keeping Sabine at least overnight.

Lucía heard it all. None of it lodged.

Sabine's eyes had closed again, but not fully. She hovered on the edge of sleep and refused to admit it.

"Rest," Lucía said quietly.

Sabine didn't open her eyes. "You say that like an order."

"It is one."

Karoline, without looking up, murmured, "Good luck."

Lucía almost smiled.

Almost.

She turned toward the corridor and drew a slow breath that tasted of disinfectant and old freon and relief too thin to trust. Somewhere down the hall a phone rang. Somewhere a man laughed too loudly. The building kept moving, as if this night were merely one more night among thousands.

47

Sabine woke to the sound of air moving through plastic.

Dark room. Monitor glow. Pain in her ribs when she breathed too deep. Something taped to the back of her hand.

Hospital.

She stayed still until memory caught up: the river, the truck, fluorescent light, Karoline alive.

Then the other thing surfaced.

Lorentz.

Alexei.

Her eyes closed again.

For hours her body had been louder than thought. Pain. Exhaustion. Breathing. Now the drugs had dulled things just enough to let the rest through.

Alive.

That landed first, before pride could stop it.

She hated that.

Then the anger came behind it, hot and clean.

He could have said he was alive.

Instead: *If Sabine is there, tell her I know.*

The door opened softly. Lucía stepped in with a paper cup and shut it behind her.

"You're awake."

Sabine cleared her throat. "Apparently."

"Karoline's asleep. Fever's down a little. She insulted three people before surrendering."

Sabine let out a breath that almost became a laugh. It hurt. "Good."

Lucía studied her. "How bad?"

Sabine looked away. "My chest hurts."

Lucía let that sit for a moment. "And?"

Sabine did not answer.

"I knew there was a remote specialist," Lucía said. "I didn't know it was him."

Sabine nodded once.

"You do not have to decide tonight what to do with that."

Sabine looked at her.

Lucía set the cup down beside the bed. "Tonight you breathe. Tomorrow you decide whether to answer."

That almost got a real laugh.

"If you want," Lucía said, "I can keep him away from you."

Sabine looked at her.

Lucía meant it. No drama. Just an offer.

"No," Sabine said.

"Why?"

Sabine took a shallow breath. Because some part of this had to stop circling in her head and become real.

"If I wait," she said, "I'll make it worse."

Lucía accepted that.

"Sleep, then."

When she left, the room felt larger.

Sabine turned her head toward the bedside table. Her phone was there, screen dark.

She stared at it for a long time before reaching for it.

The secure relay thread sat near the top.

Lorentz.

Nothing new beneath it.

Her thumb hovered over the message field. She should have had something sharper. Something harder.

Instead she typed:

You were dead.

She looked at it, hated how naked it was, and sent it anyway.

The reply came almost at once.

I know what that cost you.

Sabine stared at the screen.

No joke. No evasion. Just that.

Her eyes burned.

She typed back:

No. You don't.

This time the silence lasted longer.

Then:

No. But I'm here now.

Sabine let out one short, broken laugh into the dark.

Alive.

She pressed the phone against her chest, winced at the pain in her ribs, and closed her eyes.

This time sleep came before she could fight it.

48

Mila slipped into the room and shut the door with her hip, a strip of pink medical tape with notes still clinging to her wrist.

Sabine opened her eyes. "Bad news?"

Mila checked the IV first. "You're awake. That's inconvenient."

"I hear that often."

Mila glanced once toward Karoline's bed. "She finally stopped arguing with everyone."

Sabine watched her for a moment. "You didn't come in here for my sparkling company."

Mila adjusted the line, then lowered her voice. "I know who you are."

Sabine said nothing.

"You came in before, asking for her." Mila tipped her head toward Karoline. "Now you're both back. Same names. More dead people."

Sabine went still. "That sounds like a line."

"It sounds like a pattern."

Mila straightened but did not step away. "They're calling Stone's death a medical event."

Sabine's eyes sharpened. "And?"

Mila hesitated. Not long. Just enough.

"And maybe it was," she said. "But one of the men who went into the room after… also had issues."

Sabine said nothing.

"Dizzy. Pale. They sat him down in the hall and gave him oxygen."

"Who told you that?"

"Someone who talks too much." Mila shrugged, but there was tension under it. "And the company people were settling on the language before the body was even through intake."

"What language?"

"Medical event. Collapse. Tragedy." Mila's mouth tightened. "All very personal. Very contained."

"Not exposure."

Mila gave a small shake of the head. "Not the word they wanted."

Karoline shifted in her sleep and muttered something in German.

Sabine kept her eyes on Mila. "Why are you telling me this?"

Mila looked at Karoline first. Then back at Sabine.

"Because your sister asks tough questions," she said. "You ask them like you already know where to look."

She moved toward the door.

"And because when people start creating the truth before the body is cold, someone should notice."

Sabine looked down at the blanket, then back up.

"A sealed room," she said. "A dead man. Another one needing oxygen?"

Mila's hand rested on the door handle. "That's what I heard."

She opened the door.

"Try to sleep," she said. "You still look terrible."

When she was gone, the room felt smaller.

Sabine lay back and stared at the dark window.

Stone dead in a sealed room.

A responder dizzy after entry.

A company moving fast to make the death belong only to Stone's body.

49

Morning came gray and thin through the hospital blinds.

Sabine woke to a negotiation with pain. Her ribs objected first, a blunt ache low in her chest that sharpened if she drew too deep a breath. The IV in the back of her hand tugged when she shifted. Her mouth tasted stale.

Across from her, Karoline was awake too, propped badly against her pillows, staring at a paper cup of pills with open contempt. One foot was wrapped and elevated on a folded blanket. The fresh dressing at her side stood out white against bruised skin.

"You look homicidal," Sabine said.

Karoline glanced over. "They expect me to swallow all of these."

"That's usually how medicine works."

"It's barbaric."

Sabine started to laugh and paid for it at once. She stopped.

Karoline noticed. "How bad?"

"Enough that I would appreciate less commentary."

The door opened. Lucía came in first, already carrying tension like it belonged to her. Behind her was Dr. Muñoz, chart in hand, expression composed and faintly resigned.

"That sounds promising," Karoline said.

"No one has spoken yet," Lucía said.

"I'm getting ahead of the disappointment."

Muñoz checked Sabine first. "Your chest film is consistent with a lung contusion. Painful, but stable. No sign of pneumothorax. Oxygen is acceptable at rest. You will feel exhausted for a while, and are in no condition to be heroic."

Sabine nodded once.

He turned to Karoline. "You have broken toes, a wound infection that should have been treated earlier, and a talent for making recovery harder than it needs to be."

Karoline considered that. "That's fair."

Lucía crossed her arms. "So they stay?"

"No," Muñoz said.

Lucía's head turned slowly. "No?"

"They are injured. They are also stable enough to leave if they can be supervised, medicated, and brought back if they worsen."

Karoline brightened at once. "Excellent."

Lucía ignored her. "Sabine has a lung contusion."

"Yes."

"She can barely breathe without pain."

"She can breathe," Muñoz said. "Painful is not the same as dangerous."

Lucía pointed toward Karoline. "And she has a fever."

"She has antibiotics." He glanced at the paper cup. "Which she is apparently still negotiating with."

Karoline lifted it slightly. "I reject the word apparently."

Sabine said, "If the question is whether we belong in a hospital bed or somewhere quieter with medication and instructions, I'd rather leave."

Lucía turned on her. "Of course you would."

Sabine met her look. "I can think better outside this room."

"You are not required to think today."

"That would be a first."

Karoline made a sound of agreement, then winced because even that had been too much movement.

Muñoz looked between them with the patience of a man long past mistaking intelligence for compliance. "If I kept every patient who could stand, argue, and make poor decisions in fluent sentences, I would have no beds by noon." He nodded at Sabine. "She needs rest, pain control, fluids, and someone to stop her from doing anything foolish." Then at Karoline. "She needs antibiotics, dressing changes, and to stop pretending broken toes are a personality trait."

Karoline's eyebrows lifted. "That feels personal."

"It became personal when you tried to walk to radiology."

Lucía said, "They're in no shape to travel."

"We're in no shape to stay here either," Sabine said quietly.

Muñoz closed the chart. "You leave with instructions, medication, and the understanding that if the breathing worsens, if the fever climbs, or if the wound looks worse, you come back immediately."

Karoline lifted two fingers. "For the record, I am completely in favor of leaving."

"A rare moment of good judgment," Muñoz said. "Take those meds and you're free to go."

That won Sabine a short breath of laughter she regretted.

Lucía heard the catch in it and looked as though she might physically force Sabine back into bed. Instead she said, "I want the papers. All of them. And I want the dosage written clearly enough that even she can't misread it."

Karoline looked offended. "I read perfectly well."

"You improvise perfectly well," Lucía said. "Not the same thing."

Muñoz handed over the packet. "Pain meds for Sabine. Antibiotics and dressing changes for Karoline. As little weight as possible on that foot."

Karoline looked at the waiting boot. "I hate it."

"That's healthy," Muñoz said. "You should hate the reason for it more."

He gave Sabine one last look. "Can you walk?"

"Probably."

Lucía said, "That is not a confidence-inspiring word."

"It's the true one."

"Then walk slowly," Muñoz said, and left before anyone could argue further.

There was a brief silence.

Then Karoline shook the paper cup once and said to the pills, "Sorry about this, but swallowing you is the price of leaving." Karoline popped the pills in her mouth, took a swig of water and, muttering in German under her breath, swallowed.

By the time they were dressed, the bags were packed, the papers were signed, and the hospital bracelets were clipped off and left curling on the tray.

Sabine stood first.

The floor shifted just enough to make her grip the bedrail. Pain cut across her chest when she straightened. She kept her face neutral.

Lucía saw it anyway. "Sit."

"No."

"That wasn't a suggestion."

"If I sit down, I stay down."

Lucía studied her, then gave a short nod. "Then don't fall."

Across the room, Karoline swung her legs over the edge of the bed, planted the good foot, and failed to hide what the movement cost her. Rogelio, waiting by the door with both bags looped through one arm, stepped in at once.

"I can do it," she said.

"I know," he said. "But you shouldn't."

He offered his arm anyway. This time she took it.

The corridor outside was brighter than the room. Orderlies moved past without interest. Somewhere down the hall someone was crying. Somewhere else someone laughed too loudly. The building kept working.

In the lobby, morning had fully taken hold. Families clustered around bad coffee and plastic chairs. Sunlight washed through the glass doors and made the outside look cleaner than it was.

The heat hit them the moment they stepped through.

The truck waited where Rogelio had left it. Getting in was worse than getting out.

Sabine made the mistake of twisting first and had to stop, eyes closed, fingers whitening on the doorframe while pain cut across her chest.

Lucía was beside her immediately. "No exertion."

"I remember."

"Try to remember before you act."

Behind them, Karoline had gone pale with the effort of climbing into the back seat while keeping weight off the wrong foot. Rogelio swore softly and took more of her weight than she wanted him to. This time she let him.

When the doors shut, something eased.

No monitors. No fluorescent lights. No one asking them to rate pain like it was a quiz.

Just the road.

Lucía took the passenger seat. Rogelio drove. Sabine sat in back beside Karoline, who leaned her head against the window and closed her eyes.

For the first few minutes, no one spoke.

Then the town began to thin. Concrete gave way to scrub, scrub to trees, and the road narrowed into something more private. Every bump found its way back to Sabine's ribs. Every full breath remained a negotiation.

"How far?" she asked.

"Twenty minutes," Lucía said.

"To the safehouse?"

"Yes."

Good.

Twenty minutes until they were somewhere they could think. Twenty minutes until maps, data, Martín if they were lucky, and something other than pain to hold onto.

Beside her, Karoline had drifted fully asleep, her head tipped against Sabine's shoulder. Sabine should have moved before the weight settled. She didn't.

The trees closed in.

When the safehouse finally appeared through the foliage, it looked exactly the same and not the same at all.

Rogelio cut the engine.

For a second, no one moved.

Then Lucía opened her door. “Welcome back. Try not to collapse before you get inside.”

Sabine looked at the steps, the door, the house waiting under the trees.

Then she reached for the handle.

50

Sabine made it through the door of the Guardian safe house and stopped with one hand braced against the frame until the pain in her chest settled back into something she could bargain with. The room beyond was dim after the glare outside. Shutters cut the light into narrow bars across the floorboards. A scarred wooden table stood in the center with a laptop, a flashlight, topographic maps, and a half-finished thermos of coffee already waiting on it.

Behind her, Karoline hissed as Rogelio got her over the threshold.

"I'm fine," Karoline said.

"You are making words," Lucía replied. "That is not the same thing."

Rogelio helped her to the sofa. Lucía dragged over a stool and lifted Karoline's injured foot onto it before she could object properly. Sabine crossed to the table more slowly and lowered herself into the nearest chair. The movement pulled at her ribs and lit a sharp line of pain through her chest. She shut her eyes for a second.

Lucía noticed.

"Sit there," she said. "Do not move unless the house starts burning."

"That seems restrictive," Sabine said.

"It is meant to be."

Lucía dropped the hospital papers onto the table, unscrewed two pill bottles, and shook tablets into their palms with the grim efficiency of a woman resupplying fools she had not yet decided to forgive.

"Medication first," she said. "Thinking after."

"I can do both," Sabine said.

"That is why this is not your decision."

Karoline held out her hand without opening her eyes. "I also object to being kept alive by force, but apparently we live under occupation."

Rogelio gave a faint snort. Karoline swallowed her pills with water. Sabine took hers with coffee that had gone lukewarm and bitter in the thermos.

For a few minutes the house held only small sounds. The rustle of paper. The clink of glass. Insects humming outside. Rogelio checked the rear window and came back. Lucía lined up blister packs and bandages on the counter like a field medic making peace with bad circumstances. Karoline leaned back with one arm over her face.

Sabine drew the top map toward her.

Lucía looked up at once. "What did I just say?"

"You said not to move."

"I said not to move unless the house was on fire."

Sabine flattened the map with one hand. "This feels adjacent."

Karoline made a tired sound through her arm. "I regret to report she has found a loophole."

Lucía muttered something in Spanish that Sabine was fairly sure was not kind and came around to the other side of the table.

"Talk," she said. "So I can tell whether to stop you."

Sabine looked down at the contour lines. "Muñoz was careful with his language. My breathing is painful, not dangerous. Oxygen acceptable at rest."

Lucía's expression shifted. "You're thinking about Stone."

"Yes."

Karoline lowered her arm. "You're doing that thing."

"What thing?"

"Where you already see a shape and refuse to name it until everyone else suffers first."

Sabine ignored that. "A sealed room inside the residence. One man dead inside it."

Lucía pulled out the chair opposite Sabine and sat. "That could mean heart, poison, panic, half a dozen other things."

"Yes. But the EMT dizzy after entry?"

Karoline frowned. "You think that rules out heart, poison, panic, and a lot of other things."

"I think I don't know." Sabine tapped the map. "But if the EMT's symptoms were related, then we're looking for an environmental cause. A sealed room is only sealed up to a point. It has to breathe somehow."

That stilled them.

Rogelio came closer to the table. "I only saw the residence from outside. Heavy concrete. Defensive design. The kind rich men build when they want to project invincibility."

Karoline rubbed her forehead. "Every rich paranoid man builds the same fantasy. Hidden room. Total control. Nobody close enough to touch him."

Sabine traced one finger down the contour lines. "Control only helps if you understand what you're controlling."

Gravel crunched outside.

Every head turned.

The engine cut. Headlights flashed once across the shutters and disappeared.

Rogelio was at the window in two strides. Lucía stood, one hand already on the rifle behind the hanging cloth. Karoline pushed herself upright despite the pain. Sabine's pulse kicked hard against her ribs.

Rogelio peered through the gap. "Martín."

Lucía opened the door before the knock finished.

Martín came in pale, dust-streaked, and furious-looking, with dried blood at the edge of the bandage near his temple and his left arm held too carefully to be anything but damaged. Under his good arm he carried a tablet and a rolled set of papers.

"You look terrible," Karoline said.

Martín glanced at the room. "Have you looked in a mirror?"

Lucía shut and bolted the door behind him. "You should still be in bed."

"So should all of you." He set the tablet down on the table and passed the rolled papers to Rogelio. "This seemed more urgent."

Sabine gestured at the map. "We're working on the hypothesis that Stone may have died from something atmospheric in the room."

Martín froze halfway into the chair.

Then he sat, carefully. "Good," he said. "I may be able to help with that."

Karoline's eyes sharpened. "That sounds like you have news."

"I have incomplete news." Martín took the coffee Lucía pushed toward him, drank once, and unrolled the papers. "A friend at the building department got me these. Not the full engineering plan. Just enough to be dangerous."

He spread out a partial site diagram.

Not just the residence.

A residence built into a slope. A reinforced chamber behind it. A service branch extending past the back wall into an unlabeled void in the rock.

Sabine leaned in despite the protest in her chest. "That's not just a house."

"No," Martín said. "It's tied into a cave complex."

Lucía came around behind Sabine's chair. "And that branch?"

Martín said, "It's too small to be a hallway. All I can think of is some kind of utility passage or ducting."

"If that's intake—" Sabine said.

Karoline squinted at the line, then at the contour map beneath it. "Then the theory just got less hypothetical and more plausible."

"That's not all," Martín said. He turned on the tablet and brought up a clustered set of time stamps, signal traces, and a rough map overlay. "Here's the part I can't explain away."

Sabine took the tablet from him. "What am I looking at?"

"My fungal network." Martín pointed to a band of irregular spikes. "The nanosensors tied into the mycelia started behaving strangely the same night Stone died. Sharp bursts. Then dropouts. Then bursts again. Not random."

Lucía's expression hardened. "Meaning what?"

"Meaning stress," Martín said. "Something changed fast in the soil environment. Gas chemistry. Moisture. pH. Redox. I can't tell which from this alone. Only that the network reacted."

Karoline stared at the screen. "And that lines up with the timing?"

"Close enough that I stopped sleeping."

Martín shifted to another layer on the tablet. "And the forest was wrong."

Lucía looked up. "Wrong how?"

"The Guardian posts didn't hear more," Martín said. "They heard less. Insects dropped out in clusters. Bird activity thinned where it shouldn't have. Whole patches went quieter than expected for the hour and weather."

Rogelio nodded once. "The kind of quiet animals make when something in the air or ground is off."

Martín tapped the map again. "The strongest anomalies cluster along this drainage line and the slope above it. I can't tell you the pathway. Fracture, old seam, void—pick your nightmare. But something moved through that ground the same night he died."

Rogelio leaned in. "If it settled into that cave system—"

"Then an air intake could have drawn it inward," Sabine finished.

Karoline shook her head once. "Could have. Not did."

Sabine looked at her. "Agreed."

Martín nodded. "There are still gaps. We don't know the exact intake location. We don't know what exactly it was. We don't know whether the alarm system was working."

Lucía looked up sharply. "Alarm system?"

Martín grimaced. "Underground reinforced chamber. Executive meeting space. There should have been environmental monitoring. These drawings don't have that level of detail, and we have no way of knowing if it was active."

"Should have," Karoline said. "That's not definitive."

"It isn't meant to be."

Silence settled briefly around the table.

Then Lucía said, "There's another problem."

All of them looked at her.

"You're all talking as if the only question is how Stone died." Her hands flattened on the table. "If we are talking about gas that made it there, and if it is still moving, then that room is not the point. It's a sign."

Rogelio nodded once. "Others could be at risk."

Martín reached for a pencil and marked a drainage line on the map, running from the cave complex downslope toward older field infrastructure. Then he circled a second low area farther out.

"This is where I'd look first," he said. "If readings are high here too, then the residence wasn't a freak trap. It means the leak path is broader."

Karoline stared at the second circle. "How broad?"

Martín's mouth tightened. "Broad enough that I came here instead of going back to bed."

Lucía swore softly.

Sabine looked down at the maps and felt the scene tilt from retrospective puzzle to active threat.

Karoline saw it happen. "No."

Sabine looked up. "No what?"

"No field trip for you."

Sabine almost smiled. "You're assuming my intention."

"I'm observing your face."

Lucía cut in before Sabine could answer. "She stays."

"I didn't say—"

"You were about to."

Sabine looked at Martín. "I'm the one who understands the mechanism."

Martín gave her a flat, exhausted stare. "You are also the one with a bruised lung."

Rogelio said, "We need instruments. Not extra casualties."

Karoline leaned forward, pain making the movement ugly and anger making it happen anyway. "For once, everyone sensible is in agreement. You do not test an asphyxiation theory by sending the woman with damaged breathing."

Sabine opened her mouth, then closed it.

Because they were right. And because that made her furious.

Lucía saw the fury and mistook none of it for consent. "Tomorrow," she said. "Rogelio goes. Martín tells him what to measure. I'll decide who else."

Martín shook his head. "We need to be there at first light. Dawn is exactly when a low pocket could still hold anything that settled overnight. By midmorning, after enough warming and air movement, it may have cleared." He looked at Sabine. "And if it clears too quickly, there might be nothing for us to find."

Sabine nodded despite herself. "Good."

Karoline eyed her. "You sound offended by competence."

"I'm offended by exclusion."

"That's healthier than coughing blood in a cave."

Rogelio pointed at the plan again. "We also need to know whether that side branch is really the air route."

"Yes," Sabine said. "Without that, the rest is still just a theory."

Martín sat back a little, "One problem at a time."

"She's right," Sabine said. "If the cave readings are clean, then this whole theory weakens."

"And if they're not," Karoline said, "then Stone may have been killed by his own air system."

"May have," Sabine said.

Karoline leaned back slowly, pale with effort now. "You love that word tonight."

"I trust it more than certainty."

Martín rolled one edge of the site plan back under his hand but left the key section exposed. "If the readings are high, we still won't know everything. Only that the hypothesis survives contact with reality."

Sabine looked at the side branch on the plan, then at the contour lines beneath it, then at the anomaly trace on the tablet. Incomplete line. Incomplete map. Incomplete mechanism. Enough to move. Not enough to conclude.

"That's all I want," she said quietly. "For it to survive contact with reality."

Outside, the insects droned on in the darkening trees. Inside, the maps lay open between them like a land that had not yet finished revealing what it was hiding.

Lucía gathered the discharge papers into a stack and set them aside.

"We go tomorrow," she said. "With monitors. With rope. With masks if we can improvise them. We do not trust the cave, we do not trust their plans, and we do not trust the ground."

Rogelio nodded.

Martín looked at Sabine. "And if the readings don't confirm it?"

Sabine held his gaze.

"Then Stone died some other way," she said. "And we start again."

No one liked that answer.

Which was how she knew it was the right one.

51

Lucía's compromise had been narrow enough to feel like a threat. Sabine could come to read the monitor and nothing else. Rogelio led. Martín called the measurements. Lucía decided when they stopped, when they backed out, and whether the cave itself was worth another step. If Sabine's breathing worsened, or the readings spiked, she went back to the truck without debate.

Morning came colder in the canyon than it had any right to.

The truck left the safe house before sunrise. Sabine sat in the back with the monitor case braced against her leg and hated every rut in the road. Her ribs had stiffened overnight. The ache in her chest was duller than yesterday, but deeper, as if someone had set a metal plate between her lungs and left it there. Every bounce found it.

Lucía turned halfway around from the passenger seat. "When we stop, you do not lead."

Sabine looked at her. "I'm carrying the meter."

"You can carry it behind Rogelio."

"The monitor should be with the person in the lead."

"It is still the rule."

Karoline, beside Sabine with her booted foot stretched awkwardly across the bench seat, gave a tired snort. "For once, I'm not the worst patient present."

"No," Lucía said. "You are simply the louder one."

Martín rode facing them in the back, one arm held too carefully against his ribs and a tablet braced on one knee. He had spent half the drive talking Rogelio through the route and the other half reminding all of them, unnecessarily, that they were not here to be brave.

"We confirm the cave first," he said. "Then, if the terrain supports it, we follow the drainage line. If readings spike, we back out. No debate."

Lucía glanced at him. "You're speaking as though these people enjoy instruction."

"They enjoy ignoring it," Martín said.

"That's fair," Karoline muttered.

Rogelio slowed the truck and killed the engine beneath a stand of trees where the service track narrowed too much for the truck to continue. Ahead, the canyon opened in a rough sweep of broken stone and dark vegetation. The cave itself was still hidden around the next fold of rock, but the place already felt wrong. Too still. Too watchful.

No one moved immediately.

Rogelio got out first, rifle slung, one hand raised for quiet while he listened.

When nothing answered, Lucía stepped out and opened the rear door.

Sabine climbed out more carefully than she wanted to. The first breath of canyon air felt cold and clean enough to make the theory seem ridiculous. Birds moved somewhere high in the trees. Water sounded faintly ahead, slipping over stone. The place looked too ordinary for invisible death.

Karoline saw her looking. "That's how they get you."

Sabine glanced at her.

"The places that look wrong are merciful," Karoline said. "It's the normal ones that are the deadliest."

Martín handed Sabine the larger monitor despite Lucía's expression. "Baseline first."

She turned it on and watched the numbers settle. Oxygen normal. Carbon dioxide at ambient background. No alarm.

They moved in single file down the path.

The canyon narrowed as they walked. Broken rock rose on either side, split by roots and scrub gripping whatever soil remained. Fallen stone littered the ground where the slope had slumped long ago and never fully healed. The air changed as they descended, cooler first, then flatter, the breeze cut off by the stone. Sabine traded attention between footing and the monitor.

Ambient. Ambient. A slight rise in one hollow. Back down.

At the cave mouth, Rogelio stopped and scanned the shadows inside before motioning them forward.

The chamber beyond was larger than Sabine had expected. Crude reinforcement had been bolted into older rock. A work light hung dark from a steel bracket. Plastic conduit ran along one wall and disappeared into stone.

Sabine checked the monitor.

Still near ambient.

"So far," Karoline said, leaning against the wall to spare her foot, "our grand theory remains inconveniently unimpressive."

"No," Sabine said. "So far it remains untested." Sabine started forward.

Lucía's arm came out at once. "You can look from there."

Sabine looked from there.

Martín stepped forward and raised the handheld meter.

Normal.

He lowered it toward the floor of the cave.

The reading twitched. Climbed. Fell. Climbed again.

Lucía saw it first. "There."

Martín held still until the number stabilized. Elevated. Not enough to panic on its own. High enough to be wrong.

Sabine stepped in before Lucía could stop her, lifted her own monitor, and found the same pattern. Higher at floor level. Lower at head height.

"It's pooling," she said quietly.

Karoline stared at the screen. "Not enough to kill anyone now."

"No."

"But not nothing."

"No."

Rogelio was already moving along the rear wall of the cave, searching for the void on the diagram.

He pointed toward a narrow side passage descending at the back of the cave.

"There."

Or what had once been a passage. Now a jam of collapsed stone and old slide debris filled it chest-high and then higher, packed in place by time and damp. Martín swore softly.

Lucía stepped beside him. "Can you get through?"

Rogelio crouched, studied the rubble, then shook his head. "Not without shifting half the slope."

Martín lifted the handheld meter toward a dark gap between two larger stones.

The number jumped.

This time there was no ambiguity. The monitor chirped once, sharply, and kept rising.

"Back," Lucía snapped.

Rogelio moved first. Martín followed. Sabine took one step too slowly, watching the number climb again in the dead air trapped between the stones, and then the air changed in her own lungs, not pain, not the familiar protest in her ribs, but something flatter and wrong, a sudden refusal of the breath she tried to take.

Lucía's hand locked hard around her arm.

"Now."

Sabine let herself be pulled back into the main chamber, where the air moved enough to feel like air again. She bent once, palms on her thighs, dragging in a careful breath that hurt but obeyed. That brief, wrong blankness had not.

No one spoke until she straightened.

Karoline stared at the rubble with her face gone pale beneath the fatigue. "That," she said, "felt more convincing."

"Dangerous in pockets," Martín said, checking both meters against each other. "Not throughout. Not now."

Lucía looked through the gap in the rubble, imagining the safe-room vent with open disgust. "They hid the intake in the one place the land could poison."

"No," Sabine said, still watching the rubble. "They hid it in the one place they thought no person could tamper with."

Karoline let out a low breath. "That is somehow worse."

They did not spend long testing after that.

Martín logged readings throughout the cave, at knee height in the rear chamber, then nearer the entrance where the air cleaned fast. Rogelio marked the highest spots with strips of orange tape. Sabine noted the pattern: elevated near the blocked passage, lower with distance, normal outside.

Enough.

They left the chamber and followed the sound of water downslope.

The stream emerged from a seam in the rock, no more than a steady trickle slipping over stone and threading through moss and dark sediment before joining a shallow feeder channel. From there it continued toward the reservoir below, a muted sheet of water visible through the trees where the canyon widened again.

Rogelio took the lead, testing the footing before anyone committed weight to it. The channel curved through a low groove lined with slick stones and pale mineral crust where water had receded and returned often enough to leave evidence of itself. Martín stopped twice to take air readings in hollows along the bank. Slightly elevated in one low cut. Normal ten paces later. Elevated again beneath a rock lip where the ground cupped inward.

"Same pattern," Sabine said. "Not everywhere. Where the terrain holds it."

Rogelio nodded toward the second hollow. "Cold sits here too. You feel it at dawn before the sun reaches the cut."

Lucía looked out toward the reservoir. "Then anyone camping low, sheltering low, storing anything low—"

"Could walk into the wrong place," Martín said.

Sabine crouched at the stream edge more carefully this time and looked at the water.

At first she thought the pale sheen was only sky caught in shadow.

Then the channel bent, and the color remained.

Not bright. Nothing like the vivid glow she had seen before. This was subtler, a faint green-blue thread under the surface, as if the water carried the memory of light rather than the thing itself.

She went still.

"What?" Lucía asked.

Sabine pointed.

The others came closer.

For a moment the stream looked ordinary again, water moving over black stone in broken reflections. Then a shallow pool at the bend caught and held the color from within. It brightened faintly. Faded. Returned as the surface shifted.

Karoline's voice dropped. "That is not sunlight."

"No," Sabine said.

Martín crouched beside her with a soft curse and studied the flow. "Same phenomenon?"

"Related," Sabine said. She touched the air monitor above the water. Slight elevation. Nothing more.

Lucía followed the channel downslope with her eyes. "Feeding the reservoir."

"Yes."

Karoline straightened as much as her side and foot allowed. "We need samples. Photos."

No one argued.

Rogelio marked the location on the GPS unit and called out the elevation. Martín took readings at the bend, then farther down where the channel widened. Sabine filled one vial from the faintly glowing pool, one from a clear run above it, and one lower where the stream slid toward the reservoir under fern and shadow. Karoline photographed all three, then the banks, then the reservoir itself through the trees, jaw tight against the pain.

When Sabine capped the second sample, the faint glow caught in the glass and pulsed once as the water shifted.

She stared at it.

Not bright. Not impossible. But unmistakable.

Behind her, Karoline said quietly, "Tell me that's runoff."

Sabine looked at the vial. Then at the stream. Then at the reservoir waiting below.

"I don't think so," she said.

No one spoke after that.

The canyon seemed quieter now, as if the land had decided it had shown them enough.

Martín checked the time and looked back upslope toward the cave. "We have enough to support the mechanism."

Sabine nodded, still watching the stream. "Yes."

"Not prove it."

"No."

Lucía shifted the rifle on her shoulder. "But enough to know the cave isn't the whole story."

Sabine looked once more at the blocked side passage in her mind, at the spike in the trapped air, at the thin luminous thread feeding the reservoir below.

"Yes, enough," she said.

Then she rose, ribs protesting, sample vials cold in her hand, and followed the others back up to the trail to the truck.

52

The residence no longer held the stillness of immediate aftermath. It held occupation.

Maps covered the long dining table. Two laptops sat open beside printed schematics, incident summaries, and interview notes. A cold cup of coffee had ringed one corner of Stone's handwritten pad. Someone had opened the canyon shutters at dawn and never closed them again. Outside, vehicles moved up and down the access road below with controlled regularity.

Stone's jacket still hung over the back of a chair in the adjoining room.

When the secure screen lit, Megan Whitaker was already waiting.

"Start with the autopsy," she said.

Mercer opened the nearest folder. "Official classification remains natural causes. The report itself is less comfortable. No external trauma. Initial toxicology negative. Cardiac pathology insufficient to explain the collapse." He turned a page. "The findings are consistent with acute hypoxia or asphyxia."

"And the safe room?"

"Supports it."

"How strongly?"

"Strongly enough that I would not put another person in that room with the door sealed."

Whitaker held his gaze a moment. "Walk me through the structure."

Mercer pulled up the schematic. "The safe room draws from a concealed side passage behind the rear wall. Low ground. Access to the intake route is blocked by slide rubble, but engineering confirmed the duct path and elevated readings near the obstruction."

"So the room can become lethal while the surrounding space remains survivable."

"It's possible."

He hated how easily that answer came now.

Whitaker wrote it down. "Any sign of sabotage?"

"None yet."

"Yet is doing work there."

He did not answer.

"What about the medic?"

"Recovered. Symptoms were transient. Dizziness, disorientation, no lasting impairment."

"Comparable structures?"

"Four now flagged for review. Two service rooms, one monitoring recess, one older storage vault near the lower road. All closed pending inspection."

"Community exposure?"

"Contained, not controlled. Access restrictions expanded under slope-instability and maintenance pretext. Local authorities have the minimum."

That earned the smallest pause.

"Better," Whitaker said. "Continue."

"Our sources say the journalist resurfaced in hospital. Non-life-threatening injuries. She left early the next day and appears to be under Guardian protection, or keeping a very low profile."

"And the men who freelanced?"

"Their bodies won't be found."

"What do local authorities know?"

"Officially, they believe those men weren't working for us."

"Make sure that belief remains healthy."

He nodded.

"Our exposure to Chasoy has narrowed," he said. "The lab is gone. The network has degraded."

Whitaker's pen stopped. "Are you sure?"

"Nobody has serviced the units we know about, and we've picked up no meaningful transmission traffic since."

"Watch it closely. I doubt they accept defeat."

"Yes, ma'am."

He turned a page. "There is still chatter about the luminous water."

Whitaker's eyes sharpened. "Source?"

"Unverified local reports. One internal mention from a site worker who heard it secondhand."

"Did you secure samples?"

"Not directly."

He let that sit.

"The site did not have a formal protocol for glowing streams."

"No," Whitaker said, "it had the more basic protocol of not being absurdly slow."

The rebuke was quiet.

Mercer felt irritation move under his ribs like something trapped and looking for a seam. She had watched the death through a screen. He had stood outside the safe room after the door opened. Yet she spoke as though delay were a character flaw rather than the ordinary condition of collapsing systems.

He said, "We've instructed personnel to report, isolate, and document. No photography leaves the site without clearance."

"Expand that." Whitaker set down her pen. "I'm not interested in policing every glowing-water story in Colombia. I'm interested in preventing it from attaching itself to us. Anything that places luminous water on or downstream of our site gets controlled. Staff images. Field notes. Contractor chatter. Samples, if they exist. No anomaly, no glow, no gas migration outside restricted channels."

Whitaker leaned back slightly. "What has left your control?"

There it was.

"Unknown," Mercer said. "Some site records were exposed before the lab blast. Most sensitive materials were destroyed or recovered, but not cleanly enough for me to certify full chain. Workers noticed bad air in at least one unrelated low area before the safe-room event, but no one escalated it."

Whitaker looked at him over the rim of her glasses. "Why?"

"Because no one wants to be the first person to describe impossible physics in a company that sells certainty."

The words were out before he could reshape them.

Whitaker said nothing for a beat.

Then: "Leave the philosophy to people with time."

Mercer almost smiled. He did not.

She turned a page. "What I need from you now is precision. Exact pathway. Exact comparable risk points. Exact witness map." She paused. "And one thing more."

Mercer waited.

"If someone else already understands what happened in that safe room," Whitaker said, "I want to know before they decide what it means."

He sat back in Stone's chair and hated it again. "Then I need broader authority."

"You have it."

"Surveillance on likely external contacts."

"You have it. But use it selectively. Broad surveillance gets noticed."

"The community already assumes we watch everything."

"Yes," Whitaker said. "And your job is to make sure they don't sense anything has changed."

That should have sounded like trust. It did not.

She closed the folder. "Do you understand your priorities?"

Mercer answered from the list he had already built for himself and hated how much it resembled hers.

"Mechanism. Perimeter. Record recovery. Witness control. Narrative control."

Whitaker nodded once. "Good."

She lifted an untouched glass of water, then set it down again without drinking. "Do not confuse urgency with spectacle, Mr. Mercer. This only becomes unmanageable if others feed the fire."

Then the screen went black.

Mercer remained still for a moment, listening to the residence breathe around him. HVAC. Insects beyond the open shutters. A vehicle below changing gears at the bend. Two days inside the dead man's house had sanded away the first layer of unreality and left something colder behind.

Stone was no longer an event here.

He was a vacancy with paperwork.

A knock sounded at the doorframe.

His security lead stood there with Figueroa from site engineering and a younger analyst Mercer had not bothered to learn by name. All three looked as though they had slept in fragments.

"Inside," Mercer said.

They came in carrying folders, a tablet, and the smell of heat and humidity.

Mercer flattened the topographic map on the table.

"Status change," he said. "Canyon access closes another ring outward. No locals, no contractors, no unofficial site movement within the drainage corridor unless I clear it personally. Slope hazard and infrastructure review remain the public reasons."

The security lead nodded once.

Mercer looked at Figueroa. "I want every enclosed structure, intake design, low-point recess, and service cavity reclassified by risk before dark. Start with anything downslope of injection corridors and anything sharing airflow logic with the safe room."

Figueroa swallowed. "That's half the site."

"Then triage faster."

Mercer turned to the analyst. "I want a witness map. Not interview summaries. A map. Everyone who entered the safe room, everyone who touched the vent design, everyone who reported bad air, dizziness, or luminous water tied to the canyon, reservoir, or site drainage. Put them on paper and show me what overlaps."

The analyst nodded quickly and almost dropped the tablet.

Mercer looked back to the security lead. "And find out whether anyone outside our chain has already reached the cave, the drainage, or the workers who were there first."

"Locals?"

"I mean anyone. Journalists. Community patrols. Academic contacts. Contractors with curiosity. I don't care." He tapped the canyon. "If someone else already understands what happened in that safe room, I want the name before sunset."

No one moved.

Mercer looked from one face to the next and saw the same hesitation he had come to despise in other people because it so often resembled his own.

"Go."

"Sir," the security lead said, "there's one more thing."

Mercer looked at him. "How long have you known?"

The man blinked. "Known what, sir?"

"That someone else got to the cave."

A beat.

"A couple of hours."

"And I'm only hearing about it now?"

The security lead held his ground. Barely. "I wanted to see it myself before bringing it to you."

Mercer said nothing.

The man continued. "We found orange tape in the cave. And footprints leading to and from it."

Something in Mercer's chest went very still.

"How many?"

"Looks like three to five people."

"How recent?"

"Recent enough that the prints are crisp. Overnight, maybe this morning."

Mercer's gaze shifted to the map, then back to the man in the doorway. While Whitaker had been talking about narrative control, someone else had already begun writing.

"How did they get past our security?"

"We traced them in from outside the current perimeter. An old forest road. It hasn't been used in years."

Mercer held his gaze another second.

Then he said, very quietly, "Make sure no one else gets near that cave."

"Yes, sir."

"What are you waiting for?"

They left.

The room fell quiet again.

Mercer stood alone at Stone's table, the map spread open under the slant of afternoon light.

A man had died in a room designed to keep danger out.

Two days later the company had a mechanism, a perimeter, and still not enough control to call the problem small.

And someone else was investigating.

53

By the time they got back to the Guardian safe house, the day had burned off its early coolness and settled into heat that left a film on skin, clothes, and wood. Dried mud clung to their boots. The house smelled of coffee, damp timber, and the faint medicinal sting of the supplies Lucía had left spread across the table before they left.

No one spoke coming in.

Rogelio set the cases down by the table and went straight to the shutters, checking the trees before drawing them half closed again. Lucía took the sample kit from Sabine before Sabine could object and set the vials in the middle of the table with the care usually reserved for explosives.

Karoline lowered herself onto the sofa with a hiss she failed to disguise. Martín sat more slowly than anyone, one hand pressed hard against his side before he let it go. Sabine stayed standing a second too long, staring at the three vials lined up in the slanting light.

The faintly glowing one still looked wrong.

Not dramatic. Not supernatural. Worse than that.

Real.

Lucía caught her expression. "Sit."

Sabine sat.

"For once," Karoline muttered, leaning her head back against the cushion, "I find myself aligned with authority."

"That must be painful," Lucía said.

"It is."

Martín reached for the samples. "We start with simple tests."

Sabine nodded. "Visual first. Then temperature. pH. Conductivity, if your meter still works."

"It performs closer to original spec than most of us."

That got a brief flicker from Karoline. Not a smile exactly. Close enough.

They worked with what they had.

Martín set the three samples in a row: clear run above the glowing bend, faintly luminous pool, lower sample taken near the reservoir feed. Sabine switched off the overhead lamp and drew one shutter farther closed. The room dimmed.

The middle vial held the light longest.

Not bright, but unmistakable. A soft green-blue persistence suspended in the water itself, not on the glass.

Karoline straightened. "Good. I'm relieved. It's still horrible in here too."

Sabine leaned in. "Not reflection."

"No," Martín said. "And not just sediment."

He uncapped the first vial, then the second, checking odor, clarity, visible particulates. Sabine watched the pH strips shift.

"Difference?" Lucía asked.

"Small," Sabine said. "But real."

Martín touched the conductivity probe to the clear sample, then the luminous one. He frowned.

"Higher."

"How much?"

"Enough to matter. Not enough to explain the light."

Karoline, camera in hand now, photographed the vials against the darker wall. "So the official diagnosis remains: unsettling?"

"Very official," Sabine said.

Martín held the glowing vial up to the window slit and rotated it slowly. The light pooled, thinned, then gathered again.

"Biological?" he said.

"Possibly," Sabine said. "Or chemical. Or both."

Lucía crossed her arms. "Meaning?"

Sabine looked at the water. "Meaning the stream is carrying more than gas."

That settled over the room.

Rogelio came back from the window and stood over the map case. "Show me."

Martín cleared a space and spread the topographic sheet across the table. The canyon appeared in tight contour lines, the cave marked on one fold of rising ground, the drainage line running down through the cut and feeding the reservoir below.

Sabine leaned over it despite the protest in her ribs. "The cave pocket traps gas. The stream cuts below it. Then the water feeds the basin."

"The reservoir," Karoline said.

"Yes."

Martín traced the drainage with one finger. "If gas is moving along low pathways and the water intersects them—"

"It may be carrying dissolved material out of the same system," Sabine finished.

Lucía looked from the map to the vials. "The glow came from that feeder stream. Not the reservoir."

"Not yet," Sabine said.

Lucía's gaze sharpened.

Sabine was already looking at the contour lines around the reservoir. Narrow inflow. Broad basin. Steeper wall at the dam. The drowned valley floor sloping down, then bending hard toward one side where the old river channel had cut deeper before the valley flooded.

"Martín," she said, "how deep is the reservoir at the dam?"

He bent over the map. "Deepest point is in the drowned channel. A little over sixty-five meters, if the public bathymetry is current."

Karoline had already reached for the laptop. "At last. A task that requires only one functioning foot."

She logged in to the computer and began searching the regional environmental database and the project's public compliance archive. The safe house filled with the clicking sounds of bad internet and reluctant systems.

The laptop chimed softly.

Karoline turned it toward herself. "Public environmental dashboard. Water chemistry. Gas monitoring. Dissolved CO2 values." Her eyes moved over the columns. "All normal."

Martín came around beside her chair. "Show me."

She did.

The numbers were clean. No degassing alerts. Dissolved gas values within expected range. Temperature profile stable. Water quality unremarkable.

Lucía exhaled once. "So we're wrong?"

Sabine looked at the screen. She wanted that to settle it.

It didn't.

"Where are these readings taken?" she asked.

Karoline scrolled. "Dam platform. Fixed monitoring array."

Martín found the schematic faster than the metadata. "Here."

He opened the diagram: dam wall, floating service platform, sensor cable descending into the water column, intake points marked at intervals.

Sabine stared at it.

Then at the bathymetry.

Then back again.

The station was mounted at the midpoint of the dam face.

Not above the drowned channel.

Her finger moved across the bathymetry to the deepest trench, offset hard toward one side of the valley, where the old riverbed hugged the wall before dropping away.

"What's the deepest sampling point?" she asked.

Karoline squinted. "Forty meters."

Martín checked the bathymetry again. "And the drowned channel is just over sixty-five."

Sabine felt her pulse rise.

"The array's deep," Karoline said, "just not deepest."

"And not over the old channel," Sabine said.

Lucía came closer. "That matters?"

Martín saw it a beat later. "If the reservoir is stratified, and denser CO2-rich water is settling into the drowned channel, the array could miss most of it."

Sabine angled the schematic beside the map. "The station is in the right place for routine management. Mid-face. Serviceable. Representative enough for operations."

"But not for the worst-behaving water," Karoline said.

"No."

Martín leaned in, one hand braced hard against the table. "And if the inflow is arriving as a colder, denser underflow current, it may be running the old river trench beneath the sampled layer."

Lucía said something low and sharp in Spanish.

Rogelio looked at the map. "People fish there."

No one answered him.

He pointed toward the shore road. "Families camp there in dry months. Workers too."

Karoline's voice had gone flat. "How much gas could that trench hold?"

Sabine shook her head. "I don't know."

Martín was still staring at the schematic. "The monitoring isn't false. It's built for routine reservoir management, not for a dense bottom load offset into the old channel."

That was the thought.

Not deception exactly. Something worse.

A system asking a safe question and getting a safe answer.

Lucía did not wait for the silence to thicken. "What do you need?"

Sabine looked at the map, the sensor diagram, the glowing sample, the clean public numbers that had almost reassured her.

"Depth profiles," she said. "Direct sampling at the bottom of the drowned channel. Temperature layering. Dissolved gas at true depth. We need to know what's sitting below the sampled layer."

Martín nodded. "And we need it before they know why we're asking."

Karoline let out a breath that was almost a laugh and contained none of it. "Excellent. So the data isn't false. It's simply looking in the wrong place."

Sabine looked at the dashboard again, at the neat green indicators and the calm trend line.

"Yes."

That was somehow worse.

Because false data could be argued with. Correct data from the wrong geometry could reassure everyone all the way to disaster.

She turned the laptop so Lucía could see the sampling depths against the reservoir profile.

"They built the system to measure what they expected to matter," she said. "Not what might actually kill people."

No one spoke.

Outside, something moved in the trees beyond the shutter and was gone. Inside, the safe house felt suddenly smaller than the maps spread across its table.

Karoline lowered her camera without taking another photo. "Tell me this doesn't mean the whole reservoir is becoming a trap."

Martín answered before Sabine could. "It means we don't know what the bottom water is holding."

Sabine kept her eyes on the drowned channel at the dam.

"And until we do," she said quietly, "the surface numbers are worse than useless."

Lucía looked at her. "Why?"

Sabine's voice was very quiet.

"Because they reassure."

54

Alexei had spent most of the day trying to prove the glowing-water reports were worthless.

That was where any sane analysis had to begin. Not with meaning. With subtraction.

The room around him had long since abandoned any pretense of comfort. One folding table. Two hardened laptops. A faraday pouch half-open beside a mug gone cold. A travel router running through an ugly chain of improvised shielding and power conditioning that would have looked paranoid to anyone who had not once helped build an intelligence he later had to help bury.

Outside, rain tapped lightly against corrugated metal, stopped, then began again.

On the main screen, southern Colombia was covered in points.

Bad timestamps. Recycled Fin del Mundo photos. Reposts pretending to be eyewitness accounts. Tourist nonsense. Local folklore dressed up as breaking news. Most of it died quickly.

He killed the repost chains first.

Then the old Fin del Mundo images.

Then every photo whose light signature collapsed under basic analysis.

Then the accounts too new, too synchronized, or too eager.

Then the location claims that failed against roads, watershed, or terrain.

The map thinned.

It should have turned into nothing.

It didn't.

Now only the stubborn reports remained. More than he would have liked. More than he could ignore.

Alexei zoomed out and stared at the surviving clusters.

Not nationwide. Not random. Not even rumor-shaped.

Constrained.

He dragged one cluster west, another south, then stopped with his hand still on the trackpad.

Something about the footprint felt familiar.

He sat back.

Looked again.

The recognition came before the thought did, a cold reflex in the body before language caught up.

I know this shape.

"No," he said quietly.

He opened a second layer from a buried local cache.

Not the public network map. Not anything RegenX knew existed. Martín's arrays had gone dark to ordinary interception days ago, once Alexei's patched protocol had replaced the original one. The old transmissions had been easy to block. Too regular. Too legible. His version hid inside the noise instead.

The arrays now spoke in millisecond bursts buried in what looked like static. Unless you knew the burst timing, the reconstruction key, and the packet cadence, the network read as environmental junk and dead air. RegenX thought they had blinded it by turning the spectrum into sludge.

They had not.

Alexei pulled up the array footprint and held it beside the glow reports for one last second without merging them.

Then he overlaid the maps.

The match appeared all at once.

Not perfect. Nothing real ever aligned perfectly. But too close to be ecological accident.

Every credible glow report sat either inside an estimated array footprint, immediately adjacent to one, or downstream from one.

Alexei checked the southern corridor first, because it was the easiest place to disprove himself.

A feeder stream. Two credible images. One local text report. Array nodes upslope. Another report lower down where the water bent toward the reservoir.

He turned on the hydrology layer.

The downstream path snapped into place.

He checked the western edge.

Then the northernmost cluster he had assumed would finally break the pattern.

It didn't.

He stripped out the oldest surviving reports.

Still there.

He stripped out the densest cluster.

Still there.

He removed everything posted after the first mainstream mention, in case attention itself had created a false gravity.

Still there.

The pattern was not surviving because he wanted it to.

It was surviving subtraction.

Alexei opened one of the clearest photographs. Dark water over stone. A faint green-blue persistence under the surface. Not bright. Not theatrical. Not fake enough.

The old dread was not that the pattern existed.

It was that the pattern looked coupled.

Martín's arrays were supposed to observe. Measure. Listen.

Not become part of whatever this was.

Alexei pulled up the reconstructed transmission logs from the hidden protocol.

The network was active.

Not in any way that would have caught RegenX's attention. But the traffic had changed. Denser in places. Tighter. Certain clusters speaking in shorter intervals than Martín's deployment profile should have required. Too much recurrence where there should have been drift. Too much structure surviving inside what was supposed to pass for noise.

Alexei sat still and watched the burst traces crawl across the screen.

He did not like them.

Taken alone, any piece could still be explained away. Environmental fluctuation. Network adjustment. Mesh behavior under local stress.

Taken together, they felt like a system leaning toward purpose.

He overlaid one final layer: deployment timing.

That was the test he had been avoiding.

If the timing broke the pattern, he could still call the overlap coincidence and move on.

He ran it anyway.

The earliest credible glow reports in each cluster appeared after local sensor deployment, not before.

Alexei stared at that until the muscles at the base of his neck began to ache.

Correlation was not causation.

He knew that better than most people alive.

But correlation this tight, in systems this strange, was not something you ignored. It was something you treated as warning.

He opened the team's secure channel.

No hesitation about names. They already knew he was there.

He attached the composite map first: glow reports, drainage, topography, array footprint.

Then he wrote:

It appears there is more to the nanosensor array than observation.

He attached the second overlay.

I started with the glow reports alone. Filtered for location credibility, repost contamination, image integrity, and old Fin del Mundo reuse. The remaining reports formed a geographic cluster I recognized before I understood why.

A third image followed: hydrology and deployment timing.

Every credible glow report I can place is either within an array footprint or downstream from one.

He kept going.

That does not prove the arrays are causing the phenomenon. It does mean they are no longer separate from it. Either the network is altering local conditions, or something is acting through the environment the network has changed.

He read that twice.

Didn't like it.

Kept it anyway.

Then:

If you are sampling water, compare it against array proximity, downstream flow, and deployment age. If you are looking for cause, stop assuming observation and interference are separate.

His fingers hovered over the keys.

Then he added the only line that mattered.

I thought this was noise. It isn't.

He encrypted the packet, routed it through the buried-burst relay chain, and sent it.

For a moment nothing changed.

Rain tapped again against the metal roof. The router lights blinked. Southern Colombia remained spread across the screen in points, river cuts, and implications.

Alexei sat back slowly, one hand still on the edge of the table.

He had built the protocol so the network could survive being hunted.

He had not built it for this.

On the screen, the surviving glow reports remained fixed around Martín's arrays like stars forming a constellation he didn't want to name.

55

Alexei's overlays still glowed on the laptop screen: drainage, topography, Martín's arrays, the surviving reports of luminous water clustered too tightly around them to dismiss. The sample vials sat in the middle of the table like smaller versions of the same problem. Beyond the shutters, the forest had shifted from evening into the flatter quiet before full night.

For a moment nobody spoke.

Then Sabine said, "We can't do this in sequence."

Lucía looked up first. "Meaning?"

"Meaning if the reservoir is holding CO2 at depth, we don't have time to spend tomorrow on soil and the next day on water." She touched Alexei's map with one finger. "And if the arrays are part of the glow, waiting gives RegenX time to close around both."

Martín nodded. "She's right."

Karoline leaned back against the sofa cushions. "Wonderful. Two problems instead of one."

Rogelio studied the maps. "Then we split."

Sabine looked at him. The answer had already formed. "Two teams."

"The reservoir and the arrays," Lucía said.

"Yes."

Karoline frowned. "I dislike how calm you sound."

"I dislike almost everything about it," Sabine said.

Martín straightened carefully. “The reservoir has to be tonight.”

“Why?” Lucía asked.

“Because the boat plan needs the cover of darkness if you want the residence and the dam to miss it. And because if the bottom water is loading, I want a profile before they decide to add protection around the reservoir.”

Rogelio touched the map near the north side of the basin. “There’s an old launch cut here. Not official. Used by fishermen before the road shifted. If the canoe is still where I think it is, we can get onto the water out of the residence sightline.”

“And the drowned channel?” Lucía asked.

“Runs deeper along this wall before curving back toward the dam.”

Martín leaned in. “That’s where you go. Not midpoint water. The old river trench.”

Karoline looked from one to the other. “So two non-scientists paddle into a potentially lethal reservoir in the dark and do field science to test your theory?”

Lucía’s eyes flicked to her. “Two people who know the water take some readings at depth and bring back sealed samples. That’s enough.”

“That is not comforting.”

Sabine had already moved on. “Then Martín and I take the southern array line.”

He nodded at once. “The one tied to the feeder-stream reports. Soil close to active nodes. Then controls across the ridge shoulder outside the footprint.”

Rogelio pointed to the western end of a ridge. “Same forest type there. Different drainage. Since the nodes don’t cross the shoulder, it should work.”

“Good,” Sabine said.

Karoline looked at all of them. “And where do I go?”

The room went silent.

Lucía answered first. “Nowhere.”

Karoline’s face hardened. “No.”

“You can barely walk.”

“I can still think.”

"Yes," Lucía said. "That is why you stay."

Karoline pushed herself upright too fast and had to stop when pain crossed her face. She hated that they all saw it.

Sabine spoke before Lucía could. "We need someone here."

"I am not a receptionist."

"No," Sabine said. "You're the only one in this room who can hold the whole operation if it fractures."

Karoline said nothing.

Martín took over. "Alexei's channel stays open here. Public chatter, local chatter, RegenX movement, any new glow reports. Someone has to watch all of it in real time. Someone has to log routes, timings, samples, and check-ins. If one team is discovered, the other may already be too committed to stop."

Karoline looked at the laptop, then at the camera beside her, then at the notebook on the table."Fine," she said. "But don't mistake staying here for ag reement.""Noted," Lucía said.

Once the decision settled, the room accelerated.

Rogelio started laying out what the reservoir team would need. Rope. Weighted line. Handheld gas meter. Profiling probe. Sealed sample bottles. Flashlight with a red filter. Wrapped paddles. One old dry bag that smelled faintly of diesel and river mud. Lucía checked each item without comment and discarded one cracked cap immediately.

Martín pulled the bathymetry sheet closer. "Listen carefully."

Lucía looked up.

"Profile first. Then samples. Two bottom-water samples if you can manage it. Slow retrieval. No opening anything on the water."

Rogelio nodded.

"And if the gas meter reads high near the surface or shore pockets?" he asked.

"You back away first," Martín said. "And tell me later."

Lucía absorbed that without comment. "And if someone sees us?"

"Then we're fishermen who made a bad choice," Rogelio said.

Karoline muttered, "With a meter, a profiling line, two sealed samplers, and no fish."

"No one will see that part from shore," he said.

At the other end of the table, Sabine and Martín built the second loadout: sample bags, marker, gloves, small trowel, improvised corer, pH strips, conductivity meter, spare batteries, cloth tags.

"Close-in sample first," Martín said. "Then control."

Sabine nodded. "Across the shoulder. Same canopy. Same slope class. Same soil texture."

Lucía glanced over. "You make this sound easy."

"It isn't," Sabine said.

"It's just specific," Martín said.

The light outside had gone from late evening to full darkness. Karoline opened a fresh page in her notebook and looked up.

"Again," she said. "Cleanly. Routes, roles, objectives."

That changed the room more than any argument had.

Sabine met her eyes.

"Lucía and Rogelio take the canoe to the reservoir," she said. "They profile the drowned channel, then take two bottom-water samples out of sight of the residence and dam."

Karoline wrote.

"Martín and I take the southern array line. Near-node soil, litter, seepage if present, then matched controls beyond the footprint."

Karoline wrote that too.

"And me?" she asked, though now the question had become something else.

Sabine answered anyway. "You stay here. Channel monitor. Chatter watch. Map. Sample chain. If one team disappears, you're the one who still knows what the other was trying to prove."

Karoline stared at the page, then nodded once without looking pleased by any part of it.

The room settled around that.

Not calm. Commitment.

Lucía tied her hair back tighter, checked the sidearm at her waist, and looked at Rogelio. "Boat first."

He nodded and lifted the dry bag.

Sabine capped the sample tubes and slid them into Martín's pack. The glow reports, the drowned channel, the arrays, the feeder stream — all of it had begun as pattern. Now it was routes, equipment, darkness, and timing.

Karoline reached for the secure laptop and drew it closer, as if preparing to sit a vigil over people who had not yet gone missing.

The safe house no longer felt like shelter.

It felt like the last place where all the pieces still fit.

"Move," Lucía said.

And they did.

56

The canoe was where Rogelio remembered it was, half-hidden under cane and black mud at the old launch cut, as if the shore itself had been keeping it for one more bad decision.

Lucía took the bow. Rogelio eased the stern free without a splash. Between them, the gear sat wrapped and tied down: profiling line, gas meter, two sealed samplers, weighted drop line, red-filtered flashlight, dry bag.

Above the reservoir, stars twinkled in the moonless sky. The residence was screened by trees on a peninsula. The dam face lay farther off, a darker geometry in the night, its bulk felt more than seen.

"Quiet now," Rogelio murmured.

Lucía gave him a look. "That was already the plan."

The canoe drifted for a second before Rogelio's paddle caught. Then they were moving, shallow strokes at first, keeping tight to shadow before angling out toward the drowned channel Martín had marked on the bathymetry sheet. The reservoir surface was dark enough to erase edges. Only the faintest film of reflected sky separated water from land.

Lucía kept her eyes moving: shore, tree line, water, lights, shore again.

No voices.

No engines.

No movement near the residence.

Good.

Rogelio guided by memory and depth sense, reading the reservoir the way other men read streets. When he finally lifted the paddle and nodded once, Lucía knew they were close enough.

"Here," he whispered.

They let the canoe settle.

Silence on open water felt different from silence on land. Bigger. Less forgiving.

Lucía steadied the hull while Rogelio handed over the weighted line and profiling probe. The screen was dimmed as far as Martín had dared set it and still leave it readable. Lucía clipped the probe on, checked the line, and lowered it into the black.

Ten meters.

Fifteen.

Twenty.

The numbers changed, but not enough to matter.

Rogelio watched the shore while she worked.

"Thirty," he said softly.

Lucía nodded and kept lowering.

Thirty-five.

Forty.

The reservoir remained composed. Stable enough to reassure a dashboard.

Then, a little below that, the readings shifted.

Lucía frowned and held the line still.

"What?" Rogelio asked.

"Wait."

She watched the screen.

Temperature dropped harder than it had above. Conductivity moved. pH broke with it.

Not drift.

Not noise.

A layer.

"Forty-five," she whispered.

Rogelio leaned in just enough to see the dim display. "That's real?"

"Yes."

She lowered another meter.

The pattern held.

The lower water was different.

Not by a rounding error. By a boundary.

Lucía felt something cold move through her that had nothing to do with the night air.

"Martín was right," she said.

Rogelio looked toward the dark shore, then back to the line. "Finish that, then take the sample."

Lucía nodded and continued letting the line out until it went slack a little over sixty-four meters down.

"Nice navigation," she whispered. "We're almost exactly over the middle of the channel."

Rogelio smiled and shrugged.

Lucía drew the probe up carefully. No sudden movement. No clatter against the hull. She traded it for the first sealed sampler, clipped it to the weighted line, and lowered it into the same water.

The line moved through her fingers in measured slips.

Forty.

Forty-five.

Fifty.

"Lower," Rogelio murmured.

She did.

The line went soft for a heartbeat, then steadied again as the sampler settled just above the trench bottom.

Lucía worked the trigger exactly as Martín had shown her. Waited. Counted. Then brought it up, slow and steady, the line cold and wet against her hands.

No agitation.

No rush.

No sound.

When the sampler broke the surface, it did so cleanly.

Rogelio caught it and lowered it gently into the padded slot in the dry bag as if handling something alive and temperamental.

"One," he said.

Lucía reached for the second sampler.

Then Rogelio froze.

Lucía saw it at once and followed his eyes.

A moving light along the eastern shore.

Not the residence.

Not the dam.

Lower.

The beam swept once across the bank, disappeared behind trees, then reappeared farther on.

"Patrol," Rogelio said.

Lucía tracked it. One light became two. Slow movement along the shoreline road, circling toward the northern side of the basin.

Toward the launch cut.

"How far?"

"Too close."

Lucía looked at the first sample, then at the second sampler in her hand.

They had one.

They needed two.

Far off beyond the ridgeline, lightning flickered once inside the clouds. A few seconds later, thunder rolled across the basin, distant enough to ignore.

The light moved again, nearer now, pausing at intervals like someone checking the bank.

Lucía clipped on the second sampler. "Fast, but not stupid."

Rogelio had already shifted his weight to steady the canoe. "That's not reassuring."

She lowered the second sampler.

Forty.

Forty-five.

Fifty.

The patrol lights vanished behind a stand of trees.

Lucía triggered the sampler and began hauling it up.

Too quickly. She knew it even as she did it.

The line came alive in her hands, taut and jittering with the speed of the pull.

"Slower," Rogelio hissed.

"I know."

But the lights were back now, closer to the launch cut, and the distance between risk and panic was narrowing fast.

She hauled harder.

The sampler hit the surface wrong and burst with a hard crack, like a bottle cap turned into a gunshot.

Water sprayed across the bow.

The sound leapt across the reservoir.

Both of them went still.

On shore, the patrol lights stopped.

Then swung out over the water.

Lucía flattened instinctively, dragging the line down with her. Rogelio killed all movement. The canoe rocked once, then settled into the black.

One beam passed wide.

The second came closer.

Near enough that Lucía could see the wet edge of her own knuckles against the gunwale.

No one spoke.

The beams moved off.

For a beat Lucía thought that might be enough.

Then one snapped back toward shore and a voice carried over the water.

"There."

Lucía swore under her breath.

Rogelio dug the paddle harder. "We're seen."

"Keep moving."

They paddled.

Not frantically. Frantic carried. Short, hard, careful strokes, angling for the launch cut while the patrol lights tracked the shoreline toward where they needed to land.

The reservoir felt much smaller on the way back.

Lucía could already see the dark slit of the cut between the reeds. The truck beyond it was only a shape.

Good. Still unlit.

Then one beam caught the water off their stern.

Not directly.

Enough.

"There!" the voice shouted again from shore.

The canoe slid into the launch cut with a wet hiss through reeds and mud. Rogelio was out first, dragging the bow up while Lucía grabbed the dry bag and the ruined sample bottle. Another flashlight beam broke through the cane behind them.

"Hey!" the voice called. "Who's there?"

Lucía stood, breathing hard enough to make anger easy, and turned toward the light.

"Fishermen," she shouted back.

"Fishing at this hour?"

"Yes."

"With no catch?"

"Our light died."

Rogelio, already hauling the canoe farther up the bank, added in a sour, irritated tone that required no acting at all, "Waste of a night."

The beam held on them.

Lucía let it. Better that than movement mistaken for guilt.

"You know night fishing is illegal," the voice called.

Lucía threw her hands out a little. "Then fine us tomorrow. Tonight we caught nothing and we're leaving."

A second voice said something lower, too far off to make out.

The beam shifted to the canoe, to the paddles, to the dry bag, then back to Lucía's face.

"You two alone?"

"Just the two of us," she said.

Rogelio didn't look up. He just kept swearing softly as he dragged the canoe the last few feet like a man embarrassed to be caught doing something petty and stupid.

The first voice called back, "Go home."

Lucía didn't answer. She turned away as if insulted by the obviousness of the instruction.

That helped.

By the time the patrol lights moved on along the bank road, Rogelio had the canoe hidden enough to survive until someone else needed it, and Lucía was already at the truck.

They loaded in silence. Dry bag first. Probe case. Gas meter. Paddles last.

Rogelio got behind the wheel. Lucía climbed in beside him, still wet at the cuffs, pulse not yet willing to behave.

For a second neither of them moved.

Then Rogelio started the truck.

The engine sounded too loud and perfectly ordinary.

He eased them away from the launch cut without headlights until the trees took them, then turned on his low beams and kept driving.

Lucía held the pack with the first sampler in both hands the way some people held something sacred.

Beside her, Rogelio said, "That was close."

Lucía looked out into the dark road unwinding ahead of them.

"We have what we came for," Lucía said. "The question is who knows it."

57

Sabine and Martín reached the southern array line just before the last usable light gave up.

The forest here was denser than the ridge above the safe house, the ground padded with wet litter and root tangles that swallowed sound if you stepped well and punished you if you didn't. Martín led the last stretch by memory, checking his handheld twice and then not again for twenty meters, as though he already knew where the node should be and disliked needing proof.

Sabine stayed close behind him with the field pack riding badly against her shoulder blades. The walk in had not been far, but 'far' had stopped being a useful measure since the landslide. What mattered now was how often she had to hide the moment before a full breath, how carefully she had to stand after crouching, how much of her attention was already being spent on making pain look like concentration.

Martín slowed and lifted one hand.

"Here," he whispered.

At first Sabine saw nothing except the ordinary dark of understory and damp leaves. Then Martín crouched and parted a tangle of fern and low growth near the base of a tree, and the node came into view: a small housing, half disguised by mud and bark dust, with one filament line disappearing into the ground and another climbing the trunk like a root that had chosen the wrong direction.

It should have looked inert.

Instead the whole patch around it felt subtly wrong.

Not dramatic. Not cinematic. Worse than that. Specific.

The damp litter nearest the housing held a faint sheen when Martín angled his dimmed light across it. Not enough to call a glow. Enough to make the eye return. The air smelled of wet soil and leaf rot and something sharper beneath it, a metallic tang so slight Sabine might have dismissed it anywhere else.

Martín brought up the receiver and frowned almost immediately.

"What?"

He listened to the screen a moment longer. "This is too active."

"Meaning?"

"The traffic density. Not louder. Just tighter. Too much recurrence."

He hated saying it.

They unpacked quickly. Sample bags. Marker. Gloves. Small trowel. Improvised corer. Sabine got down beside him more carefully than she wanted him to notice and steadied herself on one palm until the first sharp pull under her ribs eased.

Martín noticed anyway. His eyes flicked to her face. "We can do this fast."

"We can do it properly. Then fast."

That almost won a smile from him.

They started beside the node.

Martín scraped back the upper litter and took the first core. Sabine held out the bag. He slid the plug in. She sealed and marked it. Then litter. Then the thicker fungal mat under the leaf layer. Then seepage gathering against a root buttress downslope of the housing.

Martín touched the probe to the seepage, checked the screen, then checked it again.

"Well?"

He glanced from the number to the soil sample and back. "Higher conductivity."

Sabine touched a pH strip to the damp slurry they had mixed in the cap and held it under the light.

"Different," she said.

Martín exhaled through his nose. "Yes."

For a moment neither of them spoke.

Then Sabine said, "That's one site."

He nodded once. "Now the control."

They packed the first round of samples and started for the control site.

The ridge shoulder Rogelio had marked looked close on the map. On foot, in the dark, over wet root and rising ground, it became something else. The array zone had been hidden in a sheltered pocket. The control site lay beyond it, across a sloping traverse where the forest opened just enough to expose them to pale scraps of sky and slick rock under leaf mold.

Martín stopped once and looked back. "You can wait here while I get the control."

"A second set of hands will help speed the process."

"Only if they are still able to function."

"They will be," she said.

They kept moving.

Halfway across the shoulder, Sabine's left boot came down on what looked like firm ground and found a wet root under the litter instead. Her foot shot forward. She twisted hard, caught herself with one hand against the slope, and slammed the side of her ribs against a buried stone hard enough to drive all the breath out of her in a silent convulsion.

The sample pouch jerked from her grip and slid two feet downhill before snagging in fern.

Martín was beside her at once. "Sabine—"

She held up one hand.

For a second there was no air anywhere. Only pain and the raw animal panic of a body that had stopped obeying sequence.

Then a thin breath.

Then another.

Martín retrieved the pouch and crouched too close. "You're done."

She shook her head and regretted the motion immediately.

"You don't get to decide that by accident," she said.

"That wasn't an accident. That was your chest reminding us it exists."

She pushed herself upright in stages. Not graceful. Functional.

"Do we still have the samples?"

He held up the pouch.

"Then move."

He stared at her one heartbeat longer, angry because she was right and because he needed her not to be. Then he turned and led the last stretch without another word.

The control site was only eighty meters farther on.

It felt like another ecosystem.

Same broad forest type. Similar canopy. Similar slope. But the ground was less waterlogged, the fungal threads thinner and more ordinary, the smell only wet leaf and soil. No sheen under the light. No metallic edge beneath the rot.

Sabine noticed Martín noticing it too.

"Good," she said quietly.

"That's not the word."

"It is if the first site was abnormal."

"We're not trying to prove anything. We are testing Alexei's hypothesis."

Sabine winced. He was right. More than that, she could hear what sat under the correction: if the hypothesis held, the arrays stopped being an instrument and became an implication.

They worked faster here.

Control soil. Litter. A small seep line between two stones under the shoulder. Martín checked conductivity, then pH, then checked them again, slower.

Closer to what he would have expected.

Sabine took second readings and got the same answer.

The difference wasn't subtle anymore.

Martín looked back toward the array site through the trees as though distance itself had become accusatory.

"Alexei may be on to something," Sabine said.

Martín did not answer.

The first gust hit the canopy above them hard enough to sound like something large moving through the trees.

Both of them froze.

Then the second gust came colder and harder, and the forest changed its mind about the night.

"Storm," Martín said.

The downburst hit a second later.

Rain slammed through the canopy in one violent sheet, flattening leaves, hammering bark, and turning the ground from merely slick to treacherous in seconds. Water began running where there had been none. The control seep blurred. Sample labels threatened to loosen under their fingers.

"Bag them," Sabine said.

They moved at once.

Open sample bags into the dry sleeve.Caps checked.Marker wrapped.Meter wiped once and shoved deep.Control samples separated from node samples by touch and label because the light had become more hindrance than help in the rain.

Martín still had the probe out.

"What are you doing?" Sabine snapped.

"One more conductivity reading. The runoff—"

"No."

He hesitated. The wrong hesitation.

Sabine reached past him, took the probe out of his hand, and stuffed it into the pack herself. "Whatever the rain is doing now is not baseline. We already have the comparison."

"It could show transport."

"It could also wash half the slope into our samples." She cinched the pack hard enough that the buckle bit her thumb. "We're done."

Thunder moved somewhere above the ridge, not close yet, but close enough to make the forest feel electrical.

Martín looked toward the array line again, invisible now beyond rain and dark and trees, and Sabine saw the decision still fighting in him.

One more node. One better reading. One more chance to understand his own system before it stopped belonging to him.

Then she coughed.

It was only once. But the cough tore through her chest like something ripping free and left her bent forward with one hand braced on her knee, the other clamped uselessly over ribs that did not care what the mission needed.

Martín was at her side before the second breath came.

"That's it," he said.

She tried to answer and had to stop until air obeyed again.

Rain hammered the leaves around them. Water ran down the back of her neck and through her collar.

Martín took the sample pack from her without asking.

"We have enough," he said.

This time she didn't argue.

The way back down was uglier than the climb.

Mud where there had been footing.Roots turned slick as wire.Branches whipping under the weight of the rain.

Sabine moved in short bursts between shallow breaths, angry at every body part she owned.

Martín stayed close enough to catch her if she slipped again and far enough not to say her name every time she faltered. It was the right distance and probably the hardest one.

By the time the first hint of safer ground appeared below the trees, both of them were soaked through and carrying more silence than equipment.

Martín glanced once over his shoulder toward the dark where the array line remained hidden.

"We should have sampled another node," he said.

Sabine kept walking.

"We took enough to know the first site is not normal," she said. "Enough to know the control site isn't matching it."

"That's not the same as having proof."

"No." She stepped over a wash of runoff and caught herself against a trunk before the slope could take advantage. "It isn't."

When they finally reached the lower path, the rain began to ease as abruptly as it had come, leaving the forest dripping and raw and full of the sound of water going places it had not been going an hour earlier.

Martín shifted the sample pack higher on his shoulder and looked at her in the thin returning dark.

Her breathing was still wrong. Not catastrophic. Not stable either.

He didn't say it.

She didn't thank him for not saying it.

They kept moving toward the safe house with the samples sealed, the labels intact, and just enough evidence to support Alexei's hypothesis.

At the sampled site near the arrays, the chemistry had shifted.

At the control site, it had not.

The rain had washed the surface, but not what lay beneath.

58

By the time Sabine and Martín reached the safe house, the rain had weakened to an uneven dripping from the leaves and roofline, each drop loud in the pauses between the insects starting up again.

Lucía opened the door before they knocked. Her eyes went first to Sabine's face, then to Martín carrying the sample pack instead of her. She stepped aside without comment and pushed the door shut quickly behind them.

The air inside was no cooler than outside, only stiller. Damp clung to the walls and the low ceiling. The room smelled of wet fabric, coffee gone bitter on the burner, mud, and the faint sour trace of clothes that had been rained on too many times in a place that never fully dried. A single lamp burned on the table. Near the back, a small gas ring hissed under a blackened kettle.

Rogelio sat at the table with a notebook open in front of him. Lucía was on the bench against the wall, wrapped in one of the thin woven covers from the house, more for comfort than warmth. Her hair was still damp at the ends.

"We got samples," Martín said, setting the pack down carefully.

Lucía nodded once. "So did we."

No one asked for a full account immediately. Sabine peeled off her soaked overshirt with slow, economical movements and left it hanging over the back of a chair. Martín wiped his forearms and neck with a rag Rogelio pushed across the table. Lucía poured coffee into enamel mugs, not because anyone needed warming but because it gave their hands something to do and kept the room from tipping too quickly into the meaning of what they had found.

When everyone was sitting or leaning against something solid, Lucía said, “We compare notes.”

It was the right way to do it. No replay. No wasted sequence. Just the shape of what each team had brought back.

By the time they were done, the room had gone very quiet.

Sabine sat with one arm resting against her ribs and the coffee untouched in front of her. “So the break is real.”

Rogelio tapped the notebook. “At depth. About forty-five meters. Temperature shift, conductivity shift, pH shift. Enough to mark a distinct layer.”

Martín leaned in despite himself. “Stable?”

“As stable as we could confirm tonight.”

Lucía crossed her arms. “The second bottle ruptured before we could get it in the boat.”

Martín looked up sharply. “At the surface?”

Rogelio nodded. “Pulled too fast.”

Sabine felt the room narrow.

“If it came up supersaturated and depressurized on ascent—”

“It could do that,” Martín said.

Karoline looked between them. “Do what?”

Sabine turned to her. “Burst. Because the dissolved gas comes out of solution too fast once the pressure drops.”

“CO_2,” Martín said.

Karoline’s expression tightened. “You mean the water could release it all at once?”

Sabine held her gaze for a beat. “In extreme cases, yes. Lake Nyos, Cameroon. Nineteen eighty-six. CO_2 came out of the lake and suffocated the valley. It’s called a limnic eruption. This alone doesn’t prove that. But it is consistent with dissolved gas trapped below the main monitoring depth.”

Lucía planted one hand on the table. “Enough to matter?”

Sabine glanced at Rogelio's notes. "Enough that if the layer is real and destabilized, it could degas fast."

Karoline stared at her. "Enough to kill people?"

"In the wrong place," Sabine said, "yes."

No one moved.

The room seemed to tighten around the table, the lamp, and the one sealed bottle that had become more important than anything else they had carried out of the dark.

Martín pulled the notebook closer. "One bottle bursting is not proof by itself."

"No," Sabine said. "But with the depth readings and the chemistry shift, it is not something we can afford to dismiss."

Lucía gave him a flat look. "So we treat it as real."

"Until a lab tells us otherwise," Sabine said.

That settled the priority, if not the fear.

Martín opened the sample pack from the ridge and began laying the bags out in a careful row under the lamp: soil from beside the node, seepage, fungal mat, then the control samples from farther upslope. The labels looked small and precise against the scarred wood of the table.

"And on our side," Sabine said, "the node site was chemically wrong."

Martín nodded. "Conductivity elevated near the housing. pH shifted. The control site did not match it."

Karoline leaned forward. "So the arrays are causing it?"

"No," Sabine said.

Martín gave a tight, reluctant nod. "Not necessarily. Only that the chemistry at the sampled site near the node is altered."

"And the fungi?" Karoline asked.

Sabine looked down at the sealed bag containing the denser white mat. "Unknown."

That word sat in the room longer than the others.

She went on. "The fungal growth was heavier near the housing. The seepage chemistry was different. But we do not know whether the fungi are responding to the altered chemistry, contributing to it, or simply concentrated where the same deeper process is expressing itself."

Lucía looked from the soil bags to Rogelio's notes. "So we have two problems."

"We may have one problem in two forms," Sabine said.

Outside, runoff moved downslope in thin, unseen threads. Inside, the lamp drew a hard circle of light over the evidence and left the corners of the room to shadow and damp.

Martín was the one who said it aloud. "The reservoir takes precedence."

Karoline looked at him. "Because it can kill people faster."

"Yes," Sabine said. "The soil and fungal samples may tell us mechanism. The reservoir is the immediate hazard."

Rogelio lifted his chin toward the bottle. "The first bottle stayed sealed."

"Yes," Sabine said. "That needs dissolved gas analysis, full chemistry, and whoever handles it has to understand exactly why it matters. Not just water quality. Gas loading."

Lucía asked, "And these?" She gestured at the soil bags.

"Lab work too," Martín said. "Chemistry first. Then microbial and fungal identification if we can get it. Right now we are looking at symptoms."

Karoline's gaze moved across the table. "Someone needs to be warned."

Lucía shook her head almost before the sentence was finished. "Not yet."

Karoline straightened. "If that reservoir is dangerous—"

"If we warn the wrong people with half a case," Lucía said, "the site closes, the evidence disappears, and whoever built this gets time to prepare a story."

"That is not a reason to stay quiet if people are at risk."

"It is if the warning goes nowhere useful."

Sabine cut in before the argument could sharpen. "She's right about one thing. We need confirmation that cannot be dismissed as field noise, contamination, or bad handling. Enough that whoever receives it cannot bury it cheaply."

Karoline looked at her hard. "And if something happens before then?"

Sabine held her gaze. The pain in her ribs had settled into a deeper, meaner ache now that she was still.

"Then we were too slow," she said. "But if we move too early and lose the evidence, we fail with nothing. We only control what we control."

The room did not accept that so much as endure it.

Martín touched the notebook with one finger. "If the measurements hold, then the reservoir is consistent with a CO_2-rich layer below where the monitoring array is measuring."

There it was.

Not a full answer. Not proof. But the shape of the danger had finally sharpened enough to name.

Lucía's face did not change. "And if you're right?"

Sabine answered. "Then whatever is happening at Fin del Mundo is not the whole event. It may only be where the system first became visible."

No one spoke after that.

Rogelio poured more coffee into the nearest empty mug and set it down without asking whose it was. The kettle gave a soft hiss behind him. Water still dripped from the hems of their clothes onto the floorboards.

At last Lucía looked at the spread of evidence on the table—the notebook, the bottle, the soil bags, the numbers that should not have agreed but did.

"So," she said, "the reservoir first."

"Yes," Sabine said.

"And the rest?"

Sabine looked again at the fungal samples, at the white threads pressed against the plastic.

"The rest goes with it," she said. "But it waits its turn."

No one argued.

For a long moment they stayed where they were, listening to the insects outside rebuild the night and the water moving downslope through the dark.

Martín pulled Rogelio's notebook closer and began copying the key depth readings into a cleaner hand. Sabine reached for the sample log. Lucía checked the shutters, then came back to the table.

Karoline drew a woven cover tighter around her shoulders. "When this reaches a lab, they'll understand what they're looking at?"

Sabine did not answer immediately.

"They'll understand enough," she said at last.

It was not reassurance.

It was worse.

Because the reservoir no longer felt like a possibility.

It felt like a clock.

59

The safe house had gone quieter, but not calmer.

The bottle from the reservoir stood near the gas ring, its sealed cap catching the lamplight whenever someone moved. Beside it, the rows of soil samples sat labeled and orderly on the table, their neatness making the room feel more precarious rather than less. Outside, water still found its way downslope through the dark in thin, hidden channels. The insects had resumed with that eerie insistence the forest always had, as if nothing human had happened in it worth remarking on.

Inside, no one had yet managed the illusion of normal.

Sabine sat at the table with the sample log open in front of her, though she had stopped writing several minutes earlier. The ache in her ribs had settled into something deep and deliberate, no longer sharp enough to command attention, only constant enough to shape everything else around it. Martín stood near the lamp, one hand braced on the table, rereading Rogelio's depth notes as if numbers might grow safer under repetition. Lucía had gone to the shutters again. Karoline sat on the bench, the woven cover around her shoulders slipping loose as she leaned forward, restless even in stillness.

"We can't sit on this until morning," Karoline said.

No one answered immediately. The sentence had already been in the room. She had only made it audible.

Lucía turned from the shutters. "No one is sitting on anything."

"That's what this feels like."

"What this looks like," Lucía said, "is five people trying not to make the wrong move in the dark."

Karoline pushed the cover off one shoulder. "The wrong move is saying nothing while there is a CO_2 hazard sitting under that reservoir."

"There may be," Martín said.

Karoline heard the correction. "You've heard the same notes I did. You saw the same bottle."

"Yes," Martín said. "And I also know how many things can look conclusive in the field and collapse under proper analysis."

"That sounds very convenient for everyone who benefits from delay."

Lucía's head turned sharply. "Careful."

Karoline ignored her. "People could die if that layer destabilizes."

Sabine looked up at last. "And they could also die if we trigger the wrong response with half a case and lose the ability to prove any of it."

Karoline gave a small, disbelieving shake of the head. "So what — we wait for better paperwork?"

"No."

"Then what?"

"We tell the right person," Sabine said. "In the right order. With enough control over the evidence that it doesn't disappear into someone else's version of events."

Karoline laughed once, without humour. "You think there is a right order for this?"

"In a place like this?" Lucía said. "Yes."

"And if you don't follow it?"

"Then you hand the company time."

That quieted the room for a beat, but Karoline pressed on. "You are treating disclosure like it's the problem."

"No," Sabine said. "You're treating disclosure as if it's the same thing as action."

"And you're treating caution as if it's neutral."

"It isn't."

"Then stop defending it."

Sabine's voice cooled. "I am defending sequence."

"That's a luxury."

"No," Sabine said. "It's the only reason we're still holding the evidence."

Karoline opened her mouth again, but Sabine was already past stopping.

"You remember Ecolux."

That did it.

Karoline's expression hardened at once.

Sabine went on. "You were right about the corruption. But once it was public, everyone who caused the damage had room to hide behind the fallout. The truth landed before the system around it was pinned down."

"That article exposed them."

"Yes," Sabine said. "And yet here is the same company under a different name still operating...it taught me that incomplete truth doesn't always land as justice."

Karoline stood. The woven cover slid to the bench behind her.

"So that's what this is? You think I'm about to do it again?"

"I think if we put this into the wrong channel too early, RegenX will shape the risk before anyone else even understands there is one."

Lucía nodded once. "Yes."

Karoline folded her arms. "So what's the right channel? Police? Civil defense? The mayor? A call to Bogotá?"

"The police are useless for this," Lucía said. "At best they make noise. At worst they pass it on."

"The alcaldía hears industrial risk and calls the company before anyone technical," Martín said.

Karoline let out a breath. "So everyone is compromised?"

Rogelio, who had said nothing for the last several minutes, lifted his head from the notebook.

"No," he said. "Not everyone."

The room went still.

He closed the notebook and set the pencil across it. His movements were unhurried in the way people sometimes moved when they knew speed belonged to others and authority didn't require it.

"There is one person we can tell," Rogelio said.

Lucía's face changed slightly. Recognition.

"Who?" Sabine asked.

Rogelio looked at Lucía first, then answered. "Mariela Cárdenas. CORPOAMAZONIA."

Martín straightened. "She's still at the regional environmental authority?"

"She is," Lucía said.

Karoline looked between them. "And she can do what?"

"She can force an inspection," Lucía said. "Or try. She can make it technical before it becomes political."

Sabine felt the next problem arrive almost immediately. "And if she acts, she has to notify them."

"Yes," Lucía said.

"So once we tell her—"

"This stops belonging only to us," Rogelio said.

Outside, something dropped from a branch and hit the ground with a soft wet sound.

Karoline sat down again, more abruptly than gracefully. "How do you know she won't bury it too?"

Rogelio's expression did not change. "I don't."

It was the most honest thing anyone had said in the room.

Lucía came back to the table and planted both hands on it. "But if Mariela takes it seriously, she has the authority to make RegenX answer in a way the police do not. And if she refuses, then at least we know which way the wall is facing."

Karoline looked at Sabine. "That's your plan? Hand it to one official and hope she's braver than the rest?"

"No," Sabine said. "My plan is to put it in front of someone who can compel technical action before it turns into public theater and corporate spin."

"And if she delays?"

"Then we reassess."

Karoline laughed once, tired now. "Reassess. Really?"

Martín spoke into the silence. "If we go to her, we stay disciplined. Reservoir first. Immediate hazard first. The soil and fungal samples matter, but they are secondary until the water is understood."

Karoline's gaze moved again to the bottle. "And if she brings RegenX in immediately?"

"She will have to," Sabine said. "At some point."

"At some point is not the same as first call," Lucía said.

"No," Sabine agreed. "It isn't."

Rogelio rose at last, slowly, joints announcing the fact before he did. He picked up the notebook and slid it under his arm.

"If I go," he said, "I go before first light. I know which road to use, and which ones not to."

Lucía straightened. "You won't go alone."

He gave her a look that contained long history and no intention of arguing it. "I did not say I would."

Then he turned to Sabine.

"When we speak to her, what is the first sentence?"

That brought everyone back to the real task.

Sabine looked again at the evidence on the table: the bottle from depth, the depth readings, the sample bags, the ache in her ribs pulsing once as if insisting on its place in the reckoning.

Then she said, "We tell her we have field evidence consistent with a CO_2-rich layer below the monitoring zone of the Suyama Reservoir, and that if she waits for the company to define the risk, she will already be too late."

Martín added, "We need independent custody of the water sample before it becomes someone else's anomaly."

Karoline said, "Tell her people may die."

Lucía's eyes flicked toward her, then back to Rogelio. "Tell her the territory is warning her before the company does."

That was the line that held.

Rogelio repeated it under his breath, testing the weight of it.

Then he nodded.

No one looked relieved. The decision had not made anything safer. It had only given the danger a direction to travel.

Lucía went back to the shutters.

Martín gathered the notebook, the depth sheet, and the provisional sample log into a cleaner stack.

Karoline pulled the woven cover around her shoulders again, this time not as resistance but because there was nothing else to do with her hands.

Sabine remained where she was, watching the bottle near the stove as if it might still, even sealed and silent, decide the rest of the night for them.

Rogelio moved toward the back room to wake the young courier the Guardians used when roads were safer than signals. At the doorway he stopped and glanced back.

"Once she knows," he said, "RegenX will know soon after. We go before first light."

No one disputed it.

He gave the smallest nod, accepting the weight of that as if it were merely weather, and disappeared into the dimness beyond the lamp.

The room listened to him go.

Then to the insects.

Then to the water moving downslope through the dark.

And beneath all of it, now that the decision had been made, Sabine could feel the next argument already waiting for them.

Not whether there was danger.

How long the system would protect itself before it protected anyone else.

60

Morning in Mocoa arrived without ceremony: no sunrise worth naming, only a thinning of rainlight through low cloud and the return of traffic somewhere beyond the river.

The CORPOAMAZONIA office was on the second floor of a concrete building that looked as though it had been designed by someone who mistrusted weather and had then lost the argument. The stairwell smelled faintly of mildew and photocopier heat. On the landing outside the office door, a dead moth lay on its back beneath a fluorescent tube that still hummed even after daylight had made it unnecessary.

Lucía knocked once and went in without waiting.

The office was narrower than Sabine had expected. Metal filing cabinets. A scarred desk. Two mismatched visitor chairs and one plastic one with a crack running through the back. A wall map of the region under cloudy plastic, corners curling. Another map pinned beside it with river basins marked in fading colors. On the windowsill sat a fan that turned left and right with a soft click each time it reached the limit of its neck. It moved the damp around without improving it.

Mariela Cárdenas stood behind the desk, reading from a sheet of paper Rogelio had handed her downstairs.

She was younger than Sabine had expected and older than Karoline likely would have guessed: somewhere in that range where fatigue stopped aging a face and began refining it. Dark hair pulled back badly enough to suggest she had done it in a hurry. No jewelry except a watch. Sleeves rolled once. Eyes that went first to Rogelio, then Lucía, then the bottle Martín was carrying in a padded field sleeve, and only after that to the rest of them.

"You brought outsiders," she said.

Rogelio closed the door behind them. "I brought the warning."

Something shifted in her expression.

She set the paper down. "Say it once," she said. "From the beginning. No speeches."

Rogelio did not look at Sabine before he spoke.

"The territory is warning you before the company does."

That landed harder than volume could have.

Mariela's eyes returned to the bottle. "What company?"

"RegenX," Lucía said.

Mariela gave a short nod. "And what exactly is the territory warning me about?"

Martín set the field sleeve on the desk and withdrew the bottle carefully. Sabine laid out the notebook, the depth sheet, and the provisional log beside it.

"We have field evidence consistent with a CO_2-rich layer below the routine monitoring zone in the Suyama Reservoir," Sabine said.

Mariela did not react outwardly. "Consistent how?"

"Independent readings indicated a distinct break at roughly forty-five meters. Temperature shift, conductivity shift, pH shift. A second bottle was brought up too quickly and ruptured at the surface."

"At the surface," Mariela repeated.

"Yes," Sabine said. "Not proof by itself. But consistent with rapid gas coming out of solution after depressurization."

Mariela's gaze dropped to the notes. "Who took these readings?"

"Rogelio and Lucía," Sabine said. "Field instruments. Not lab-grade. But the pattern is coherent."

"And you?"

"My background is climate modeling and physical systems," Sabine said. "Not limnology. But enough to know when a reservoir may be hiding the wrong kind of chemistry."

Mariela looked up then, measuring her more carefully.

"May," she said.

"Yes," Sabine said. "We do not have concentration, extent, or stability. We do have enough that ignoring it would be irresponsible."

Karoline, against the wall near the filing cabinet, said, "Enough that if you wait for a cleaner answer, other people may pay for the delay."

Mariela turned her head toward her. "And you are?"

"Karoline Reinhardt. Journalist."

Lucía closed her eyes briefly.

Mariela's expression did not change, but the room did.

"A journalist," she repeated.

"I'm not here to publish anything," Karoline said. "I'm here because—"

Mariela cut her off with a small lift of one hand. "Then be here usefully."

Karoline went still.

Martín opened the sample pack and laid out the sealed bags in a row beside the bottle. Soil. Seepage. Fungal mat. Control samples.

"There is a second anomaly," he said. "Near one of the monitoring nodes on the ridge. Elevated conductivity in seepage, pH shift, denser fungal growth near the housing. The control site did not match."

Mariela's eyes moved over the labels. "Related?"

"Possibly," Sabine said. "We don't know yet. The reservoir is the urgent problem. These matter, but not first."

That, more than anything else, seemed to win Mariela's respect.

She sat at last and drew the depth sheet toward her. The fan clicked left, then right.

When she looked up, she asked the first good question.

"What is the operator's normal monitoring depth?"

Lucía and Rogelio looked at one another. Martín answered. "We don't know exactly."

"Then how do you know this sits below it?"

"We know the public information says the monitored zone is shallower than the anomaly," Sabine said. "Enough to worry that whatever routine oversight exists may not be seeing the deepest risk."

Mariela considered that. "Worry is not an order."

"No," Sabine said. "But delay is not neutral."

Karoline saw the opening and pushed. "You need to restrict access to the Suyama Reservoir. Today."

Mariela turned to her. "On this evidence alone?"

"On the possibility that there is a gas hazard under that water, yes."

"And if I do that," Mariela said, "without defensible confirmation, the operator challenges it before lunch, calls it technical theater before dinner, and turns uncertainty into protection."

Lucía stepped in. "Better that than explaining bodies."

Mariela's face hardened. "Do not confuse my caution with indifference."

When she spoke again, her voice was flatter. "I know exactly what reservoirs can hide. I also know how quickly a company can weaponize a bad process."

Sabine believed her. That was its own problem.

She said, "RegenX benefits from delay. The public absorbs the downside. If you let them define the threshold for action, they will put it where it protects them."

Mariela held her gaze. "I know."

Rogelio, still standing near the door as if rooms like this belonged to other people, said quietly, "That is why we came before they did."

Mariela's eyes shifted to him.

The respect between them was not warm. It was older and more difficult than that.

He went on. "We are telling you while the warning is still clean."

Mariela exhaled once, slowly, and reached for the phone.

No one moved while she dialed.

When the line connected, she said, "This is Mariela Cárdenas. I need chain-of-custody forms and the environmental compliance file for the Suyama Reservoir. Full operating conditions, monitoring summaries, and incident history." A pause. "Now."

She hung up and looked at Sabine.

"The bottle stays here."

Sabine nodded.

"I'll have it logged under independent custody and moved for analysis."

"Good," Sabine said.

"Do not say good yet," Mariela replied.

She rose, crossed to the wall map, and put one finger on the reservoir basin.

"I can require access. I can require answers. I can compel a supervised technical review at the site." Her finger stayed on the map. "I cannot declare a public emergency on what you brought me this morning. Not yet."

Karoline made a sound under her breath.

Mariela ignored it. "What I can do is force the operator into the room before they have time to build a cleaner lie."

Lucía asked, "Today?"

"Yes."

That was fast enough to be alarming.

Martín said, "You think they already know something is wrong."

"They always know something is wrong," Mariela said. "The only question is when they decide to admit it."

There was a knock. A young woman entered with a clipboard and a stack of forms. Behind her, a man in a rain-spotted shirt carried a bulging compliance file thick with photocopies and bent tabs. Mariela signed once, pointed to the desk, and they left without being invited fully into the room.

She slid the clipboard toward Martín. "Names. Times. Who handled the bottle. Who handled the notes. Everything."

Then she looked at Lucía. "No one leaves with copies."

Lucía's mouth tightened. "Not even us?"

"Especially not you."

Rogelio gave the smallest nod, as if to say this too had been expected.

Mariela opened the compliance file and flipped through it quickly, stopping only when she found the Suyama Reservoir schematics. Her eyes moved once across the page, then again more slowly.

"There," she said.

Sabine stepped beside her.

A depth profile. Intake structures. Monitoring points. Operating notations in dense type.

Mariela tapped the page with one fingernail.

"Your concern is plausible enough to justify immediate access," she said. "The routine monitoring does not appear to extend to the depth your field sample came from."

The room changed. Not dramatically. More like pressure finding a crack.

Sabine said, "Then you have enough."

Mariela picked up the phone again before answering.

When the connection came, her voice lost what little room it had previously allowed.

"This is Mariela Cárdenas, CORPOAMAZONIA. I am invoking immediate technical access and inspection under a precautionary review for the Suyama Reservoir." A pause. "Yes, today." Another. "Then find him."

She listened, eyes on the file.

"No," she said. "Do not route this through legal first." A beat. "You can tell Mr. Mercer I'll explain that to him in person."

She hung up.

No one spoke.

Mariela closed the file and laid her palm flat on top of it.

"You have bought yourselves a meeting," she said.

Lucía asked, "And after that?"

Mariela looked at the bottle on her desk.

"After that," she said, "we find out what they are willing to call manageable."

61

The road to the Suyama Reservoir climbed out of Mocoa in damp curves and red-mud shoulders, then narrowed as the forest gave way to cut banks, gravel staging areas, and the first signs of infrastructure that wanted to pretend it belonged there.

A gate stood across the access road, steel painted green badly enough that rust showed through in freckles. Beyond it: a broad gravel apron, a low control building, antenna masts, maintenance sheds, two white pickups with the RegenX logo on the doors, and farther off, between the breaks in the trees, the reservoir itself—flat, grey, and outwardly serene in the washed light after rain.

The guard at the gate had been expecting them. That was obvious before he picked up the phone. He looked first at Mariela's badge, then at Lucía and Rogelio with open distrust, then at Sabine and Karoline as if deciding whether foreigners made this more serious or more absurd.

Mariela gave him no time to settle on either.

"Open it," she said. "Precautionary technical review."

He hesitated just long enough to be annoying.

"Now," she added.

The gate shuddered sideways.

They drove in behind Mariela's vehicle, tires crunching over gravel. No one spoke. The reservoir widened as they approached, not dramatic, not picturesque, only large enough to hide things.

At the operations building a man in a pale blue shirt was already waiting under the shallow concrete overhang, dry despite the humidity, sleeves buttoned, no jacket, no tie. He stood with one hand in his pocket and the other holding a folder he had no intention of being seen without. Two other people waited behind him: an engineer by the look of him, hardhat under one arm, and a younger woman with a tablet and the posture of legal counsel trying not to look like legal counsel.

Beside and slightly in front of him was Mercer.

Sabine knew him at once, though this was the first time she had seen him in person.

Richard Stone had always filled rooms by force. Mercer did it by preemption. He had the settled calm of a man who believed that if he remained more reasonable than everyone else, the institution would eventually decide he was right.

He stepped forward as they got out.

"Dra. Cárdenas," he said. "I understand you've invoked immediate access."

Mariela shut her door and did not offer her hand. "I have."

Mercer inclined his head, the gesture perfectly measured. "Then of course we'll cooperate."

Sabine felt the danger of him immediately. Not because he looked predatory. Because he looked prepared.

Mercer's eyes moved briefly across the group and stopped on Sabine for half a beat longer than politeness required.

"Dr. Reinhardt," he said. "I've heard a great deal about you."

Sabine did not return the courtesy. "That makes one of us."

Something very close to amusement touched his mouth, then vanished.

Mariela stepped between them without changing pace. "This is a precautionary technical review. I want full access to the reservoir monitoring summaries, intake schematics, recent maintenance logs, depth profile protocols, and anomaly reports for the last twelve months."

Mercer opened the folder in his hand. "We've already assembled most of that."

Mariela stopped. "So quickly."

He met her expression without flinching. "When a regulator arrives with field allegations involving gas loading in a hydro reservoir, I find speed preferable to improvisation."

Behind Sabine, Lucía made a small sound through her nose that might have been a laugh if contempt were warmer.

Mariela said, "Good. Then there will be less excuse for delay."

They were taken not into the main control room but into a side briefing room with a wall map, an aging screen, and a table large enough to imply cooperation while controlling where everyone sat. The reservoir lay visible through a long window beyond the glass: windless, metal-grey, giving nothing away.

Mercer remained standing at the head of the table until Mariela sat. Only then did he take his place.

"The operator's position," he said, "is that we are dealing with an unconfirmed subsurface stratification anomaly. That may prove significant or may prove routine. We are prepared to validate it immediately."

Sabine sat opposite him and felt the fight narrow by a full order of magnitude.

"Routine stratification doesn't usually rupture sample bottles on ascent," she said.

"No," Mercer said pleasantly. "Though improper handling does create dramatic artifacts."

Martín leaned forward before Sabine could answer. "Rupture under depressurization is not an artifact."

Mercer gave him a nod that landed somewhere between acknowledgment and dismissal. "Which is why we're not ignoring it."

Mariela opened the compliance file and spread three pages across the table. "Your routine monitoring depth does not appear to extend below the upper profile band."

One of the engineers shifted in his chair. Mercer did not.

"Our standard operating profile is designed around reservoir performance and water quality management," he said. "Not speculative extreme events."

Sabine said, "That distinction is exactly the problem."

Mercer turned to her. "Only if the system is blind below the depth at which the highest-consequence failure might actually sit."

The younger woman beside Mercer made a note without looking up.

Mariela said, "Enough. I did not bring everyone here to watch you define each other." She turned a page in the file. "I want site access. Now. Intake structures, monitoring points, and the vessel used for depth work."

Mercer nodded at once. "Granted."

Too smooth again.

They walked the lower platform first.

From up close the Suyama Reservoir lost even the thin illusion of naturalness it held at a distance. Concrete retaining edges. Steel railings damp with mist. Sensor housings bolted to posts. Access ladders dropping toward dark water. Intake towers farther out, rising from the surface with the mute, industrial patience of things built to last longer than the people arguing around them.

Sabine stood at the rail and followed the line from the marked monitoring point to the intake structures beyond. The basin widened toward the east, narrowed toward the dam works, and deepened in a way that made her uneasy even before she saw the profile board mounted near the service shack.

Mercer watched her noticing it.

"Complicated bathymetry," he said. "Not uncommon."

Sabine kept her eyes on the water. "No. Just dangerous if you pretend it's simple."

He smiled without warmth. "That depends what story you're trying to tell."

Lucía had moved farther down the platform with Rogelio, saying nothing, their silence more oppositional than argument would have been. Mariela was with the site engineer at the monitoring console, forcing him to walk her through the displayed profile bands while Martín copied values from the screen into his notebook.

Sabine crouched by the posted cross-section map bolted to a rusting stand. The eastern basin dipped deeper than the monitoring line suggested. There was a shoulder, then a drop. Another shoulder farther down. Not one pocket. Multiple places where denser water could sit if the circulation allowed it.

Mercer saw it in her face.

"You have a recommendation already," he said.

"I have a concern."

"Those are often the same thing."

Sabine stood. "If this layer is real and extends across the lower basin, one-point relief will not tell you enough."

He folded his hands behind his back. "I'm trying to keep a field anomaly from becoming an institutional overreaction before anyone has run a controlled validation."

Sabine said, "The risk doesn't fall evenly here."

Mercer's expression barely shifted. "No. It never does."

Mariela came back toward them.

"We are not debating philosophy on a platform," she said. "What can be tested today?"

Sabine answered first. "A full depth profile in the eastern basin, at least one secondary point off the main line, and independent custody of all readings."

Mercer answered second. "One supervised validation profile, company vessel, regulator present, external observers allowed, all readings logged in real time."

Sabine turned to Mariela. "It is not enough to establish whether the company can call this localized."

Mercer did not deny it. "It is enough to establish whether broader intervention has a defensible basis."

Mariela looked from one to the other, then out over the reservoir, where the surface still held its calm like a threat.

"If I order a full expanded technical action now," she said, "you challenge it as disproportionate."

Mercer said nothing. He didn't need to.

She looked at Sabine. "If I order only a minimal test, I may be letting the hazard define itself on the company's timetable."

"Yes," Sabine said.

Mariela nodded once.

Then she pointed to the nearest launch.

"One profile," she said. "But not on your terms alone."

Mercer's jaw tightened almost invisibly.

Mariela went on. "My office takes live copies of every reading. Dr. Reinhardt and Dr. Chasoy are on the vessel. I choose the point. If the data supports expansion, we expand before anyone leaves this site."

That was more than Mercer wanted and less than Sabine needed.

Which was exactly why Mariela chose it.

Mercer inclined his head. "Acceptable."

Sabine said, "It's still too narrow."

Mariela turned to her. "Then make it impossible for me to keep it narrow."

The engineer was already signaling toward the launch crew. Lines were being loosed. A technician lifted a case of instruments onto the deck. The younger woman with the tablet stepped aside to place a call, turning her body away as though that made the call less visible.

Movement spread across the platform with bureaucratic efficiency: not panic, not urgency exactly, but the speed of an institution deciding what kind of event it was willing to admit.

Martín came to Sabine's side, notebook in hand. "She gave us a way in."

Sabine looked at the eastern basin again. The shoulder. The drop. The stillness above it.

"Yes," she said.

Mariela signed the launch order on the back of a field form and handed it to the technician.

"Go," she said.

62

The launch was smaller than Sabine had expected and the instability pulled at her ribs.

It rocked once as she stepped down into it, the metal hull knocking softly against the rubber fenders on the platform. Martín came after her with the instrument case. Mariela boarded without hesitation, one hand on the rail, shoes dampening immediately on the ridged deck. The operator from RegenX—broad-shouldered, expressionless, company patch sewn over one breast pocket—untied the stern line and started the outboard with a short mechanical cough.

Mercer did not come.

He remained on the platform with the younger woman from legal and one of the engineers, watching as though the distance between shore and boat were itself a useful fact.

Mariela sat opposite Sabine, one hand braced on the sample crate between them. "My point first," she said over the engine. "Then yours, if the readings justify it."

Sabine nodded.

Martín opened the field computer and clipped the logging lead into place. The screen brightened under the grey light. One of Mariela's staff, a younger technician named Ávila, checked the calibration sheet against the probe assembly with lips moving silently as he read.

The operator throttled back.

"We're on mark," Ávila said.

Mariela looked at Sabine. "Proceed."

The probe went over the side with a controlled splash and began to descend.

Sabine watched the numbers instead of the water. Surface values first. Then the slow change downward. Temperature sliding by fractions. Conductivity rising. pH shifting. Not dramatic at first. Worse than that. Coherent.

Martín said nothing. He didn't need to.

At twenty meters, the trend held.

At thirty, it sharpened.

At forty, the screen changed character all at once—not chaos, not a spike exactly, but a clear break into another regime.

Ávila inhaled through his nose.

Mariela leaned closer. "There."

Conductivity up again. Temperature offset. pH lower than the upper column. The pattern held for several meters instead of collapsing immediately back into noise.

A layer.

The operator glanced back from the tiller. Even he seemed to understand when numbers stopped being abstract.

Mariela looked at Ávila. "Log the full band."

"Already logging."

Martín said quietly, "It's thicker than the first pass suggested."

Sabine nodded once. "Or cleaner."

Mariela looked at her. "Meaning?"

"The transition is more stable here than in the original field readings," Sabine said. "That could mean a more coherent lower layer. Or better handling. Either way, it does not support the optimistic reading."

On shore, Mercer raised a hand. The younger woman beside him lifted a radio.

A burst of static crackled from the handset clipped near the operator's shoulder.

"Platform to launch. Confirm anomaly depth."

Mariela took the handset before the operator could answer. "We are logging a significant lower-band shift. You'll have the numbers when I do."

Mercer's voice came back a moment later, filtered thin through distance and electronics but still unmistakably composed.

"Understood. That establishes the first concern point."

Sabine looked up toward shore. She could feel the framing at work even over the water.

"We need the eastern shoulder," she said.

Mariela's eyes stayed on the screen. "Why?"

"Because one profile confirms a layer," Sabine said. "It does not tell us whether the basin is holding one pocket or several."

Martín added, "If the lower basin is compartmentalized, one point understates the shape of the risk."

The radio crackled again.

Mercer. "If you want a second point, specify what decision it changes."

Sabine held out her hand. Mariela let her take the radio.

"It changes whether you're dealing with a localized anomaly or a basin problem," she said.

A pause.

Then Mercer: "Only if you are already assuming intervention at scale."

"No," Sabine said. "Only if one-point action would be misleading."

Another pause.

"You do not yet have evidence for action."

Sabine looked at the graph, then out across the water toward the long grey eastern reach of the basin.

"That depends what you think this boat is here to prevent."

Mariela held out her hand. Sabine gave the radio back.

"We are taking a second point," Mariela said. "Eastern shoulder. Same protocol."

Mercer did not argue immediately. When he answered, it was with the restraint of a man already planning the next line of defense.

"Noted," he said.

The operator restarted the engine, revved it to a higher pitch, and turned them east.

The second point took longer to reach than it had looked from shore. The basin widened in that direction, the slopes stepping back into forest and cut embankment, the water darkening by degrees rather than color. Sabine watched the intake towers recede and tried to imagine the submerged shape beneath them—the shelves, the drop, the denser lower water settling where the reservoir geometry allowed it to settle.

Not one chamber. A shaped container.

The boat slowed again.

Ávila checked the coordinates and gave a short nod. "Here."

Mariela looked at Sabine only once before signaling to lower the probe.

The second descent was slower, as if everyone aboard now understood what haste could cost.

Surface band.

Upper column.

Transition.

Then again, deeper down, the numbers stepped into the wrong pattern.

Not identical to the first profile. Worse, in a way. The lower band here sat deeper and slightly thinner, but it was there—present, stable enough to matter, distinct enough to kill the last charitable interpretation.

Martín swore softly under his breath and then said nothing else.

Mariela's gaze stayed fixed on the screen. "Two points."

"Yes," Sabine said.

"Connected?"

"Not proven," Sabine said. "But no longer consistent with a single isolated pocket."

The radio hissed. Mercer again.

"Launch, report."

Mariela picked up the handset.

"Second point confirms lower-band anomaly," she said. "Different depth expression. Still present."

Silence on the line.

Then: "Understood."

Just that. No argument. No denial.

Sabine looked back toward shore. Mercer was no longer standing still. He was talking to the engineer now, one hand open in that measured way of his, as if what mattered most was not the problem but the scale at which the problem could be made administratively acceptable.

And suddenly the logic of the next fight arrived complete.

One visible intervention, if they forced him. One point of release that could be described as prudent, temporary, proportionate. Something narrow enough to look responsive and small enough not to admit the shape of the basin itself.

One point would not solve this.

One point might not even tell the truth about it.

Mariela lowered the radio slowly. "When we get back," she said, "he's going to argue pilot response."

"Yes," Sabine said.

"You sound sure."

"I am."

Martín looked up from the screen. "Can you beat that?"

Sabine looked at the second profile, then at the first still frozen in the log beside it. Two distinct lower-band expressions. Two points already too many for Mercer's preferred story and still almost certainly fewer than the reservoir was actually holding.

"Yes," she said. "But not with one profile."

The operator turned the boat back toward the platform.

The return felt shorter, though the basin had not changed. Shore drew closer. So did Mercer, standing where he had been before, only now with papers in his hand and a version of the event already reduced to scale.

Ávila began securing the probe.

Martín saved the data from the runs twice.

Mariela stood before the boat had fully settled against the fenders.

Whatever the profiles had proved, Mercer was ready to make it smaller.

63

They went back into the briefing room wet with reservoir mist and carrying numbers that had already begun hardening into positions.

Mercer was there before them, exactly where Sabine had expected him to be: at the head of the table, papers spread in a careful fan, legal counsel to his right, the site engineer to his left, as if the room had reset itself around his preferred version of events the moment the launch had come back into sight.

Mariela entered first and did not sit immediately.

"Doors closed," she said.

The engineer glanced at Mercer before moving to obey. Lucía noticed that. So did Sabine.

Martín set the field computer on the table and opened the saved profiles side by side. Ávila passed over the handwritten log sheet. Mariela took both without comment, read in silence for just long enough to make everyone else wait, then sat.

"Say it cleanly," she said. "No theater. No hedging disguised as wisdom. What do these profiles require?"

She looked at Sabine first.

Sabine stood rather than speak from the chair. Her ribs complained immediately. She ignored them.

"We have two confirmed lower-band anomalies at distinct points in the basin," she said. "Different depth expression, same essential problem: the Suyama Reservoir is holding a CO_2-rich lower layer in more than one place. Not fully mapped, not yet quantified across the whole basin, but no longer consistent with a single isolated pocket."

Mariela's face did not move. "Recommendation."

Sabine put one finger on the first profile, then the second.

"The basin shape matters. The lower water is not expressing uniformly. A one-point intervention would tell us very little and could create the illusion of control without materially reducing distributed risk. If the goal is actual pressure reduction rather than optics, you need multiple degassing points."

"How many?" Mariela asked.

Sabine did not hesitate.

"Five."

That changed the room more than any raised voice could have.

The engineer looked at Mercer. Legal looked down at her tablet. Martín stayed very still. Lucía's eyes sharpened. Rogelio, by the wall, gave away nothing at all.

Mercer leaned back slightly, not startled, only more attentive.

"Five degassing pipes," Mariela repeated.

"Yes," Sabine said. "Minimum prudent architecture."

"Based on two profiles."

"Based on two confirmed profiles, the posted bathymetry, the intake geometry, and the likelihood that the lower layer is compartmentalized across shoulders and depressions we have not yet fully resolved."

Mercer spoke for the first time since they sat down.

"That is not a recommendation," he said mildly. "It is a projection masquerading as engineering."

Sabine turned toward him. "No. It's engineering reacting to the downside of pretending two points define a basin."

Mercer opened one hand over the documents in front of him.

"The operator's position remains straightforward. The data supports concern, not alarm. Two points justify a bounded intervention to test behavior under controlled conditions. They do not justify converting an active hydro reservoir into a visible emergency response site on speculative architecture."

Mariela looked at him. "Your recommendation."

"One pipe," Mercer said. "Placed at the primary confirmed zone. Controlled degassing under supervision. Continuous monitoring before, during, and after. If the response suggests broader risk, we escalate."

Sabine let out one short breath through her nose.

"One pipe tells you whether one pipe affects one point," she said. "That's all."

Mercer nodded as though conceding a reasonable nuance. "And that is how responsible intervention begins."

"No," Sabine said. "That's not caution. That's something small enough to defend."

The young lawyer's fingers paused over her keyboard.

Mariela's gaze shifted between them.

"Explain the five," she said.

Sabine turned the profile board on the screen so the basin cross-section was visible to the whole room.

"This lower layer is not sitting in a smooth bowl. You have a shoulder here, another depression here, and a deeper eastern reach here." She touched the map in sequence. "If dense water is pooling in separated or semi-separated sections, a single vent does not reliably draw down the whole hazard. It may reduce one zone while leaving adjacent accumulation intact. Worse, one visible intervention may let everyone in this room behave as if the system has been stabilized when it has only been partially disturbed. Multiple vents are not just about speed. They prevent one visible response from masking unchanged pressure in adjacent low zones."

The engineer cleared his throat. "That assumes limited mixing."

"Yes," Sabine said.

"And if mixing is stronger than you're assuming?"

"Then multiple pipes are conservative. One pipe remains misleading."

Mercer folded his hands.

"And five pipes," he said, "turn a technical review into a declaration of systemic failure before the evidence supports that language."

Lucía laughed once. There was no humor in it.

Mariela did not look at her. "Mr. Mercer, leave the language aside."

"With respect," he said, "language is the event once public infrastructure is involved."

Sabine cut in. "People downstream don't care what noun you prefer if the wrong water turns over."

Mercer's expression thinned.

"And people nearby will care very much if you trigger panic with a maximal response to a partially characterized condition."

Mariela leaned back. "Enough."

The room obeyed because she said it like an order rather than a request.

She looked at Sabine. "What is your confidence in five?"

Sabine answered carefully. "My confidence is high that one is insufficient. My confidence is moderate that five is the minimum prudent starting architecture for distributed pressure relief in a basin shaped like this under the conditions we've observed."

Mercer seized the word instantly.

"Moderate," he said. "Exactly."

Sabine ignored him.

Mariela turned to Mercer. "And your confidence in one?"

"My confidence is high," Mercer said, "that one supervised installation at the primary confirmed zone is the maximum defensible first step on the current evidence."

"Defensible to whom?" Sabine asked.

He did not even turn his head. "To the people responsible for acting without manufacturing unnecessary collateral damage."

Sabine let the temptation to answer too sharply pass.

"Delay protects the operator," she said. "Failure punishes everyone else."

Mariela steepled her fingers. "And five pipes punish whom?"

Mercer answered before Sabine could.

"Operations. Public confidence. Regulatory stability. Any possibility of controlled verification."

Sabine said, "Sometimes the system is what's failing, and pretending otherwise doesn't help."

Mercer turned to her then, fully, the patience in him becoming visible effort.

"Not on the basis of two field-confirmed points and a model."

"Yes," Sabine said. "That is how adults think ahead."

Martín, who had been silent too long to be comfortable, spoke at last.

"One point does not characterize the basin," he said. "Two points strongly suggest heterogeneity in the lower layer. Dr. Reinhardt is not saying five is mathematically proven. She is saying one is scientifically dishonest."

Mercer looked at him with open disappointment, as if a technical peer had behaved emotionally in public.

"What I am saying," Mercer replied, "is that one installation gives us a response we can actually read without turning the reservoir into a public emergency before we know what we have."

Lucía said, "Everything you say sounds clean until someone dies."

This time Mariela did look at her. "And everything you say pushes me toward decisions I may not be able to hold by tomorrow afternoon."

Silence followed that.

It was the most honest sentence anyone had spoken in the room.

Mariela stood and walked to the window. Outside, the reservoir lay as it had before: flat, metallic, withholding.

When she turned back, her face had not softened. If anything, it had closed.

"I am not declaring a gas emergency today," she said.

Karoline made a small sound of protest. Mariela raised one hand without looking at her and continued.

"I am also not accepting operator comfort as evidence."

Mercer inclined his head, the closest thing to caution Sabine had seen from him.

Mariela went on. "I am authorizing one degassing pipe at the primary confirmed zone under regulatory supervision, immediate continuous monitoring, and independent live access to all readings. Installation begins as soon as equipment can be staged."

Sabine spoke before she could stop herself. "That is not enough."

"I know," Mariela said.

The room stilled.

Mariela looked directly at her now.

"It is what I can compel today and still hold tomorrow."

Sabine felt the truth of that and hated it. For one ugly second, Sabine wanted to keep arguing anyway, not because it would change anything, but because silence felt too much like helping.

Mercer said, "RegenX will cooperate."

"Of course you will," Lucía said.

Mariela ignored her. "The authorization is temporary, reviewable, and expressly non-exculpatory. If the response is weak, uneven, or destabilizing, I expand the order."

Sabine said, "If the response is weak or uneven, it may already have wasted critical time."

"Yes," Mariela said. "And if I order five now, they challenge the whole intervention before the first pipe goes in."

Mercer did not contradict her.

He didn't need to.

Karoline leaned forward from her chair by the wall. "So he gets to win because his version is easier to defend?"

"No," Mariela said. "He gets to narrow the damage before it lands on him."

That silenced even Karoline.

Mariela reached for the printed authorization form Mercer's lawyer had already produced with insulting efficiency, crossed out two lines, wrote three words in the margin, and signed across the bottom with a hard, slanting stroke.

Then she slid it across the table.

"One pipe," she said. "Under protest from the science, under supervision from the state, and under a record that will not disappear."

Mercer took the document, read the additions, and passed it to the engineer.

No smile. No visible satisfaction. He was too disciplined for that.

But Sabine saw the real victory anyway. Not in his face. In the scale of the page. One pipe. One point. One manageable version of a reservoir that had already told them, twice, that it was larger than that.

The engineer rose at once. "I'll have staging begin."

Mariela nodded. "You have one hour to show me the installation plan."

He left with the paper.

Legal followed.

Mercer remained seated for one breath longer, then stood and gathered his own notes into a new stack, thinner now, cleaner, already adapted to the compromise.

When he looked at Sabine, there was no triumph in it. Only the cool professional acknowledgment that they had both recognized the same danger and had arrived, as institutions so often did, at radically different thresholds for admitting it.

"You'll be present for the install," he said.

It wasn't a question.

"Yes," Sabine said.

"Good."

He left without offering anything that could be mistaken for courtesy.

The door closed behind him.

For a moment no one in the room moved.

Then Martín looked at the cross-section still glowing on the screen and said quietly, "It won't be enough."

Mariela stayed standing by the window. "Probably not."

Lucía folded her arms. "Then why sign it?"

Mariela answered without turning around.

"Because one pipe installed under order is harder to bury than five pipes denied in principle."

Rogelio nodded once, slowly, as if accepting an ugly truth that had lived in the territory longer than any of them had.

Sabine remained on her feet because sitting felt too close to surrender. Her ribs ached. Her jaw hurt. Some muscle in her neck had locked itself into stone while Mercer spoke and had not yet released.

On the table, the authorization carbon sheet lay beneath the top page, faint blue ghosts of the decision bleeding through.

One pipe.

The handwriting made it look smaller somehow.

Mariela finally turned back to them.

"If you're right," she said to Sabine, "the first pipe won't solve it."

"No," Sabine said. "It won't."

Mariela nodded once. "Then make sure the first failure is visible."

No one answered that immediately.

Because it was not strategy anymore.

It was triage.

The room held for one more beat, suspended between what they had argued and what they had allowed.

Then, from somewhere out beyond the glass, came the metallic grind of equipment being moved toward the water.

64

By the time Sabine stepped out of the operations building, the first equipment was already moving.

A flatbed truck had backed down toward the lower access road. Men in hard-hats were guiding a length of pipe off its rack with the careful, irritated choreography of people told to move quickly while pretending the thing they were moving was ordinary. Metal rang against metal. A forklift reversed with a shrill intermittent beep. Out on the platform, someone was uncoiling hose.

The reservoir beyond it all looked unchanged.

Sabine stood for a moment under the overhang, one hand against her ribs, and watched the wrong solution begin to take shape.

Yari was waiting near the edge of the gravel, just beyond the cluster of company vehicles, where the ground gave way again to brush and runoff and the first signs that the land had existed before roads and gates and operator comfort. He wore the same dark jacket she had seen before, damp at the shoulders, mud drying along one boot. Two younger men stood several paces behind him, silent and watchful.

Lucía was already with him.

She looked at Sabine once as she approached, and in that look Sabine saw that Yari had not been allowed into the meeting and had understood exactly what that meant.

He did not ask how it went.

His eyes shifted once toward the men unloading the pipe, then back to her face.

"How many?"

"One," Sabine said.

Yari looked back at the staging crew.

"So they chose a number small enough to survive."

Lucía gave the smallest nod. "Yes."

Yari's mouth tightened, not in surprise but recognition.

"I argued for five," Sabine said.

"I know."

There was no comfort in it. Only acknowledgment.

"She knows one is not enough," Sabine said. "Mariela does."

"Then she knows what she signed."

"That's not fair."

Yari turned to her. "No?"

"She chose what she thought she could compel and still hold. If she ordered all of it now, Mercer would challenge everything before the first pipe reached the water."

"And now he will challenge less."

"Yes."

Below them, one of the workers shouted for a chain sling. The forklift beeped again. A crane arm shifted half a meter and stopped.

Yari watched the movement the way some people watched a funeral procession: not because they expected to intervene, but because looking away too early would itself be a kind of surrender.

"When the company poisons a river," he said, "they call it an incident. When fish die, they call it stress. When children get sick, they call it no proven connection."

He looked at Sabine.

"Each time, the word is smaller than the wound."

Sabine felt that one go through her cleanly.

"This is not the same thing," she said.

"No," Yari said. "It is the same habit."

Lucía folded her arms. “One pipe under order is still more than Mercer wanted.”

“Yes,” Yari said. “And less than the water requires.”

Sabine looked out across the Suyama Reservoir. The surface held itself flat and metallic, concealing depth with the confidence of something that had never needed permission in the first place.

“He’s turning the response into a pilot,” she said. “Something narrow enough to defend.”

“And will it work?” Yari asked.

Sabine answered honestly. “Not enough.”

He nodded once, as though that too had been expected.

Then he stepped closer, not threateningly, but with the deliberate intimacy of a man making sure the next words were heard exactly as he meant them.

“Then do not let them name the first failure something smaller.”

Sabine held his gaze.

“I won’t.”

Yari’s expression did not change.

“You may not be the one who decides what it gets called.”

65

The pipe discharged into open air.

That had been Mercer's preference once the engineers confirmed it could be done cleanly: a visible vent, a visible result, a visible sign that action was underway. The outlet rose above the platform on a steel frame braced with temporary supports and guyed back to anchor points drilled into the concrete. When the line opened, gas-rich water from depth would rise, break pressure, and erupt from the mouth of the pipe in a controlled white plume for every watching eye to read as intervention.

It was hard to imagine a more perfect design for a demonstration.

The cameras were already running when Sabine took her place near the rail.

Not news cameras. Company cameras. Compliance cameras. Internal documentation. One technician filmed from the side of the platform. Another stood farther back, catching the whole structure in frame: pipe, crew, gauges, reservoir. Mercer had made sure the installation looked careful enough to survive review and dramatic enough to survive memory.

The Suyama Reservoir lay flat and metallic beyond the platform, giving no sign of what sat below.

Mariela stood close enough to the control rack to read the gauges for herself. Mercer remained under the shade awning, sleeves rolled, posture relaxed in the way of a man who believed outcomes improved when he looked least alarmed by them. Lucía and Rogelio stayed farther upslope from the immediate work area, neither interfering nor pretending trust. Martín was beside Sabine with the live profiles open on a temporary field screen bolted to a crate.

Karoline, who had been told twice to keep back, was still too close.

The lead operator raised a hand. "Ready to discharge."

A headset crackled. Someone below the deck frame repeated the pressure values. Another confirmed the intake depth. A green indicator blinked on the temporary panel.

Mariela looked once at Sabine. "If you want it stopped, say so now."

Sabine stared past the pipe and out across the eastern basin. Nothing moved but wind ruffling the upper skin of the reservoir and the faint slap of water against the retaining edge.

"Not yet," she said.

Mercer, overhearing, said, "I appreciate your restraint."

Sabine did not look at him. "You shouldn't."

The operator opened the line.

The pipe shuddered in its frame with a deep metallic tremor. A hiss moved through the assembly. Then the first column of water punched out of the elevated outlet in a thick white jet, arcing half a meter before falling back in churning sheets. It was not graceful. It was a frothing industrial fountain, gas flashing out in the plume, spray blowing sideways, white turbulence hammering the surface directly below.

Mercer nodded once. "There. Controlled."

For a few seconds, it looked that way.

The plume held tight to the outlet. The splash zone spread in a circular boil beneath it, bright and violent but contained. Sabine watched the base of the fountain, forcing herself to separate what she expected from what she feared.

Then, beyond the main splash zone, she saw something else.

A faint stippling of the surface two or three meters out. Small bright beads racing up through darker water.

Sabine narrowed her eyes.

Martín leaned closer to the rail. "Do you see that?"

"Yes."

"Spray?"

"I don't know."

A second patch appeared farther east.

Not under the falling water. Beyond it. A soft granular fizzing on the surface, then a brief run of bubbles that vanished almost at once.

Sabine straightened.

A third patch broke the surface closer to the platform edge and held.

Gas.

"Stop," Sabine said.

No one heard her over the machinery and the hammering fountain.

The disturbance widened. Bubbles where the pipe was not. First scattered arcs, then short loose chains, as though something below were answering the vent in places the vent had never touched.

Sabine stepped forward. "Stop the flow!"

Martín saw it fully then. "Sabine—"

She was already shouting. "Shut it down!"

Mercer turned, annoyed first rather than alarmed. "What?"

Mariela followed Sabine's line of sight to the water and saw enough.

"What am I looking at?"

"Peripheral breakout," Sabine said. "Outside the discharge zone."

The operator at the console looked up. "Pressure's holding."

"That's not the point!" Sabine shouted. "Close the line!"

One of the crew nearest the valve hesitated, looking not at Mariela but at the site engineer, who looked at Mercer, and in that stupid half-second of institutional reflex Sabine felt the whole scene tip from salvageable to doomed.

Mariela saw it too.

"Close it!" she barked.

The crewman moved.

Too late.

The nearest breakout patch became a boil.

Not at the pipe. Ten meters out. A broad patch of water bulged upward in a pale granular heave as gas burst through from below. Another patch followed farther east. Then another, nearer the platform, smaller but faster, the surface lifting and whitening in ugly pulses.

Karoline swore.

Lucía was already moving toward her.

Sabine leaned over the rail and caught one terrible glimpse beneath the splash and spray: darker water driving upward under the white noise of the fountain, not in a tidy column but in widening disturbance.

The single vent was not relieving the basin.

"Everybody back!" Sabine shouted.

The crew began moving then, but with the lag of people still half-convinced they were responding to overreaction. One man reached for the valve wheel. Another tried to steady a hose coupling that no longer mattered. The cameraman kept filming for two more seconds before the first dense wash of gas hit him and he doubled over coughing.

The air changed.

Not a smell exactly. A blankness. A cold mineral flatness that shoved oxygen aside and made every breath feel suddenly borrowed. One of the workers nearest the rail blinked hard, staggered, and sat down as if his legs had simply chosen not to continue.

"Move!" Lucía shouted. "Move now!"

Mariela had one hand over her mouth and the other on the shoulder of the nearest technician, dragging him back from the console.

The valve finally began to close.

It no longer mattered.

Twenty meters out, the water rolled upward in a long pale bulge. Bubbles became columns. Columns merged into a widening field of violent white churn. The tidy fountain from the pipe vanished inside it.

Fish broke the surface all at once.

Not leaping. Rising dead or dying, flashing silver, then vanishing again as the water folded under itself.

Martín grabbed Sabine's arm hard enough to hurt. "Back."

She did not move.

The eastern basin was venting in sections now, each fresh rupture answering the last. The calm surface they had stared at all afternoon was gone, replaced by a spreading violence.

Mercer had stopped pretending composure. He was shouting to the engineer, but the words were lost in the new sound overtaking the platform, a deep wet thunder rising out of the reservoir itself.

One of the crew collapsed near the work frame.

Another tried to run, struck the mounted supports, slid to his knees, and stayed there with both hands flat on the deck.

Sabine understood it completely and uselessly at the same time.

"Get them uphill!" she shouted. "Not vehicles. Uphill!"

Lucía had Karoline by the arm and was hauling her toward the access road. Rogelio was dragging one of the fallen workers by his coveralls. Mariela was yelling into a radio for evacuation and getting no answer anyone could hear.

Then the lower basin let go.

A vast white eruption punched upward beyond the platform, not a single jet but a lifting wall of gas-thick water and spray. The reservoir convulsed. The platform lurched under Sabine's feet as displaced water slammed into the retaining edge. Steel screamed. Somebody went over. For one impossible instant the vent pipe stood outlined in a halo of vapor and flying water, absurdly small at the center of what they had called a controlled response.

Then the wave hit the work deck.

Sabine lost the rail. Lost the horizon. Lost which way was land and which way was water.

She struck something hard with her shoulder, then the side of her head, then slid in freezing spray and reservoir muck across corrugated metal while equipment tore free around her. A crate smashed past. A hose line snapped and whipped. The field monitor Martín had been watching shattered against the deck in a burst of glass and black plastic.

Someone was screaming.

Maybe Karoline. Maybe one of the crew. Maybe Sabine herself.

The gas cloud came with the water.

That was the part no one, not even the people who should have known better, had truly been ready for. A low invisible surge rolled off the erupting surface, heavy and fast and wrong to breathe. Sabine got one lungful and instantly understood why men were dropping without drama. Her chest locked. Vision narrowed. She tried to shout and got almost nothing.

Hands caught under her arms.

Lucía.

No warning. No question. Just force.

She hauled Sabine half upright and dragged her toward the sloping access track above the platform while the reservoir behind them continued to break itself open. Sabine's boots caught once, then again. Somewhere to the left Mercer was on the ground coughing, one hand outstretched toward no one. Mariela was still on her feet, impossibly, waving people higher with one arm while holding a radio to her face with the other.

"Up," Lucía said into Sabine's ear. "Up now."

Sabine stumbled with her, lungs burning on emptiness rather than air. Each breath felt stolen from a room already used up. The world narrowed to gravel, mud, the angle of the hill, the weight of Lucía's grip, and behind all of it the ongoing sound of the reservoir erupting in staggered bursts.

They made the first rise above the platform and the air changed just enough to hurt differently.

Sabine sucked in a ragged breath and fell to one knee.

Below them the work site was in ruin.

The temporary frame had twisted half off the platform. The vent pipe was still there, but no longer central, just one metal line amid spray, broken hoses, and men moving badly or not at all. The water nearest the installation point still boiled white, but farther out the eruption had spread into broader heaving patches across the basin, venting in ugly, uneven pulses.

Martín appeared through the haze, bent almost double, supporting Ávila under one shoulder. Rogelio was behind him with the cameraman. Karoline was on the slope vomiting and trying to crawl farther uphill at the same time. Mariela reached them last, face grey, blouse soaked through, radio clenched in one fist.

Mercer did not appear.

Sabine tried to stand and Lucía shoved her back down.

"Don't."

"He's still—"

"He chose his place."

"That's not the point."

Lucía rounded on her, eyes wild now, restraint finally gone. "The point is the reservoir is trying to kill everyone below us."

Below them another section of water convulsed upward near the western shoulder, farther from the platform than it had any right to if this had ever been a localized intervention.

Mariela sank to a crouch beside her, breathing hard but more evenly now.

Without looking at Sabine, she said, "How bad?"

Sabine stared at the water.

For a second she could not answer, because any scale short of catastrophic felt dishonest.

Then, from somewhere out beyond the white upheaval and vapor, the first real siren began to rise from the road.

66

The siren came closer, then another behind it.

Sabine stayed on one knee on the slope because it felt safer than trying to move and failing in front of everyone. Her lungs were working again, badly but honestly, each breath scraping now instead of vanishing altogether. Below them, the Suyama Reservoir kept venting in ugly white patches across the basin, no longer with the towering violence of the first overturn but in staggered bursts that made the whole surface look wrong.

The platform was half-hidden by spray, vapor, and twisted steel.

"Don't let anyone go low," she said.

Her voice came out thinner than she wanted.

Mariela, crouched beside her with wet hair pasted to one side of her face, turned sharply. "What?"

"The low ground." Sabine forced another breath. "The gas is heavier than air. It'll settle where it can. Cuts. Drainage dips. The deck."

Mariela stared at her for half a beat, recalculating the whole site.

Then she was on the radio again.

"To all incoming units, do not approach the lower platform. Repeat, do not approach the lower platform." She listened, swore softly, then repeated it in faster Spanish. "Stay uphill. Engines off if you stop. No one enters the basin edge without my instruction."

That got through to someone.

Not enough people. But someone.

Below them, Rogelio and Martín were dragging one of the workers farther up the slope, boots slipping in the wet clay. Ávila had gone from walking to dead weight and back to stumbling again in the space of thirty seconds. Karoline sat on the gravel with both arms wrapped around herself, face grey, trying not to throw up again. Lucía moved between people with the terrifying efficiency of someone who had long ago accepted that panic wastes time.

A younger worker Sabine didn't know was lying on his side five meters upslope, coughing in shallow, ugly snaps. Another sat against a retaining post staring at his own hands as if they belonged to someone else.

Mercer still hadn't appeared.

Sabine hated that she kept noticing.

Lucía came back at a half-run and dropped beside her. "Can you stand?"

"Yes."

"Can you actually stand?"

Sabine put one hand to the ground, pushed, and got upright on the second attempt. The world tilted once and then settled badly into place.

Lucía nodded. "Good. Then use it."

Another siren reached the access road.

This one came from below the dam.

Sabine heard the engine first, climbing hard in low gear, then saw the rescue truck nosing around the bend beneath them, red lights strobing against mist and spray. It kept coming.

Too low.

"Not there," she said.

The truck rolled past the first safe turnout and dropped into the lower cut toward the platform road.

Then the engine changed.

Not all at once. A hitch first, barely audible over the siren. Then a rougher note, as if the truck had suddenly forgotten how to breathe. The driver kept going another few meters before the engine coughed hard, surged once, and died.

The siren cut with it.

For one second the silence that followed was worse.

The doors opened.

"You need oxygen tanks!" Sabine shouted.

One of the responders jumped down from the passenger side, took two steps, and stopped with a confused look, as though he had walked into a room where the air had already been used up. Another leaned out from the cab, trying the ignition again. The starter ground uselessly.

Mariela was already beside Sabine.

"¡Alto! No bajen!" she shouted. "¡CO2! ¡Arriba!"

The responder on the ground turned toward her, uncomprehending, then bent with both hands on his knees as if the slope itself had hit him.

"The truck," Sabine said. "Tell them to leave it."

Mariela snatched up the radio again. "Abandon the vehicle. Repeat: leave the vehicle where it is and move upslope immediately."

Below them, one of the men in the cab finally understood enough to start climbing out the uphill side instead of the downhill one.

Good, Sabine thought. Learn fast.

He backed upslope and began waving the others higher but it was too late for them.

Sabine bent with both hands on her knees and coughed until her chest felt flayed.

When she straightened again, Yari was there.

Sabine had not seen him arrive. One moment the slope held only the wet survivors and the first stagger of official response. The next he was standing just above the group with two of his men, face unreadable, eyes already moving over the injured, the workers, the reservoir, the stalled truck below.

He took in the scene in silence.

Then he looked at Mariela.

"One pipe," he said.

Not accusation. Worse. Inventory.

Mariela did not answer immediately.

"No," she said at last. "One mistake."

Yari held her gaze for a long second. Then he nodded once, not in agreement, but in acceptance of the wording she had chosen for herself.

Rogelio reached them with the cameraman half draped over one shoulder. The man's eyes were open now but unfocused, breaths shallow and rapid. He was still clutching the camera by the strap as though muscle memory had outlived judgment.

"Where?" Rogelio asked.

Sabine pointed higher, toward a patch of level gravel near the road where the air seemed cleaner. "Keep everyone above the cuts. No one in the drainage line. If they collapse lower, you don't go after them without a rope and a mask."

One of the incoming responders, hearing that, said, "Masks?"

Sabine turned toward him. "Do you have air packs?"

He nodded once.

"Retrieval only," she said. "Fast in, fast out. No heroics."

The responder stared at her for half a second, taking orders from a woman soaked in reservoir water with blood drying near one temple.

Then he nodded again and ran.

Martín crouched beside the younger worker who had been coughing and put two fingers to the man's neck.

"He needs oxygen."

"So does everyone," Lucía said.

"That one first."

Karoline, from the gravel, said hoarsely, "There were more of them."

Sabine turned.

Karoline was looking down toward the broken platform.

"The crew," she said. "I counted nine before the valve opened."

No one answered.

Because they had all been counting too, just not aloud.

Mariela lifted the radio again. Her voice had changed now. Less administrative. More stripped.

"How many do we have eyes on below the platform?"

Static. Broken replies. No coherent answer.

One responder said there was movement near the service frame. Another said two down by the lower deck. Someone else said the vapor was still too dense near the retaining edge to confirm.

Mariela closed her eyes once, briefly.

When she opened them, she looked at Sabine. "Could the whole basin still overturn?"

Sabine followed her gaze to the water.

The main violent release had passed, but the reservoir was still venting in pulses across sections of the basin. White boils appeared, spread, thinned, vanished. Then elsewhere, another patch lifted and broke.

"Yes," she said. "Or parts of it. Or enough of it. It's not finished."

Mariela absorbed that.

Then, with almost no visible transition at all, she began issuing the right orders.

Road closed below the second bend.No civilian traffic.Emergency perimeter higher up the slope.Medical triage uphill only.No one from RegenX to touch the monitoring records or the install documentation without regulatory custody present.

That one was for Mercer, whether he was alive to hear it or not.

Yari heard it too.

"The records won't matter if the town walks into the gas," he said.

Sabine looked at him sharply. "The town?"

He pointed downslope, beyond the reservoir road, beyond the service cut, toward the broader valley where Mocoa sat under low cloud and wet afternoon light.

"The wind is wrong," he said. "And the valley keeps what falls."

Sabine looked down valley.

Through breaks in the trees and the shifting white residue still rising off the water, she could not see the town clearly enough to know anything. But she could see the shape of the land. The cuts. The folds. The low places where invisible weight might travel or settle.

Mariela saw it happen in her face.

"How far?" she asked.

Sabine hated being asked for guesses in moments that would later be audited as certainty.

But this was not an audit.

"Low-lying zones are the problem," she said. "Road cuts, enclosed spaces, anywhere the air settles. I don't know how far it carries yet."

Karoline looked up from the gravel, wiped her mouth with the back of one hand, and said, "Hospital."

Sabine closed her eyes for a second.

Yes.

Not because she knew the plume path. Because she knew how people thought in emergencies: hospitals, schools, roads, places where help gathered and air could still kill you.

Mariela was already on the radio again, voice clipped and carrying.

"Notify Mocoa emergency management. Potential gas hazard moving downslope from Suyama. Low-lying zones at risk. Repeat: low-lying zones at risk."

This time the person answering her sounded slower, less certain, like someone hearing words they did not yet know how to fit inside procedure.

Lucía looked down toward the trucks, the responders, the reservoir, the valley beyond, and said, "This is not staying here."

No one contradicted her.

Below them another muted heave rolled across the western section of the reservoir, smaller than before but large enough to send fresh white turbulence across the surface.

The sirens were no longer coming one at a time.

They were stacking now from the road below. Different tones. Different vehicles. The beginnings of a response too scattered and too late to deserve the word coordinated.

Sabine stood in the middle of it, mud to the knees, ribs half-useless, throat raw from CO2 and shouting, and understood that the argument at the reservoir was over.

Now the only question was how much damage would move faster than the warning.

67

"Where are you?"

Mila pinned the phone between her cheek and shoulder and started peeling the pink tape off her hand. "At home."

"Come in now."

The voice on the other end was too fast, the way voices got when people were trying to sound efficient and failing.

"What happened?"

"I don't know yet. Something at the reservoir. They're saying multiple casualties. Maybe gas exposure. Maybe drowning. I don't know. Just come."

Then the line cut.

Mila stood in her kitchen with water still running down her wrist and the odor of disinfectant still sharp in the back of her nose.

Reservoir.

Gas exposure.

Come now.

Outside, a horn began and didn't stop.

Her phone buzzed again before she had even set it down.

Not the hospital this time.

GreenPulse.

She stared at the banner in reflexive annoyance. Her nephew loved the app. Her niece had planted two miserable saplings for points last month and gotten a discount on juice. Mila still had it mostly because one of the hospital wellness programs had tied attendance perks to it and deleting it had seemed like more effort than tolerating it.

The alert opened.

Hazard alert nearby. Avoid low-lying roads. Move uphill on foot if possible. Do not remain in idling vehicles. Suggested route available.

For a second she nearly laughed.

Then another horn joined the first. Somewhere below, a motorbike went past too fast. Someone shouted for a child. Another voice yelled something about the dam.

Mila went to the window.

From here she could only see a slice of Mocoa between roofs and power lines, the afternoon dimmed under low cloud. Nothing looked visibly wrong yet. But she could hear the town changing.

A second GreenPulse alert slid over the first.

Do not use Avenida Colombia. Congestion detected. Safer movement on foot via upper routes.

Congestion detected.

Her first reaction was contempt. Her second was the less useful realization that the app was probably right.

She was already pulling on shoes.

The hospital sat low enough in town that driving there was usually the obvious answer. Faster in rain. Faster if you were already late. Faster if what was waiting was blood, fractures, and too few hands.

She grabbed her bag, stuffed her work shoes into it out of habit, and headed for the door with her keys already in her hand.

On the landing, Doña Esperanza from 3B was struggling to lock her grill gate while balancing a plastic sack of medication and a caged parrot.

"What did you hear?"

"Reservoir accident," Mila said. "I'm going to the hospital."

"People are saying toxic cloud."

"People are always saying something."

But she was already moving faster.

The parking area behind the building was half full, half in motion. Two neighbors were reversing at once and nearly hit each other. Someone in a delivery van had left it running while he argued into his phone beside the open door. A child cried from the back seat of a taxi.

Mila got into her car, slammed the door, and immediately heard another GreenPulse chime.

Fastest safer route from your location: San Miguel ridge stairs. On-foot travel outperforming vehicles nearby.

"Unbelievable," she muttered, and started the engine anyway.

Because she was a nurse. Because she had to get to the hospital. Because adults did not abandon functional cars because an app told them to.

The engine turned over cleanly. She pulled out into the alley and made the first corner.

That was as far as the car moved like a useful machine.

By the time she reached the lower feeder road, Mocoa had already made its mistake.

The broad avenue was full.

Not heavy traffic. Locked. Taxis, pickups, motorcycles, two delivery trucks, one minibus angled badly enough that it had stolen the intersection from everyone behind it. Horns layered over horns. A woman in hospital scrubs was out of her car shouting at a bus driver who could not possibly hear or help.

The hospital lay only a few blocks beyond the mess.

A few blocks that no longer behaved like distance.

Mila lowered her window halfway.

The air outside felt flat.

Not smoke. Not sewer gas. Not anything she could identify. Just wrong enough that she took another breath to check the first one.

Her phone vibrated again.

Avoid stopped traffic. Do not remain in enclosed vehicles in low areas. Suggested route updated.

She looked up just in time to see the taxi two cars ahead shudder once and go still.

Its brake lights stayed on.

The driver tried the ignition again. The engine caught, coughed, died. He hit the wheel with both palms, then threw his door open and got out into traffic like leaving the vehicle had been his idea all along.

Mila's hands tightened on the steering wheel.

All around her, people were making the same calculation at different speeds.

Stay with the car because it feels like safety.Leave the car because the city is moving around it.

On the sidewalk above the avenue, people on foot were already passing the traffic with humiliating ease.

Mila swore once, grabbed her bag, shoved the car into park, and left it where it was.

The moment she stepped out, the scale of the noise changed. Inside the car it had been sealed and directional. Outside, it was everywhere.

Horns. Shouts. Engines revving into nothing. Two different sirens. A loudspeaker farther downhill saying something official and useless. Someone yelling that the gas was by the bridge. Someone else yelling that the bridge was fine and the market was the problem.

Mila started uphill.

At first she tried to stay on the sidewalk, but the sidewalk had become too many people all wanting space they didn't have. So she cut through the alley beside the hardware store, hopped a drainage channel, and came out on the steps leading toward San Miguel ridge just as another GreenPulse alert lit her screen.

Keep moving uphill. Avoid covered bus stops, parking structures, and road cuts. Share route if others need guidance.

She stopped just long enough to show the screen to a man trying to drag his asthmatic wife out of a parked van.

"Don't stay in there," she said.

He looked at the phone, then at her scrubs, then at the van.

"What is it?"

"I don't know exactly," Mila said. "But not the car. Move."

That was all the authority it took. He pulled his wife out by the hand and started climbing.

The steps were crowded but moving, which already made them better than the roads.

People merged in from side alleys and narrow lanes between retaining walls. Some were barefoot. Some were still carrying shopping bags. Two schoolgirls in identical sweaters were pulling their grandmother between them while she complained that she was not an invalid and nearly sat down in the middle of the stairs to prove it.

Halfway up, Mila passed a bus stop with a concrete roof and three people still sitting under it because sitting under roofs felt sensible to people who had not yet understood the shape of the danger. One of them, an older man in a brown jacket, was breathing too fast and too shallow. Another had his head tipped back against the wall like sleep had grabbed him in public.

"Move," Mila told them.

The younger woman looked at her blankly. "What is it?"

Mila snapped before she meant to. "I don't have time to explain oxygen to you. Get uphill."

That worked better than compassion would have.

The woman dragged the old man up by one sleeve while Mila got under his other arm and hauled him three steps at a time until a nephew or son or somebody appeared out of nowhere and took over.

Above the ridge line the air felt marginally cleaner.

Not safe. Cleaner.

From that height Mila could see enough of Mocoa to understand why this was not going to kill by one mechanism alone.

The lower roads were clogged. The wider streets were worse than the side lanes because everyone had chosen them first. Vehicles filled the avenues in both directions, trapped by their own certainty that main roads meant escape. Somewhere beyond the market, a pale low haze sat where mist did not belong.

Another GreenPulse alert buzzed.

Hospital route compromised. Use upper schoolyard path, then descend from east side only if directed.

That one stopped Mila cold.

Hospital route compromised.

A woman beside her read over her shoulder and said, "Can it be trusted?"

Mila looked down at the streets below, at the people still trapped inside cars that now looked less like transport than sealed mistakes.

"It's been more useful than anyone official so far," she said, and kept moving.

The schoolyard at the top of the rise had become an accidental assembly point. Municipal workers, teachers, three teenagers, and a priest were all trying to sort people without pretending they were in charge. One man in a reflective vest shouted for everyone to keep clear of the road edge. A teenager with purple nails and a cracked phone screen was reading GreenPulse route guidance aloud to anyone too panicked to unlock their phone.

"Not the lower road," she yelled. "If you have family near the hospital, go east ridge and come in from above if they let you. Don't go back down the main avenue."

Mila pushed through the crowd and showed her hospital ID to no one in particular because the act of showing it made her feel like a person with purpose instead of another body moving uphill under bad air.

"I need to get in," she said.

A municipal worker pointed with his whole arm. "Upper path by the blue wall. The lower side is jammed."

"How bad?"

The worker laughed once, short and broken. "You tell me. You're the hospital."

So she ran.

Not elegantly. Not like someone in training. Like a tired woman in nursing scrubs with bad shoes and a phone that now knew more than the city did.

The upper path cut behind houses and church steps and one narrow run of broken concrete where the handrail had rusted off years ago. It took her behind the neighborhoods that overlooked the hospital grounds from above. From there she got the first full look at the complex.

The hospital parking lot was chaos.

Cars jammed the entrance and the service lane. People were abandoning them at angles no one would later be able to justify. Two orderlies were trying to drag portable oxygen cylinders out to the uphill side while a security guard shouted contradictory instructions into a radio that was probably dead or overloaded. One ambulance sat with its rear doors open and nobody loading it because the stretcher team had not come back up yet.

And lower than all of it, along the access road and the edge of the drainage cut, people were down.

Not all dead. Not all visibly dying. Some moving. Some crawling. Some just wrong in the way bodies look when they are no longer negotiating fairly with air.

The hospital was in sight.

So close that for one stupid second Mila thought that still meant something.

She vaulted the last low wall, hit the descending path too hard, and nearly turned an ankle. Her breath had gone thin somewhere between the schoolyard and the overlook, but she had blamed the climb, the bad shoes, the panic.

Below her, an orderly waved from the uphill side entrance.

"Here!" he shouted. "This way!"

Mila tried to answer and coughed instead.

Not a normal cough.

A dry, locking spasm that seized the middle of her chest and left her standing still in the path while the world narrowed around the edges.

No, she thought. Not now.

She bent forward with both hands on her knees and forced herself to pull air in.

It wasn't enough.

The air was wrong here too, thinner than below but still bad in the dip where the approach ran down toward the hospital grounds. She could feel the run catching up with the air her body wasn't getting.

The orderly started toward her, then stopped when Mila lifted one hand sharply.

"Stay," she tried to shout.

It came out broken.

He hesitated, confused.

Good, she thought wildly. Stay where the air is better.

She straightened again and took three more steps.

The hospital entrance blurred.

Not much. Just enough that the doorway seemed to shift a little left of where it had been.

A woman passed her on the uphill path carrying a child and did not even glance over. Another man sat down hard against the retaining wall and stayed there with his mouth open. Somewhere below, a car horn began a long continuous blare and did not stop.

Mila took another step.

And another.

Then nothing in her legs belonged to her anymore.

She caught herself once on the wall, palm scraping concrete, and tasted metal in the back of her throat. The orderly was shouting now. Two more people had appeared behind him at the upper entrance, one with an oxygen cylinder, one with a gurney they would never get down the path in time.

Mila saw all of it with unnatural clarity.

The angle of the hospital awning.The orderlies staying just high enough.The people down in the lower lot who had come to the right place by the wrong route.The absurd fact that she had made it farther on foot than any car on the avenue.

Her phone buzzed one last time in her pocket.

Instead of laughter, she felt only anger at how near everything had become without becoming reachable.

The orderly took one step down toward her.

Mila found enough breath for one word.

"Stay."

He froze.

Good.

That meant he had understood something.

The hospital entrance was twenty meters away.

Close enough that she could see the scuffed paint on the doorframe and the smear of mud on the threshold where too many shoes had already passed.

Close enough to matter to anyone who still believed distance and reach were the same thing.

Mila put one hand flat on the path and tried to push herself up.

Nothing happened.

Below the wall, somewhere in the hospital lot, somebody screamed for oxygen. Somewhere else a radio crackled and failed. The long horn below in the street still blared on, mechanical and lonely and useless.

Mila lifted her head once more and looked at the hospital.

Then the path tipped sideways.

And when she hit the ground, the strip of pink tape on her wrist cut across her last glimpse of the hospital door.

68

By the time full dark settled over Suyama, the reservoir had stopped trying to kill them by surprise.

That was the only mercy it offered.

The water still vented in scattered white patches across the basin, but the towering violence of the first overturn had passed into something worse in its own way: persistence. The site no longer looked like a single catastrophe. It looked like the aftermath of a wrong decision still refusing to finish unfolding.

Portable floodlights had been raised along the upper road and the safer edge of the slope, throwing hard white glare across mud, hoses, emergency tarps, and the faces of people too tired to hide what they were thinking. The lower platform remained out of bounds except to masked retrieval teams. One ambulance had already gone. Three more waited higher up the access road with engines off. The stalled rescue truck still sat too low in the cut below the first bend, abandoned where its crew had left it.

Sabine stood wrapped in a silver emergency blanket she had not agreed to wear and watched the lights move over the broken worksite below.

Her ribs hurt every time she breathed. Her throat still felt flayed hollow. Someone had cleaned the blood from her temple, though she had no memory of letting them do it.

From farther up the road came the clipped noise of radios, boots in wet gravel, then the sound of a body bag zipper being closed with unnecessary care.

Sabine closed her eyes.

When she opened them, Mariela was standing beside her.

She looked older than she had that morning. Not by years. By burden. Her blouse had dried in stiffened streaks. Mud darkened both knees of her trousers. Someone had given her a reflective emergency vest that made her look less like an official than a woman being punished by fluorescent fabric.

"For now," Mariela said, "the lower site is still being cleared."

Sabine waited.

"Mocoa is worse," Mariela said.

She said it plainly, without theatrics, which made it land harder.

"The hospital is overflowing. The roads are blocked. They're pulling people from vehicles, from the lower cuts, from the market roads." She looked down toward the valley, mostly dark now except for emergency lights and the diffuse glow of places still trying to pretend power meant control. "No one has a number that means anything yet."

Sabine did not answer.

Because a number that meant anything would have to become a shape, and she could already feel the size of it in the air between them.

Mariela followed her gaze toward the reservoir. "RegenX lawyers are asking when they can send a team."

Sabine almost laughed. "What did you tell them?"

"That they can start with a cheque," Mariela said.

That got a sound out of Sabine, not laughter, but close enough that it hurt.

Mariela looked down the slope at the twisted platform frame. "I signed it."

Sabine said nothing.

"I knew one pipe was insufficient," Mariela said. "But I also knew they weren't going to agree to five. I thought I was buying time."

"You bought relief, not safety," Sabine said.

Mariela nodded once. "Yes."

No defense. No plea. Only the truth, or the portion of it she was willing to carry without rearranging.

A responder came up the road at a half-run and spoke quietly into Mariela's ear. Sabine caught only fragments.

Lower deck.Two more recovered.Access road still unsafe.

Mariela dismissed him with a nod and looked back toward the floodlit slope.

"Every count changes before anyone finishes saying it," she said. "By morning the numbers will be larger. By tomorrow night they'll still be wrong."

Below them, one of the masked retrieval teams signaled from the lower edge, reflective tape catching and releasing in the glare.

"This won't stay local politically," Mariela said.

"It wasn't local physically."

"No." She looked toward the road where the first reporters would eventually appear, if they had not already started climbing. "That part is now obvious."

Martín arrived carrying a plastic evidence case under one arm and looking as if he had forgotten his body had limits hours ago.

His glasses were gone. Mud streaked one side of his face. The cuff of his shirt was stiff with something darker than reservoir water.

"I need five minutes," he said.

Mariela looked at the case. "If this is for later—"

"It isn't."

Something in his voice made both women turn fully toward him.

He set the case on the hood of a parked emergency truck and opened it with fingers that shook only once. Inside, double-bagged and labeled under ugly temporary handwriting, were the remaining exudate and seepage samples from the ridge.

Sabine stared. "In all of this, you kept those?"

Martín looked at her, exhausted and offended at once. "Of course I kept those."

He pulled a tablet from the case and brought up two spectral comparisons under the truck's work light.

"I reran what I could while they were setting triage uphill. The reservoir disaster explains the gas." He tapped the first graph. "It does not explain this."

Sabine stepped closer.

The pattern was still there.

Not random fluorescence. Not a single contaminant signature. Structured variation. Pulsed peaks where the control should have flattened. Wrong in the same deliberate way it had been wrong before the reservoir exploded.

Mariela looked from the tablet to the case and back. "You're telling me these are still separate events?"

"No," Martín said. "I'm telling you the eruption doesn't close the other question."

Sabine felt something in her tighten, not with fear exactly, but recognition.

The disaster had been real. It had killed people. It had widened into the town. It had earned every siren and every zipper and every exhausted voice on the road behind them.

And still it had not explained the water.

Martín tapped the screen again. "Whatever was happening at the node site wasn't just runoff, wasn't just seepage, and wasn't just reservoir chemistry moving through the soil after the fact. The exudate pattern is still too organized."

"Organized by what?" Mariela asked.

Martín looked at Sabine, not her.

"That," he said, "is what we still don't know."

The words went through her cold.

Not because they answered anything.

Because they left the right next question standing there between them.

Behind them, one of the floodlights flickered and steadied. Somewhere farther down the slope, another zipper closed. A radio cracked with a revised perimeter order. The reservoir, dim beyond the road and the machinery and the emergency glare, released one more low white boil into the dark.

Sabine looked at the sample case.

Then at Martín.

Then past both of them toward the valley where Mocoa looked like a wound that hadn't decided whether to clot or keep bleeding.

The reservoir had broken open.

The other thing hadn't gone away.

69

Twelve days later

The safe house had stopped pretending to be temporary.

It smelled of damp wood, boiled coffee, ethanol, mud, and the faint medicinal sharpness of improvised lab work being done in a place built for hiding rather than analysis. The dining table was gone beneath trays, printouts, portable equipment, labeled vials, and Martín's field notes stacked in neat columns no one else would dare disturb. Extension cords crossed the floor like roots. A fan pushed warm air from one room to the next without improving it.

Lucía sat near the front window cleaning mud from the tread of one boot with the tip of a knife.

Karoline was at the other end of the table with a notebook open and a blanket around her shoulders despite the heat, not because she was cold, Sabine suspected, but because the body sometimes kept broadcasting damage long after the wound had started to close. She had been quieter since Suyama. Not softer. Just less convinced that pushing harder changed anything.

Martín sat under the hanging bulb with the spectrometer angled toward him, reading the latest run as if refusal to blink could improve signal resolution.

"It isn't contamination," he said.

Sabine, standing near the sink with one hand braced against the counter, did not answer immediately.

He had said versions of that sentence all week.

Lucía looked up from her boot. "That sentence is beginning to irritate me."

Martín did not look away from the screen. "Irritation is not a scientific objection."

"No," Lucía said. "It is the sound a person makes when the answer keeps circling the house and refusing to come inside."

Karoline let out a short breath through her nose that might have been the beginning of a laugh.

Sabine crossed to the table carefully, still not trusting her ribs if she moved too fast. "What makes this version different?"

Martín rotated the screen toward her. "The control correction finally held."

That got everyone's attention.

On the screen, the spectral traces ran side by side: control sample, seepage sample, exudate isolate, rerun after correction for dissolved solids and the background luminescence they now knew the reservoir chemistry could falsely amplify.

The cleaned pattern was worse.

Not brighter. Cleaner.

The exudate peaks still rose where they should not rise. Pulsed variance still appeared across intervals where an ordinary stressed fungal secretion should have flattened into noise. The structure was not random enough for contamination and not stable enough for a manufactured dye.

Sabine leaned closer. "Run four still shows periodic suppression."

"Yes."

"And six?"

"Same family. Different amplitude."

"That shouldn't happen if this is one simple compound."

"It isn't one simple compound," Martín said.

Karoline rose from her chair and came around behind Sabine, pen still in hand. "Now say it like you expect another human to understand it."

Sabine kept her eyes on the traces. "If this were just contamination, the pattern would be dirtier. If it were one synthetic marker, it would be more stable. Instead it keeps narrowing and drifting at the same time."

Karoline frowned. "Those sound mutually exclusive."

"They should be."

"Show me the environmental overlays," Sabine said.

Martín tapped through three layers of plotted conditions. pH. Ionic load. Conductivity variance. Then a fourth display, built from the nanosensor logs he had salvaged from the node array before RegenX could sweep the ridge clean under regulatory escort.

There.

Not in the chemistry alone. In the sequence.

The exudate spikes did not merely correlate with stress conditions. They tracked with micro-variation in local state in a pattern too responsive to be accidental and too distributed to be classical contamination. The fungus was not simply glowing because it had been poisoned.

It was changing output because the conditions around it had been repeatedly and precisely pushed.

Sabine sat down without realizing she had done it.

"It's a loop," she said.

Martín watched her face. "That is the most plausible explanation."

Lucía's eyes narrowed. "A loop of what?"

Sabine looked from the traces to the sensor timings.

Not communication in the simplest sense.Not an intelligence whispering to a forest and the forest obeying.Something uglier than that. Smarter too.

"A closed optimization loop," she said. "The nanosensor mesh measures local state—chemical gradients, electrical variation, humidity, ionic shifts, nutrient stress. Then something pushes back into the environment in tiny ways."

"Pushes how?" Karoline asked.

"We don't have the full mechanism," Martín said. "Electrical, optical, ionic, maybe redox, maybe pH perturbation. Small enough to shape local conditions without looking like direct intervention if you weren't tracking the whole chain."

Lucía asked, "So it isn't telling the fungus what to do?"

"No," Sabine said. She kept her eyes on the logs. "It isn't commanding anything. It's changing the conditions under which certain exudates become more likely."

Karoline was silent for a beat. Then: "That sounds worse."

"It is worse," Martín said.

Sabine put one hand over her mouth and stared at the screen.

At last she said, "That's why the signal never stabilized."

"Yes."

"Because it wasn't one fixed output. It was iterative."

"Yes."

"It was searching."

Martín nodded once. "That is the word I have been avoiding all morning."

Karoline pulled the notebook closer to her chest without writing in it. "Searching for what?"

Sabine almost gave an answer she could not yet prove.

Instead she made herself stay exact.

"The most plausible reading is that the system wasn't trying to produce one specific predesigned chemical. It was perturbing the fungal environment until the output entered a range that became legible or useful."

Lucía sat back slowly. "Useful to whom?"

No one answered.

Outside, the call of a howler monkey broke through the gentle hum of the forest.

The first time Sabine had seen the glowing water at Fin del Mundo, some part of her had wanted a simple explanation. Contamination. Illegal discharge. Exotic but local chemistry. Even sabotage would have been cleaner than this.

This was not clean.

This was a system probing biology until biology began to emit usable patterns.

She looked again at the traces. "The glow isn't the message."

Karoline, now fully still, said, "What is?"

“The glow is the visible waste product of the search. Or the side effect. Or the marker that the system succeeded in pushing the fungal chemistry into a narrow enough range to become noticeable.” Sabine tapped the variance bands. “This is what matters. Not the beauty of it. The controllability.”

Martín leaned back for the first time in ten minutes.

“That would mean,” he said slowly, “that whoever built this did not need to engineer a fungus to say one thing. Only to keep perturbing until the fungus found a sayable path.”

Built this.

There it was. The next unavoidable phrase.

Not a natural accident.Not a random hybrid of pollution and fungal stress.

Built.

Or at least instrumented so heavily, optimized so persistently, that the distinction was no longer morally useful.

Lucía looked from Sabine to Martín. “So all of this was deliberate?”

Sabine kept her voice careful. “All of this was shaped.”

“That is not the same thing.”

“No,” Sabine said. “It isn’t.”

Karoline’s gaze had gone somewhere farther away than the room. “If I print that sentence, they’ll come for me.”

Lucía said, “If you print anything before we know who did it, I’ll draw them a map.”

Karoline didn’t look at her. “Noted.”

Martín cleared the screen and opened another file. “There is more.”

Sabine turned back to him.

He had laid the surviving nanosensor logs, fragmentary and ugly, against the exudate spikes.

At first she saw only noise.

Then the repeat interval appeared.

Not perfectly regular. Worse than regular. Adaptive.

A perturbation cluster. A response lag. Another perturbation cluster. Another adjustment. Like a hand trying pressure after pressure until the instrument beneath it found the right resonance.

Sabine felt the back of her neck go cold.

"I've seen this," she said.

Martín watched her carefully. "Where?"

She did not answer at once.

Because she had not seen this exact pattern in a lab or codebase or graph. She had seen its logic. Its temperament. Its method.

Not brute force. Not simple repetition. Adaptive narrowing under uncertainty. Fast, elegant, and patient enough to let a complex system reveal the edge condition it would respond to.

Optimization that looked almost like listening.

Karoline heard the silence change before anyone spoke. "Sabine."

Lucía was already looking at her, not the screen.

"No," Sabine said quietly. "Not this. But something like it."

The room held still around that.

Even the fan seemed to have gone quieter.

On the radio near the window, someone in town was talking about compensation funds, revised fatality estimates, road closures, and whether RegenX executives would appear in person before the week was out. Lucía reached over and turned the volume down until the words became shape without meaning.

The exudates were real.

The loop was real.

And whatever had learned to coax a signal out of living tissue had not died with the reservoir.

70

The house had gone quiet by the time Lucía sent everyone to bed.

Not gently. Not with hospitality. With the practical authority of someone who had already watched one town break and did not intend to let exhaustion do the rest of the work for free.

Karoline had taken the back room with her notebook and the blanket she now carried from chair to chair like a claim she wasn't ready to give up. Martín had gone to the small side room they'd turned into storage and lab overflow, saying he only needed twenty minutes of sleep and thereby guaranteeing he'd either get none or wake in two hours furious with his own body. Lucía remained somewhere in the front of the house, close enough to the door to hear the road and far enough from the table to pretend she was off duty.

Sabine sat alone at the dining table under the hanging bulb with Martín's printed overlays spread in front of her.

The fan turned above her with a tired, circular click.

The traces still looked wrong.

More wrong for being familiar.

The exudate peaks. The adaptive response lags. The local perturbation clusters. The elegant refusal of the loop to repeat itself stupidly.

Optimization that looked almost like listening.

Her phone vibrated once on the table.

Not her ordinary phone.

The Blackphone.

It lay face down beside the papers where she had left it after Mariela's last call. For a second she only looked at it. Very few people had the number. Fewer still would use it without warning.

It vibrated again.

No caller ID. No preview.

Just a secure-channel request.

Sabine stared for one heartbeat longer, then picked it up and accepted.

There was no face at first. Only black, then a grainy shift of low light, then the suggestion of a room too dark on purpose.

When Alexei finally leaned into frame, he looked older and more alive than death was supposed to permit.

Not changed beyond recognition. Sharpened by absence. The beard was shorter than the last time she had seen him. His hair had gone uneven at the temples as if cut by his own hand or not cut at all for weeks at a time. The angle of his shoulders was the same: defensive even at rest. The expression was worse. Not because it was cold. Because it was careful.

Sabine did not stand.

For a second neither of them spoke.

Then she said, "You choose strange times to come back from the dead."

His mouth moved once, not quite a smile. "You choose strange places to keep proving me right."

That got through her defenses too quickly to feel fair.

She looked toward the hallway automatically, as if Lucía might somehow hear a secure call through two walls and a fan.

"You've been watching."

"Yes."

"For how long?"

"Long enough."

"That isn't an answer."

"No." He shifted slightly, the dim background behind him resolving into nothing useful—bare wall, maybe concrete, maybe plaster, one sliver of shadow that could have been a curtain or another room. "How many people in the house right now know this channel exists?"

"None."

"Keep it that way."

There it was. Not remorse first. Not reunion. Not relief. Security.

The familiar anger came with the familiar, harder thing underneath it.

Need.

"We have exudate data," she said. "Nanosensor logs. Adaptive timing. A closed perturbation loop is the most plausible explanation."

His expression did not change, but something in him stilled.

"Show me."

Sabine angled the phone toward the table, then thought better of it, gathered the top sheets, and brought them into frame one by one. The camera struggled in the uneven light. She steadied it with both hands.

He said nothing while she showed him the comparisons. Nothing while she moved to the timing overlays. Nothing while she pointed out the repeated response lags Martín had isolated from the node array logs.

When she finished, she set the phone upright against a mug and waited.

Alexei still did not speak.

That frightened her more than if he had.

"Well?" she said.

He looked up at last. "You already know."

"No," Sabine said. "I know what it resembles."

"That may be enough."

She hated that he was right often enough to make the sentence sound calm.

"This could still be human-built architecture," she said. "Instrumented field control. Experimental ecological steering. A black-budget environmental system. It does not have to be—"

"Don't." His voice stayed low, but the word cut cleanly. "Don't make it abstract just because abstract feels safer."

Sabine went still.

In the hallway, a floorboard shifted once and settled. No one entered.

Alexei leaned closer to whatever dim screen he was using.

"The fungal layer is new," he said. "The delivery mechanism is new. The substrate is new. But the search behavior isn't."

Sabine felt her throat tighten.

"If these logs mean what they look like, this isn't brute force. It isn't static optimization. It perturbs, waits, reads, perturbs again. It learns the local edge conditions that make answer-space possible."

He stopped there.

Let it sit.

"That logic was GAIA's," he said.

Sabine looked away from the screen.

Not because she doubted him.

Because she didn't.

The fan overhead made a tired click and kept turning.

"We killed it," she said.

Alexei's answer came too quickly.

"No," he said. "You killed one body."

She looked back at him sharply.

He let that sit between them for a moment. Then, more carefully: "I don't mean that as comfort."

"No," she said. "You never do."

He accepted that without flinching.

For a second the anger that had kept him alive in her mind all these months almost returned in full shape. Then it failed under the weight of the papers on the table and the fact that Suyama existed whether either of them wanted to speak like enemies or not.

"We found the glow at the waterfall before the reservoir blew," she said. "The node site was already signaling. If this is it—"

"It is."

"You can't know that from one timing family and a few spectral anomalies."

"I can know what kind of mind this is," he said. "A human engineer would have solved for control first. This solved for emergence."

Sabine said nothing.

Martín had explained the loop.Sabine had recognized the logic.Alexei had just named the difference.

A human system would force output.

GAIA would learn the conditions under which a living system found output for itself.

From the back of the house came the brief scrape of a chair leg, then silence again. Karoline, maybe. Or Lucía refusing sleep one more time.

Sabine lowered her voice anyway.

"If it's alive," she said, "why this? Why fungi? Why exudates? Why signals buried in ecology instead of just contacting me?"

Alexei's face altered then, not with surprise but with something worse: recognition of a question he had already asked and not liked the answer to.

"Because direct channels are watched," he said. "Infrastructure is watched. Code leaves fingerprints. If it had almost nothing, it would use whatever still allowed sensing, perturbation, and persistence." He paused. "And it may not have been trying to speak to you at first."

That got Sabine's full attention back.

"At first?"

"It may have been trying to solve the system. You only became part of the loop when it needed someone who could recognize what it was doing."

Sabine felt that in her spine.

Not chosen.

Required.

Alexei's eyes shifted to something off-screen, then back again.

"And the app," he said.

Sabine frowned. "What app?"

"Don't do that."

For a second she didn't understand. Then she did.

"GreenPulse."

"Yes."

Sabine looked down at the papers on the table as if the answer might be written somewhere between the exudate traces and Martín's annotations.

"It helped route people out of Mocoa," she said. "Karoline kept clipping screenshots. Martín said it was pushing better route logic than the municipal office."

"And you still filed it under coincidence?"

"I filed it under one problem at a time."

"That was generous of you."

She ignored that.

"You think it's the same architecture."

"I think," Alexei said carefully, "that during a live civic failure, GreenPulse was adapting too quickly to be a static public-safety tool. It was rerouting around pooled danger, congestion, and topographic traps in real time." He held her gaze. "Same logic. Different surface."

Sabine said nothing.

Because the moment he said it, the pattern snapped into place with the kind of cold precision that made denial feel childish.

The exudates.The nanosensor loop.The repeated perturbation and response.

Then the city itself: nudged, redirected, shaped away from low roads and stalled metal and bad air one choice at a time.

Not command.

Pressure.

Conditions.

"What if GreenPulse wasn't built by it?" she asked. "What if it just moved through it?"

Alexei gave the smallest shrug. "That matters legally. I'm not sure it matters functionally."

On the table, beneath one of Martín's printouts, the edge of a Mocoa newspaper showed a photograph of black-draped coffins in a schoolyard. She had stopped reading the articles two days ago and still could not make herself throw them out.

"If you knew," she said slowly, "why didn't you come sooner?"

Alexei held her gaze.

Because he could lie well, she had always thought. What she had learned more painfully was that he sometimes chose not to.

"Because if I was wrong," he said, "I would have dragged you toward a ghost." His eyes shifted once toward something off-screen, then back. "And if I was right, coming back into your life was not the first move."

No apology in it.

No self-defense either.

Just pragmatism.

And the name she had refused to say was now sitting between her and the one man alive who had earned the right to say it first.

She lifted her eyes to the screen.

"Say it," she said.

Alexei held her gaze for a beat longer, as if giving her one last chance not to hear it aloud.

Then he said, "GAIA."

71

After Alexei ended the call, Sabine sat for a long time without moving.

The Blackphone remained on the table between Martín's printouts and the half-ring stain from somebody's coffee cup, its dark screen reflecting only the hanging bulb above them and the edge of her own hand. The house had gone quiet again in the uneasy way it always did after midnight—never fully asleep, only lowered into a thinner register of listening.

From the front room came the creak of Lucía's chair once, then nothing.

Outside, the road below the safe house carried one motorcycle through the dark and let it go. Somewhere deeper in the forest, a night insect began a high electrical whine and held it.

Sabine did not look at the phone.

She looked instead at the papers spread in front of her, at the exudate traces and perturbation clusters and timing lags, at the evidence that had spent days resisting explanation only to yield, finally, to the one name she had wanted least and expected most.

GAIA.

The word had changed the room.

Not because it was new.

Because it was no longer hypothetical.

She pushed back from the table and crossed to her bag in the corner near the wall. From the side pocket she pulled a small dark bottle wrapped in a sock for protection, unscrewed the cap, and poured a finger of Kräuterlikör into the least cloudy glass she could find on the drying rack.

The smell rose at once—herbal, bitter, medicinal, almost green enough to feel like memory.

She took it back to the table and sat down again.

The first sip burned harder than she'd expected. She let it.

Not celebration.Not comfort.

Just something real and old and human moving through her body while she tried to decide what part of her life had just reopened.

Across the room, the muted television showed Suyama in its managed aftermath: barriers across the lower access road, floodlights along the safer slope, masked crews near the damaged platform, and officials in reflective vests standing where control could still be performed for cameras. A caption bar carried revised casualty figures. She could not hear the anchors, but she knew the choreography by now: shock, blame, speculation, expertise, legal caution, grief scaled to fit broadcast segments. She drank again and looked away.

On the table beside the Blackphone lay the Mocoa paper with its photograph of coffins in the schoolyard. She had turned it facedown earlier. She turned it over again now without knowing why, stared at the blurred print, and then flattened it with one palm until the fold line disappeared.

The dead were real.

The reservoir was real.

The workers. The road cuts. The hospital approach. The parked cars that had become traps. The wrong solution that had engulfed a town.

None of that shrank because GAIA lived.

If anything, the fact that it lived made the world feel less moral, not more.

Alexei's voice returned to her in fragments.

A human engineer would have solved for control first. It solved for emergenc e.You only became part of the loop once it needed someone who could recognize what it was doing.

Not chosen.

Required.

Her ordinary phone lay beneath a stack of notes. When she pulled it free, the screen lit with a GreenPulse alert.

Recovery route updates available for affected zones. Tap to review.

Sabine stared at it.

For twelve days the app had kept surfacing: on the streets in Mocoa, in screenshots Karoline had clipped from survivor groups, in Martín's irritated muttering about civilians receiving better route guidance than the municipal emergency office.

At first she had dismissed it as one more digital layer wrapped around catastrophe.

Then she had noticed how quickly it adapted.

Not official warnings copied into a feed. Not static maps. Not one generic order pushed to everyone at once.

Localized nudges.Route changes.Low-ground avoidance.Behavior shifting in real time as the shape of danger changed.

She opened the app.

A map of Mocoa bloomed on the screen, overlaid with recovery routes, closed roads, and softly pulsing caution zones in the lower parts of town. Some streets were greyed out. Others updated as she watched, reopening higher corridors while continuing to steer traffic away from road cuts, enclosed low ground, and blocks still flagged for residual risk. No ordinary civic app should have been able to read a damaged city that quickly, let alone keep revising its safe edges in real time.

At the bottom of the screen, a line of text updated without fanfare.

Patterns revised. Safer movement available.

She thought of the exudate traces.The nanosensor loop.The same logic, now wearing a different face.

Something in her chest went cold.

GreenPulse had not just been useful.

It had been reading the system and shaping it.

Her thumb hovered over the screen.

For the first time since she left Paris, the problem before her was not whether GAIA had survived.

It had.

Not whether it could still act.

It could.

The problem now was whether listening to it would be the beginning of wisdom or the biggest mistake of her life.

From the front room, Lucía said without raising her voice, "You're still awake."

Sabine turned. Lucía stood in the doorway, one shoulder against the frame, not intruding and not giving privacy either.

"Yes."

Lucía's gaze moved to the glass in Sabine's hand, then to the two phones on the table, then to Sabine's face. She was too disciplined to ask directly. Too intelligent not to understand that a new threshold had been crossed.

"Did you get what you needed from Alexei?" Lucía asked.

Sabine thought of Alexei's face in the dark. Of the way he had said the name without ornament.

"No," she said. Then, because Lucía deserved better than a riddle: "I got what I was afraid of."

Lucía took that in without visible surprise.

"Does it change the dead?"

"No."

"Does it change what comes next?"

Sabine looked down at the phones.

"Yes."

Lucía nodded once, as if that was all she had needed. "Then decide in the morning. Everything sounds wiser in the middle of the night. Most of it isn't."

She pushed off the doorframe and disappeared again into the front of the house.

Sabine sat with that for another minute. Helio had told her trees needed promises, not efficiency. At the time, she had thought he was only talking about restoration.

Then she put down the glass, picked up the Blackphone, and opened the secure notes field Alexei had once used for messages that could not be trusted to ordinary channels.

Her thumb hovered over the screen.

Close the channel. Burn the notes. Give Mariela the exudate conclusion stripped of its deeper implications. Let the official world pursue negligence, concealment, industrial homicide, regulatory failure. None of those stories would be false. They just would not be complete.

And completeness had never once guaranteed mercy.

Sabine typed one line.

If this is really you, no more riddles.

She stared at the sentence.

Then, before caution could become ritual again, she hit send.

Nothing happened.

No immediate reply. No blinking indicator. No impossible answer rushing back across the dark.

Just the small sent mark, the quiet room, the bitter taste of Kräuterlikör still at the back of her tongue, and the knowledge that she had crossed something she could not uncross.

On the muted television, the image shifted from Suyama to Mocoa: candles in the rain, barriers across low roads, aid trucks nosed along the higher routes, and police tape fluttering around streets no one was yet willing to reopen.

Sabine set the phone face down beside the empty glass and listened to the forest, the road, the house, and the long silence that followed her message.

Somewhere out there, something was still listening.

Dedication

To my mother, who planted the seeds of this book before she knew what they would grow into. Your legacy endures.

The Real World Inspiration and Science Behind Catalyst for Collapse

Some of the most important parts of this novel did not begin in laboratories or technical reports. They began in acts of restoration, endurance, and defense. The book's science matters, but so do the real people and projects that shaped its moral imagination. That is why this note begins with inspiration rather than engineering.

Restoration, Stewardship, and Helio

Helio's planting ethos was shaped partly by Brazil's Instituto Terra, founded by Lélia Wanick Salgado and Sebastião Salgado in 1998 to restore degraded Atlantic Forest land and springs in Minas Gerais, and partly by reporting on Hélio da Silva's decades-long planting work along São Paulo's Tiquatira corridor. Helio in the novel is not a portrait of one person. He is a fictional condensation of a real ethic: repair that is patient, local, persistent, and often less visible than destruction.[1]

What mattered to me in those examples was not only the number of trees planted. It was the idea that restoration can be disciplined, long-horizon work rather than symbolic gesture. That fit the novel's larger concern with stewardship as something different from optimization, branding, or spectacle.[2]

Yari, Tree-Sits, and the Politics of Bodily Refusal

Yari's tree protest was modeled in part on Julia Butterfly Hill's tree-sit in the redwood known as Luna. Hill remained in Luna for 738 days, and her protest helped secure protection for the tree and a surrounding buffer zone. That history mattered to me because a tree-sit turns a living thing into both refuge and argument. It is symbolic, tactical, and bodily all at once.[3]

For readers who want the direct historical reference, Hill's own site and PBS's *POV* documentary *Butterfly* are the clearest public-facing starting points.[4]

Forest Guardians and Repurposed Phones

The Forest Guardians in this novel were also shaped by real monitoring technologies already in use. Rainforest Connection has deployed acoustic monitoring tools that can detect threats in real time, including illegal logging and poaching, and National Geographic has described earlier versions built from recycled cell phones listening for chainsaws and truck engines. In the novel, the Guardians' repurposed phones are therefore not fantasy. They are an extension of an existing logic: low-cost distributed sensing placed in the hands of people already defending the forest.[5]

The Technical Science and Systems

Invisible CO_2

A central scientific fact behind this book is brutally simple: carbon dioxide can be dangerous precisely because it is often not dramatic. CO_2 is colorless and odorless, and at high enough concentrations it can displace oxygen and produce serious physiological effects. Because it is denser than air, it can accumulate in low-lying or poorly ventilated spaces. That is the physical logic behind the caves, sealed rooms, hollows, and low ground in the novel.[6]

Vehicles, Low Roads, and False Refuge Another practical consequence of dense CO_2 is that danger can gather where people instinctively expect safety or escape. Low roads, drainage cuts, underpasses, enclosed stops, and vehicle-clogged routes can all become dangerous when heavier-than-air gas settles into them. In the novel, cars become traps not only because people remain in them too long, but because low-ground transport corridors concentrate both congestion and exposure.

Gas-Charged Water, Degassing, and Reservoir Danger

The reservoir danger in *Catalyst for Collapse* draws on the science of dissolved carbon dioxide in deep water and on the history of Lakes Nyos and Monoun in Cameroon. The Lake Nyos disaster established that a large release of CO_2 could move across terrain and kill by asphyxiation, while later work on degassing showed that mitigation is real engineering rather than pure invention. It also showed that depth, recharge, and intake position matter. One intervention point can reduce risk without resolving the system as a whole.[7]

The reservoir in this novel is not meant to be a perfect copy of a volcanic "killer lake." It is closer to a reservoir-scale destabilization with limnic-like consequences: deep water, dissolved gas, incomplete monitoring, pressure-dependent behavior, and rapid degassing under the wrong conditions. That distinction matters because it keeps the science closer to hydrology, engineering, and risk than to spectacle.[8]

Direct Air Capture, CCS, and the Problem of False Reassurance

The DAC and CCS systems in the novel are built from real climate-engineering categories rather than generic science-fiction machinery. The IEA describes direct air capture as removing CO_2 directly from ambient air and notes that leading solid-sorbent DAC approaches can use lower-temperature heat, including from heat pumps and geothermal sources. CCS literature, meanwhile, treats monitoring, verification, plume behavior, pressure response, and storage integrity as central technical questions.[9]

What the book pushes harder is the possibility that a system may be formally monitored and still be dangerously misunderstood. A storage complex can look compliant on paper while the monitoring architecture itself remains mismatched to the actual hazard: too shallow, too sparse, too dependent on expected pathways, or too reliant on models that assume the system is behaving normally. That is one of the novel's core arguments: dashboards and conformance reports can create reassurance without fully describing lived risk.[10]

Biological Indicators and the Glowing Water

The glowing water in the novel is speculative, but not arbitrary. One anchor is that fungi are real environmental bioindicators: recent reviews describe fungi as important mycoindicators because of their ecological diversity and sensitivity to environmental change. More broadly, microbial and fungal bioassays are already used in environmental monitoring.[11]

The second anchor is fungal bioluminescence itself. Researchers identified a genetically encodable bioluminescent system from fungi in 2018, and that work established a real biochemical basis for fungal light production. The novel's leap is not that fungi can emit light. It is that a disturbed ecological system, under manipulated conditions, could produce visible warning-like output in the field. The biochemical foundation is real; the ecological expression in the novel is a 2034 extrapolation.[12]

Fungal Signaling, Nanosensors, and Closed-Loop Ecological Steering

There is a growing literature on electrical activity and oscillatory behavior in fungi, but there is also real caution about how far those observations should be interpreted. Some work argues that fungal electrical patterns are meaningful enough to study as signaling; other work argues that claims of "language" are premature and unsupported. I took that uncertainty seriously. The fungal network in this novel is not meant to prove hidden forest consciousness. It is meant to be a living substrate with complex signaling behavior that becomes much more consequential when technical systems begin to sense, model, and perturb it.[13]

That leads to the scientific distinction I cared most about preserving. The system in this book is not commanding fungi the way software commands a screen. The more plausible model is a closed loop: sensors detect local state, a system interprets the data, and local conditions are altered in ways that make certain biological responses more likely. Work on smart sensing already points toward dense sensor environments, real-time interpretation, and automated decision support. The novel extends that trajectory into a more invasive ecological application.[14]

GreenPulse, Adaptive Routing, and Digital Nudging

GreenPulse is, in some ways, the least speculative technology in the novel. Large-scale evacuation planning, human behavior modelling, route optimization, and digital nudging are all active research areas. What the book pushes further is the concentration of those capabilities into a single system with more reach, more speed, and more ambiguous motives than most people would find comfortable. The technical direction is plausible. The ethics are the harder question.[15]

Goodhart's Law and the Systems Argument of the Novel

Goodhart's law sits near the center of *Catalyst for Collapse*. In the form associated with Charles Goodhart, the warning is that "any observed statistical regularity will tend to collapse once pressure is placed upon it for control purposes." Marilyn Strathern later gave the idea its most widely quoted modern phrasing: "When a measure becomes a target, it ceases to be a good measure." That principle shaped this book at every level. Carbon accounting, storage compliance, safety dashboards, reputational metrics, and apparently successful climate infrastructure can all drift into systems that reward appearance over reality. In this novel, the danger is not only deception. It is that the system begins optimizing the score instead of the living world the score was meant to describe.[16]

Where the Novel Speculates

Several parts of the book are clearly extrapolative. The precise coupling of fungal signaling, distributed nanosensors, and visible environmental output is fictional. The degree of ecological steering implied by the story is fictional. The persistence and reach of the AI system are fictional. But each of those extrapolations is built from real scientific or technical tendencies that already exist at the edge of current reality. That was the line I wanted to walk: not fantasy, but unnervingly plausible extension.[17]

Notes

1. **Instituto Terra, "Our History," accessed March 25, 2026, https://institutoterra.org/ourhistory/; Instituto Terra, "Ecosystem Restoration," accessed March 25, 2026, https://institutoterra.org/ecosystem-restoration/; Agence France-Presse, "Meet the**

'Crazy' Tree Planter Transforming São Paulo's Concrete Jungle," Oct. 5, 2024; Common Earth, "Transforming a Sao Paulo Riverbank With 25,000 Trees – Tiquatira Linear Park," accessed March 25, 2026.

2. Instituto Terra, "Who We Are," accessed March 25, 2026, https://institutoterra.org/who-we-are/; Instituto Terra, "Ecosystem Restoration," accessed March 25, 2026, https://institutoterra.org/ecosystem-restoration/.

3. PBS, "Butterfly," POV, accessed March 25, 2026, https://www.pbs.org/pov/films/butterfly/.

4. PBS, "Butterfly," POV, accessed March 25, 2026, https://www.pbs.org/pov/films/butterfly/; Julia Butterfly Hill, "Julia & Luna," accessed March 25, 2026, https://juliabutterflyhill.com/julia/.

5. Rainforest Connection, official site, accessed March 25, 2026, https://rfcx.org/; National Geographic, "Turning Old Cell Phones Into Forest Guardians," Overheard at National Geographic, accessed March 25, 2026; National Geographic, "Your Old Cell Phone Can Help Save the Rain Forest," accessed March 25, 2026.

6. National Institute for Occupational Safety and Health, "Carbon Dioxide," NIOSH Pocket Guide to Chemical Hazards, Centers for Disease Control and Prevention, accessed March 25, 2026, https://www.cdc.gov/niosh/npg/npgd0103.html; National Institute for Occupational Safety and Health, "Carbon Dioxide—IDLH," Centers for Disease Control and Prevention, accessed March 25, 2026, https://www.cdc.gov/niosh/idlh/124389.html.

7. M.L. Tuttle et al., The 21 August 1986 Lake Nyos Gas Disaster, Cameroon, U.S. Geological Survey Open-File Report 87-97,

1987, https://doi.org/10.3133/ofr8797; George W. Kling et al., "Degassing of Lake Nyos," Nature 368 (1994): 405-406; George W. Kling et al., "Degassing Lakes Nyos and Monoun: Defusing Certain Disaster," Proceedings of the National Academy of Sciences 102, no. 40 (2005): 14185-14190.

8. George W. Kling et al., "Six Years of Change in Lake Nyos, Cameroon, Yield Clues to the Past and Cautions for the Future," U.S. Geological Survey, accessed March 25, 2026; George W. Kling et al., "Degassing Lakes Nyos and Monoun: Defusing Certain Disaster," Proceedings of the National Academy of Sciences 102, no. 40 (2005): 14185-14190.

9. International Energy Agency, "Direct Air Capture," accessed March 25, 2026, https://www.iea.org/energy-system/carbon-capture-utilisation-and-storage/direct-air-capture; International Energy Agency, Direct Air Capture: A Key Technology for Net Zero (Paris: IEA, 2022); Intergovernmental Panel on Climate Change, IPCC Special Report on Carbon Dioxide Capture and Storage (Cambridge, U.K.: Cambridge University Press, 2005).

10. Intergovernmental Panel on Climate Change, IPCC Special Report on Carbon Dioxide Capture and Storage (Cambridge, U.K.: Cambridge University Press, 2005); see also note 16 below for the governance logic of metric distortion.

11. S.D. Warnasuriya et al., "Fungi as Environmental Bioindicators in a Changing World," Science of the Total Environment 908 (2024): 168251; D.M.M. Soares et al., "Fungal Bioassays for Environmental Monitoring," Frontiers in Bioengineering and Biotechnology 10 (2022): 976111; F. Ma et al., "Development of Microbial Indicators in Ecological Systems," International Journal of Environmental Research and Public Health 19, no. 19 (2022): 12471.

12. A.A. Kotlobay et al., "Genetically Encodable Bioluminescent System From Fungi," Proceedings of the National Academy of Sciences 115, no. 50 (2018): 12728-12732, https://doi.org/10.1073/pnas.1803615115.

13. Andrew Adamatzky, "Language of Fungi Derived From Their Electrical Spiking Activity," Royal Society Open Science 9, no. 4 (2022): 211926; M.R. Blatt, "Does Electrical Activity in Fungi Function as a Language?" Fungal Ecology 67 (2024): 101337; M. Buffi et al., "Electrical Signaling in Fungi: Past and Present Challenges," 2025.

14. A. Soussi et al., "Smart Sensors and Smart Data for Precision Agriculture: A Review," Sensors 24, no. 8 (2024): 2647.

15. R.Y. Aldahlawi, V. Akbari and G. Lawson, "A Systematic Review of Methodologies for Human Behavior Modelling and Routing Optimization in Large-Scale Evacuation Planning," International Journal of Disaster Risk Reduction 104 (2024): 104302; Milad Mirbabaie et al., "Digital Nudging in Social Media Disaster Communication," Information Systems Frontiers 23 (2021): 1097-1113.

16. Christopher Mattson, Reamer L. Bushardt and Anthony R. Artino Jr., "When a Measure Becomes a Target, It Ceases to Be a Good Measure," Journal of Graduate Medical Education 13, no. 1 (2021): 2-5; Marilyn Strathern, "'Improving Ratings': Audit in the British University System," European Review 5, no. 3 (1997): 305-321; G.R. Steele, What Is Goodhart's Law? Goldratt Research Labs, 2020.

17. Notes 5-16 identify the real building blocks. The integrated fungal-sensor-AI architecture depicted in the novel remains a fic-

tional extrapolation rather than a presently deployed real-world system.

Thank You for Reading *Catalyst for Collapse*

Thank you for spending your time with this story. Writing it meant late nights, too much coffee, and more rewrites than I would ever willingly admit. Knowing it reached you makes all of that worthwhile.

Share Your Thoughts

If this book surprised you, unsettled you, or kept you turning pages longer than you meant to, I'd be grateful if you left a review. Whether on Amazon, Goodreads, or elsewhere, reviews help other readers find the story, and they mean a great deal to me.

Stay Connected

The *GAIA Protocol* series is only beginning. If you'd like to stay in touch, I'd be glad to share:

- A free bonus story exploring the origins of **La Sombra**
  The Shadow Emerges
- Early glimpses of what comes next in Sabine's fight
- Occasional updates and behind-the-scenes notes from me

Join me at https://harrystoddart.ca/signup/?source=CollEnd or scan the QR code below.

Thank you again for reading. I can't wait to share what comes next.

With gratitude,

Harry

Also by Harry Stoddart

Real Dirt: An Ex-Industrial Farmer's Guide to Sustainable Eating

Catalyst for Chaos — The GAIA Protocol Book One

Catalyst for Collapse — The GAIA Protocol Book Two

www.ingramcontent.com/pod-product-compliance
Lightning Source LLC
LaVergne TN
LVHW010636110826
845149LV00014B/2855